IN OVER HER HEAD

Anjelica knew she should not be swimming with the handsome Stuart Delaney so close to her in the rippling water of the jungle river. Even worse, she had gone out too far. She was treading water now, and had to gasp to Stuart, "Can I hold on to you? I can't touch bottom here."

As she grasped his shoulders, he put his hands around the bare skin of her waist. He only had to slide his fingers a fraction of an inch upward to touch her naked breasts. He kept his self-control for one excruciatingly intense moment. Then he brought her body in hard against his own.

"We shouldn't be doing this, you know," she half-moaned, even as she put her arms around his neck. "It's wrong. I belong to Nicholas Sedgwick."

"Yes, I know," he said, and then his mouth found hers . . . and she was opening her lips under his . . . and what never should happen had begun. . . .

White Orchid

WHITE ORCHID

by

Linda Ladd

A TOPAZ BOOK

TOPAZ
Published by the Penguin Group
Penguin Books USA Inc., 375 Hudson Street,
New York, New York 10014, U.S.A.
Penguin Books Ltd, 27 Wrights Lane,
London W8 5TZ, England
Penguin Books Australia Ltd, Ringwood,
Victoria, Australia
Penguin Books Canada Ltd, 10 Alcorn Avenue,
Toronto, Ontario, Canada M4V 3B2
Penguin Books (N.Z.) Ltd, 182-190 Wairau Road,
Auckland 10, New Zealand

Penguin Books Ltd, Registered Offices:
Harmondsworth, Middlesex, England

First published by Topaz, an imprint of Dutton Signet,
a division of Penguin Books USA Inc.

First Printing, May, 1995
10 9 8 7 6 5 4 3 2 1

 Topaz is a trademark of Dutton Signet,
a division of Penguin Books USA Inc.

Printed in the United States of America

For my mother, Louise King— I love you, Mom;

And for Diane Kirk and Evelyn Strong,
and all the other lovely ladies
of Rose Petals and Pearls Romance Sorority—
Thanks for being so nice!

Prologue

U nlike the other spacious rooms of Marian Foxworthy's grand mansion, her library was dim and quiet. Though seventy or more resplendently adorned guests mingled and waltzed the night away, Stuart Delaney stood alone before a bay window centered at the end of the book-lined, mahogany-paneled chamber.

Outside the frosted, diamond-shaped panes, gigantic flakes of snow tumbled and fell in a wild, wind-tossed cotillion toward the ground. He watched the lacy ice crystals whiten the long frozen lawn as the tall Chippendale grandfather clock behind him heralded the first minutes of the new year, eighteen sixty-six. As the twelve slow bongs began, he heard the wild cheers of celebration issuing from the glittering ballroom on the third floor.

He had only come tonight because Marian had begged him, and he owed her. She was as much a social creature as he was antisocial. An unamused grin touched his mouth. Marian was too much like his American mother had been—obsessed with her aristocratic lineage and inherited money. Marian's

7

wealth had come from her dead husband whom she had never loved and who had been old enough to be her great-grandfather; Stuart's mother's plantation house on the James River had been in their family for generations of Virginia bluebloods.

Twin Pines was probably gone now, no doubt burned to the ground by the Yankees when they had overrun the state of Virginia in the last few months of the war. He didn't really care, he realized with a vague sense of surprise. Twin Pines meant little to him. It was just a big, pillared mausoleum that his mother had loved more than she had her own children. His sister Cassandra had loved the place, too, but he never had.

Now his mother was dead and he hadn't seen his sister for over five years though he knew she had staunchly supported the Confederacy. His older brother, Harte, had fought for the North. Stuart doubted if he would ever see him again.

Not liking to think about his Yankee brother he grimaced and withdrew a narrow silver box from the breast pocket of his black evening jacket. He selected a square-tipped cheroot, puffed it to flame, then held it idly between his fingers.

A coach drawn by four white horses had come to a sliding stop underneath the Corinthian columns of Marian's portico. A young man in the dashing red of a British military uniform climbed out then assisted a young woman wearing a fox-lined royal blue cloak.

For the last eight months since Lee had surrendered to the North, Stuart had tried to establish a new life in England. For the last three years of the war, he had lived and worked in London as a procurer of goods to fill the holds of blockade runners destined for southern ports. He had met the beautiful Marian through his business dealings with her late husband's munitions factories and her financier friends who supplied the ways and means through their London banks. Together they had been a good team until the Americans finally decided to quit killing one another.

Marian had welcomed him into her business dealings with open arms as well as her elaborate silk-draped bed. She had been a good friend and opened plenty of doors invaluable to a Confederate soliciting funds for his cause. After the South had fallen, it hadn't been difficult to continue the same work in legal exporting. Only now his customers were shipping companies from France and Holland on the continent, and others as far away as South America.

Marian was still his lover—a rich, beautiful woman who made no demands on him. Until now. Unfortunately she had decided that she wanted to marry him and had dangled as a carrot to entice him the control of her vast business enterprises. If she didn't press too hard, he just might do it. He sure as hell had nothing left to go home to.

"So there you are."

At the sound of Marian's voice, he turned and found her silhouetted in the doorway. She always looked lovely but tonight she had outdone herself. His eyes swept down the front of her slim white gown glistening with tiny silver beads. Her skin was as creamy as the silk of her gown, and he knew from experience that one tug on the silver comb at the nape would bring her long black hair tumbling down from the regal coiffure piled in ringlets atop her head.

Marian was an insatiable lover. He wondered if that was why she had left her guests to seek him out. As she moved across the room, her long earrings swung back and forth, the gas lamps setting fire to the tear-shaped diamonds until they winked and sparkled like stars shooting through the heavens.

"You missed the stroke of midnight, darling. I looked everywhere for you." A faint hint of petulance colored her words, but not enough to anger him. She was pampered and spoiled, but she knew better than to order him around.

"I was bored with it all."

"Does that include me?" she inquired with arched brow as she reached out and touched him in an intimate way.

Stuart smiled at her brazen caress. "Not at the moment."

"You enjoy making me pursue you, don't you?" she accused in a husky whisper. She pressed herself against him and the sweet essence of the gardenias pinned in her hair drifted across his senses.

"You never tell me where you're going or what you're thinking."

"Maybe that's because it's none of your business where I'm going or what I'm thinking." He grasped the back of her neck and pulled back her head where he could press his lips on the side of her throat.

Marian moaned with pleasure. "You better stop that or I won't want to tell you about the job my solicitors have offered to you."

His interest piqued, Stuart quickly released her. "What job is that, love? Something to get me out of London for a while, I hope."

Marian's fine satin petticoats rustled enticingly as she perched a hip on the desk. "Yes, as a matter of fact, but I don't want you to go away."

Getting away sounded damn good to him, especially if it paid enough. "Where do they want me to go?"

Her lips formed the pretty pout he knew so well. "All the way to India."

Stuart was intrigued. "To India? Why?"

"To find a friend of ours who seems to have disappeared off the face of the earth. We've heard some rumors that he might have entered one of the princely states where the native kings still rule."

"Who is this man, who's looking for him, and why me?"

Marian smiled. "Why are you always so suspicious of everyone's motives?"

"Maybe because my Yankee friends still have a price on my head."

"But you don't have to worry about that anymore. The war's over in America."

"Not for all of us. I did them a lot of harm before the truce. And I'm still sending funds to the new Confederacy they're trying to set up in Mexico."

"Don't frown so, sweetheart. The Yankees have nothing to do with this job. A lot of people here in London have business affairs they need to tie up with this man. They've gone together and hired my attorneys to find him."

Stuart was still wary. "Who is he?"

"His name is James Blake."

"How long's he been missing?"

"For over five years now—"

"Five years, and they're just now starting to look for him? Finding him can't be too pressing."

"They fear he might be dead, and some of the friends are concerned about the girls."

"What girls?"

"His daughters, Anjelica and Suzannah."

Stuart sat down in the plush leather desk chair and gazed up at her. "I'm beginning to suspect there's more to this than you're telling me."

Marian smiled. "Well, there is, really. I do have a personal interest. In fact, my family's willing to double the fee Stonegate and Havenstern is offering if you'll bring the one named Anjelica back to England when you find her."

"My, my, this is sounding more interesting all the time. Have you gotten yourself in trouble again?"

"Oh, stop, it's not my problem, it's Nickie's."

"Nick, your long-lost cousin?"

"Yes, very few people know this but he was married to this girl by proxy about ten years ago."

"You're kidding. Isn't that a bit old-fashioned?"

"His mother arranged it with Mrs. Blake. They were best friends from finishing school. I don't know all the details, but Nickie doesn't even know if she's dead or alive. He's the male heir of the family, and Aunt Julia is worried he'll never settle down."

"Why doesn't he go after her himself?"

"Oh, you know Nickie, he's off on some island with his doctor friends studying some exotic disease or another. I don't think he wants to find her."

"So what's in it for me?"

Marian smiled knowingly. "Ten thousand pounds from Stonegate and Havenstern and the same amount matched by Nickie and my aunt."

Stuart's face didn't change but he was astounded at the sum. No one paid out that kind of money without a damn good reason.

"Are you sure there isn't something you're not telling me? Has James Blake done something illegal?"

Stuart knew at once that he was right. He always knew when Marian was lying to him. "Not really, but there have been rumors that he might have taken up with a native girl. Something like that could embarrass everyone concerned so I hope you'll be discreet with whatever you uncover down there."

"For that kind of money I can keep my mouth shut. I'll leave as soon as I can make arrangements."

Marian sat down on his lap. "And now for the best part. I'm coming with you, darling. It could be a wonderful honeymoon for us—"

"I'm going alone, or I'm not going."

"Stuart, please, I'll be so lonely here with you gone so long."

"There're plenty of men around for you to charm until I get back."

"You don't care a fig about me, do you?"

"And that's precisely why you like me, isn't it, love?" he murmured, standing up then taking her wrists and pulling her close against him.

"Yes."

Her answer was low, husky, her words cut off as she parted her lips beneath his probing tongue. Twenty thousand pounds would set him up comfortably in London or anywhere else he had a mind to go, he thought as he bent Marian backward over the desk. A trip to India was well worth the trouble. He was damn sick and tired of ice and snow anyway.

Chapter One

Nearly two months later as Stuart Delaney swatted impatiently at the cloud of gnats torturing his ears, snow and ice sounded a hell of a lot better than the stinging flies and scorching sun of India. The heat had nearly staggered him when he had stepped off the gangplank and into Calcutta, a city overrun with suffering humanity and the stench of bodies burning in the Hindu funeral ceremonies on ghats along the rivers.

Stuart had escaped the place as soon as he could find a military attachment headed for the British compound in the city of Agra. There, over a lace-covered tea table, Abigail Coleridge, the elderly wife of the very distinguished Major George Coleridge hadn't hesitated to share with him the ugly rumors concerning the notorious Blake family.

Mary Blake had been a sainted lady who worshiped the Crown as any true Brit should. James Blake, on the other hand, had been a peculiar man, one who actually thought the poor, simpleminded Indians possessed some intellect. The two Blake daughters were nothing less than headstrong hoydens who had been allowed to run with the dark-skinned native urchins from babyhood on.

Why, the last she'd heard, Abigail had whispered behind her fan with bizarre clucks of disapproval, James Blake had taken his girls into the jungles of Udaipur and was living in sin with some young native woman inside the wicked walls of the maharajah's palace. And everyone knew what kind of things went on there under the decadent eye of that awful Maharajah of Udaipur. After sharing that last scandalous comment, Mrs. Coleridge seemed ready to expire with the horror of relating the sordid gossip, and Stuart understood why James Blake had decided to disappear forever.

He had promptly hired a guide to take him to the city of Udaipur and now sat on the bank of Pichola Lake, swatting flies and watching for any sign of anyone sporting white skin. Rubbing beaded sweat off his forehead with the back of his arm, he leaned back against the ridged trunk of a palm tree and stared across the water. The palace of the Maharajah of Udaipur stood like a romantic illusion with its high white walls, arched towers, and graceful minarets.

For a week he had been watching the elephant gate. According to his innkeeper the inhabitants of the palace used that entrance to gain access to the lake; eventually he was bound to catch sight of someone. He wished to God someone would show up soon because he damn well didn't want to walk blindly into an armed fortress without a hell of a lot more information about what relationship James Blake had with the decadent Maharajah of Udaipur. At the moment all he wanted was to get the job done and get the devil out of the godforsaken jungles where the heat alone could drive a man crazy.

The afternoon crawled by like a wounded buffalo, and as the sun dipped lower in the sky, he stripped off his shirt and boots and stepped off the bank and into the water. He waded about ten yards down to where a rippling river fed into the lake. The current was clear and strong, and he sat down in the shade of trailing willow branches and dipped a handful of the cool water over his head. He pushed back his wet hair with both hands, then froze in the motion. An absolutely huge gray elephant was splashing into the shallows a short distance upstream.

Stuart ducked back out of sight when he saw that a native rode atop the animal. The boy was dressed like many of the other Indians Stuart had observed—in a loose fitting white cotton shirt and some kind of white garment worn wrapped around the waist and sometimes tucked up between the legs similar to a loincloth.

The elephant handler called a command and the elephant sank down to his knees like an obedient slave. The trainer was speaking soothingly in one of the many Hindi dialects, and the gigantic beast fell onto his side in the rushing currents as if shot down by a hunter's gun. The tall, slim boy executed agile footwork to stay upright, then suddenly pulled loose the big white turban he wore on his head releasing long and curly white-blond hair that tumbled past his waist.

Stuart's mouth gaped but his initial astonishment soon turned to realization. The Blake girl, he thought in relief, then was shocked a second time when she stripped off the baggy shirt with one swift motion. For a brief second, he stared at firm bare breasts before she executed a perfect shallow dive into the flowing water.

Seconds later she surfaced, stood up and tugged loose the cloth girdling her slender hips. Stuart's blood stirred dangerously, and his eyes locked on her firm sun-browned flesh until she sank down to her neck, instantly snapping the spell. She had to be Anjelica Blake, and her faraway fiancé Nickieboy was one lucky bastard. He glanced around and found no one was nearby so he stepped out where she could see him.

"Anjelica?"

The girl whirled around, covering her naked torso with her crossed forearms. Her hair was slicked back from her face, making her huge gray eyes appear to glint like two silver mirrors against her tanned face. She was beautiful, and very young, but he was surprised by her dark skin. Most women he knew shielded their complexions as diligently as their virginity, especially in Virginia.

"Who are you?" she demanded breathlessly, her eyes darting around with fear.

"Don't be afraid. I'm not going to hurt you."

She didn't seem to believe him. She inched backward, deeper into the water. "What do you want?"

"You are Anjelica Blake, aren't you?"

Never taking her eyes off him, she quickly found her shirt and pulled the wet garment back over her head. "How do you know who I am?"

Stuart heaved a sigh of relief. "I've been looking for you. I've come here to take you back home to England."

"Are you Nicholas Sedgwick?" she asked cautiously.

"No, but he's the one who sent me."

Her young face changed, and he could almost see the apprehension drain away. She immediately began to wade out toward him, either unaware or uncaring how the thin cotton was plastered against her body, leaving nothing to his imagination. Stuart made a valiant effort not to take note, but Lord help him, she might as well have been totally naked. By force of will, he dragged his gaze back to her face.

Up close he found her even more striking, with small delicate features and high, finely chiseled cheekbones. He was stunned when she reached him and didn't hesitate to press her body full length against his bare chest.

"Thank God, you've finally come for us," she whispered hoarsely.

Stuart swallowed convulsively at the feel of her

erect nipples through the thin barrier and tried to listen to what she was saying in a voice thick with emotion.

"I was afraid Nicholas had forgotten all about me."

Stuart forced himself to come to his senses and concentrated on the problem at hand. He took hold of her shoulders and held her at arm's length. "Look, I'm here to take you and your sister back. Is there going to be trouble getting you out?"

She lifted incredibly beautiful eyes and presented him with the most enchanting smile he had ever seen. She glanced over her shoulder at the palace, and Stuart's eyes dipped down to the alluring curves of her body. God help him, he had been celibate too long this time to ignore a woman like her.

"You can't let them see you with me," she warned, grabbing his arm and pulling him behind the willow fronds, "or they'll probably kill you."

Stuart didn't like the sound of that. "Kill me? What'd you mean?"

"Watch out!" she cried as water splashed close behind him. Stuart dropped and turned, but not before something hit hard against his back and knocked him to his knees. He jerked his gun out of the holster, then backed off when he found the girl's elephant right behind him, making threatening sounds and swinging his massive trunk at him again.

"Get back, Prafulla Veda! He's a friend!" Anjelica was shouting, but the elephant took another violent

jab at him, then lifted his trunk in the air and gave
a hostile cry.

"What's wrong with it? What did I do?" he managed breathlessly as Anjelica pushed its shoulder
and the beast lumbered a few yards downstream,
still eyeing him with rage. He hadn't been around
elephants much—never, to be exact.

"Oh, nothing. She just gets jealous when men get
too close to me. I shouldn't have hugged you like I
did."

Stuart scowled downstream at the possessive
pachyderm. "Just keep it away from me. Now tell
me who's going to kill me? And where's your father?
I'm here to find him, too."

Her eyes darkened a deeper shade of gray, and
she looked away. "Papa died three years ago, and we
haven't been allowed to leave. That's why I'm so
glad to see you."

"You're a British citizen. Why didn't you contact
Major Coleridge at Agra?"

"The maharajah wouldn't let me."

"Why?"

"He's too fond of me," she answered simply.

Stuart could understand the maharajah's interest.
Any red-blooded man would want to keep Anjelica
Blake around. "Surely he's not stupid enough to
defy British law, is he?"

"The British cannot dictate terms here in
Udaipur. The prince is the only law, but there is a
way—"

When a bell began to peal somewhere high

above, Anjelica shot a fearful look toward the towering palace walls. "I have to go! The guards'll see
us!"

"Wait, dammit!" Stuart's low words gave her little
pause as she waded out to where the elephant was
wallowing and snorting angrily.

"Come to the Amba Pol tomorrow at noon, that's
the north gate of the walled city," she called back
softly. "I'll meet you there and tell you what to do
next."

"Wait, that's too bloody risky!"

The girl ignored his objections as she adroitly
rewrapped the cloth around her hips just before a
soldier wearing a long black coat and a small crimson turban appeared on the road leading to the
gate. Stuart concealed himself as the guard called
out to the girl in his own tongue.

Anjelica Blake replied in the same language and
immediately led the elephant by its trunk toward
the bank. When she called a command, the elephant bowed her head and allowed her to use her
trunk as a ladder up to his head. She scampered up
with easy agility and settled herself on the back of
its neck. As she urged the lumbering beast up the
road toward the guard, Stuart hoped like hell
Anjelica Blake knew what she was doing. Sum-
moning him inside the walls of the palace didn't
sound like such a great idea, especially with the
maharajah being so fond of her. But he had to trust
her judgment. What other choice did he have?

Chapter Two

L ate the next afternoon Stuart wasn't sure the
beautiful girl on the elephant was real or a
figment of his heat-crazed imagination. He had
come to the palace as she had directed and found
only a contingent of burly royal guards at the Amba
Pol who spoke no English and had no use for trying to.

Now he stood waiting in a room straight out of
the tales of the *Arabian Nights*. Everything was the
color of gold—the walls and ceiling of fine gold
leaf, the shimmering silk draperies, and carpet of a
deeper yellow hue. Hell, there was enough gold
glimmering around him to underwrite the entire
Confederate treasury.

After nearly four hours during which he alter-
nated between pacing and lounging on plush divans
covered with rich gold brocade and amber silk
fringe, he got up and prowled outside onto a narrow
iron balcony overlooking a small walled garden.
Several other windows faced the interior courtyard
from the opposite side, all tall and arched in the

Hindu design with ornate ivory screens to provide
ventilation and privacy.

The Maharajah Shashur Sikh of Udaipur sure as
hell spared no coin on home furnishings, he mused,
but was too annoyed with his state of affairs to be
overly impressed. He'd had reservations about
waltzing into the bloody place, and now he was un-
armed, too, except for the derringer he had been
prudent enough to tuck in his right boot. The sen-
tries at the first portico had taken his Colt revolver
and gun belt, and Stuart felt naked without them.
He cursed the girl under his breath.

The quiet of the garden was suddenly disrupted
as two green parakeets fluttered to perch on the
branch of an orange tree. The pair warbled and
trilled their joy in being alive and from the lush
green depths of the foliage where blue and white
mosaic-tiled paths meandered he heard the music
of a trickling fountain.

The peace and tranquillity did nothing to relieve
his growing anxiety. He was trapped inside a gigantic fortress that seemed to be inhabited by no one
other than black-coated guards posted at intervals
in the long, intersecting marble corridors through
which he had been led.

Getting out of the palace would be more difficult
than getting in had been, that was for damn sure.
To complicate matters, he had yet to meet anyone
who understood a word of English. He had repeated his name and a request for an audience with
the maharajah to at least six different soldiers man-

ning the six locked interior gates through which he
had passed, and the maze of winding halls had
been so confusing he probably couldn't find his way
out if he did manage to escape.

Stuart turned when he heard the muted sound of
a gong and found an old man standing in the
threshold. The ancient Hindu looked to be around
eighty. His skin was very dark brown and wizened
with deep grooves and pockmarks. Although slight
of stature, the man stood erect and proud in a rich
coat of shiny emerald satin that reached nearly to
his knees. He wore loose trousers gathered tight at
the ankles and embroidered all over with black silk
thread. As with nearly everyone Stuart had encountered in Udaipur, his hair was concealed by a small
turban that indicated his rank with a large, square-
cut ruby securing the folds of black satin. All in all,
the man certainly did not look like the run-of-the-
mill servant.

Without speaking, the man motioned for Stuart
to follow him. Relieved to be out of the blinding
gold room, Stuart crossed the thick Indian carpet,
hoping that he wouldn't end up in some dank dun-
geon where no one would ever find him again.
Once outside the gilded chamber he was led swiftly
along a twenty-foot-wide corridor of gold-veined,
black marble.

As far as he could see, the highly polished floor
flowed like a mirror-surfaced, ebony river into mysterious depths of the white palace of Udaipur. They
climbed one elaborate pink marble staircase with

graceful gold candelabras at the base, then two more of similar grandeur as they walked for a stretch of twenty minutes. With each step, Stuart grew angrier with Anjelica Blake for luring him into this trap. He liked to be in control, and he sure as hell wasn't at the moment.

The black turbaned Indian continued at a fast clip considering his age, passing dozens of rich chambers furnished lavishly with brocades and low silk couches and chairs. His soft satin shoes had felt soles that made no sound, only drawing more attention to Stuart's heavy black boots, which clicked sharply with each step he took, the sound echoing loudly into the unsettling silence of the marble halls.

Thank God, Stuart thought when the Indian paused before a brass-studded ebony door. The portal was at least twenty feet wide; the breadth of its passageway so vast it would sustain the girl's surly elephant. And it probably did, he mused sourly as the servant made a great show of reverence as he turned the solid gold handles. As the immense panels swung inward, the man backed away with head bowed and palms pressed together.

Warily, Stuart stepped inside, then halted on the threshold, completely awestruck by the throne room of Udaipur. He had found the maharajah's palace extraordinarily ostentatious from the outset but there was no fitting description for the opulence upon which he now looked. Even the lavish rooms of Buckingham Palace where he had escorted Marian on occasion seemed to pale in comparison.

High above his head the white ceiling was edged with gold but frescoed with scenes of gardens where maidens worshiped elephant-headed Hindu gods and fierce warriors with multiple sets of arms fought ugly, masked demons. Eighteen black marble pillars lined a center hall at the far end of which rose a dais draped in purple silk. Molded of pure gold, the throne shone brilliantly in a single shaft of light descending from somewhere high above. Two absolutely huge black men stood on either side of the throne. Naked except for black satin trousers, each held a pair of lethal-curved scimitars across his chest. No one else was evident, and the two royal bodyguards stared straight ahead as if they did not see him.

Now what the devil was he supposed to do? His fingers itched to find their way around Anjelica Blake's slender neck. He was no doubt expected to approach the throne, but he sure as hell didn't know the correct protocol concerning an Indian maharajah.

The burly bodyguards did not move a muscle, and Stuart took a deep breath and started the long walk down the black marble floor. As he drew closer, he decided he would identify himself and request an audience.

A crimson velvet bench was positioned below the throne of the mighty potentate, and Stuart stopped and debated whether he should kneel or sit down.

"Don't kneel."

The soft directive had come from his left, and he turned and stared at Anjelica Blake where she sat on a huge black cushion tasseled in gold, half hidden by a length of flowing azure silk. He blinked in disbelief. He looked again and realized he wasn't imagining the bushy black mustache just below her pert nose. Otherwise she was dressed identically to the old man who had led him through the palace except that her garments were of black silk, her black turban set with a gigantic round diamond. Easily the size of Stuart's thumbnail, it glittered fiercely, rivaling the silver beauty of her eyes. She looked lovely even with the clump of ridiculous fake hair stuck to her lip.

"It's about time you showed up," he muttered in an undertone, glancing warily at the royal bodyguards. They stared into space.

"I'm sorry, but the maharajah insisted that I entertain him throughout the morning." She didn't bother to lower her voice. Stuart took that as a positive sign. Her next remarks weren't so encouraging.

"Listen carefully, Mr. Delaney. Now that you are inside the gates, you must do exactly what I tell you. You really must, or the maharajah could very well have you beheaded. Do you understand?"

Stuart was incredulous. "Why the hell didn't you share that crucial little tidbit before I walked in here?" he demanded angrily.

"Because I was afraid you might not wish to come if you thought you might be executed."

"And you're damn right." Stuart clamped his teeth together and enjoyed the fantasy of wringing her neck.

"Don't look at me with your face all red like that, or the Nubian slaves will have to thrash you," she advised softly, her pretty mustachioed face a bit worried. Stuart began to feel as if he were trapped in some ridiculous dream, then decided he had better take the girl's advice when he found the two black men looking at him as if picturing his head on a block.

"Why the devil are you wearing that stupid mustache?" he asked with as pleasant a smile as he could dredge up.

"Because here in Udaipur I am a man."

Good God, the girl was insane. That had to be it. Maybe that was the ugly truth James Blake had been hiding from his English kith and kin.

"You could've fooled me."

Anjelica sighed as if highly exasperated. "I'm not really. The maharajah decreed me a male so that I could become an advisor and assist him with English-speaking supplicants. My father acted in that capacity before he died. He requires me to wear the mustache so no man will desire me in a carnal way."

"Well, I've got news for him. It doesn't work."

"Your voice harbors anger, Mr. Delaney," she warned with a trace of a frown. "Do you wish to be beaten with bamboo rods? Is that your wish?"

"Oh yeah, lady, a good flogging really appeals to me at the moment," he ground out tightly.

"Surely you don't mean that—"

"Of course I don't mean it, dammit!"

Delicately arched blond brows knitted in vague concern. "There's no need for such profanity, Mr. Delaney. You are acting most unwisely. You are much too intelligent to allow your male arrogance to dictate your words."

Stuart clenched his jaw so hard he could actually feel a vein pumping in his temple. She was right. He was at her mercy. He needed a moment to get hold of his anger. It took more than a moment but his voice had a degree of calm when next he spoke.

"Why don't you just tell me how I can get out of here alive, Miss Blake?"

Anjelica smiled as if pleased with his self-control. "Just trust me, Mr. Delaney. I do know what I'm doing here. The maharajah understands very little English, so you can speak freely to me without worrying. When the brass gong is struck, he will enter and take his place upon the golden throne. You must keep your eyes focused on the floor until the gong sounds a second time. Then you must rise and bow deeply from the waist. Don't kneel to him under any circumstances or he will think you of lower caste. Most importantly, you must never lust openly after my body the way you did yesterday at the river. If the maharajah senses that you desire to have congress with me in the way of a concubine or lover, he will lapse into a jealous rage. If that happens, I'm not sure I can save you from harm."

This could not possibly be happening, Stuart thought helplessly, and he wasn't thrilled to hear the prince was enamored of her. It certainly wouldn't help Stuart's quest to get her out of India. "Does that mean you're his lover?"

"Of course not. I just told you that I am a man here in Udaipur. I can't be anyone's lover until he decrees me a woman again."

She's nuts, Stuart thought, and I'm never going to get out of here in one piece.

"Please don't look at me like that, Mr. Delaney. I have a very good plan for our escape. The maharajah trusts me implicitly. Just don't show any anger toward him or any lust for me, and you'll be perfectly safe."

"I'll try to restrain myself," he agreed, any desire he had entertained for Anjelica Blake withering rapidly.

He jumped when the six-foot-wide brass gong behind the throne was struck by a black-clad servant with a mallet. Quivering metallic vibrations reverberated down the long empty hall for nearly five minutes.

"Quick, bow low and keep your face averted until I say you can look."

Stuart decided his best bet was to obey her every whim, no matter how stupid it seemed. He was trapped in her weird world with no way out. He bent deeply from the waist and held the pose as

Anjelica launched into a rapid discourse in the Hindi language. By the time she finished her lengthy speech, he wondered if he could straighten his back.

"All right, you can stand up and look but don't stare at the maharajah overly long."

Stuart did so and stared wordlessly at the little boy perched cross-legged on the golden throne.

"He's just a kid," he muttered, an aside to Anjelica.

"He'll be ten soon."

Stuart returned his attention to the boy. The all-powerful Indian prince looked small for his age. On the other hand, he was an exceedingly handsome young man and did portray a certain air of authority, even as young as he was.

While Stuart watched silently, the child lounged to one side, propping his elbow on a stack of soft crimson velvet pillows. He was dressed in gold brocade to match the rest of his palace, the gleaming satin cloth shimmering with lavish silver embroidery around the mandarin collar and down the front of his short tunic. He did not wear a turban or a crown, but a small, flat-crowned hat of matching fabric, every inch of which was adorned with diamonds, rubies, and emeralds. His little pierced ears were hung with diamonds even bigger than the one decorating Angelica's turban. Chokers of pearls, onyx beads, and gold coins encircled his neck, dozens of gold bracelets jangled on his wrists, and his fingers sparkled with ten gold rings.

Stuart inclined his head courteously, vastly relieved to find out he was dealing with a mere boy instead of a grown man. Imperiously, the prince waved a small hand. Immediately, a young, black-robed servant hustled forth from the waving silk curtains, carrying a small black-lacquered casket set with gold hinges. He placed the gift on the ground in front of Stuart, lifted the lid, then backed away with deferential respect.

Stuart stared speechlessly at the wealth of gold coins and glittering jewels.

"Say something," Anjelica prodded softly. "Anything will do, but hurry up, and try to look impressed with his gifts."

"I am bloody impressed. Is this really mine?"

Instead of answering, Anjelica lapsed into the indecipherable tongue of India again. The little maharajah inclined his head and nodded.

"What are you saying now?" Stuart asked the girl, a bit more comfortable with the way Anjelica Blake was handling the situation.

"I told him you are the great American king, Nicholas Sedgwick."

Stuart jerked a startled look at her. "What?"

"I told you not to look at me with lust."

"It's not lust, I assure you," he said, attempting a pleasant tone without much success. "Are you out of your mind telling him that? America doesn't have a king."

"I know that," she replied as if he had insulted her, "but Shashi doesn't. He's just a little boy and he's fascinated with America and the redskinned natives who roam the big plains out in the West. I told him that you're the Exalted King of Louisiana and all the Atlantic seaboard and that all the redskinned Americans are your loyal subjects."

"Good God, you can't be serious—"

Stuart's groan ended abruptly when the young maharajah spoke up for the first time.

"The maharajah has invited you to become his guest here in the palace. Nod with a lot of eagerness, then smile real big and say how honored you are to be invited."

"No, I don't want to stay here," Stuart said with a big fake grin, "say whatever you have to to get me out of here tonight."

"You will be killed if you don't stay here."

"Maybe I will then, dammit."

"You're going to have to say more than that because I have a lot more I need to tell him." Anjelica's voice had taken a sharper edge. "Remember, I'm pretending to translate what you say. You're not being the least bit helpful, Mr. Delaney."

With some effort, Stuart kept his sanguine expression but his lips were so stiff with anger that he wasn't sure he could get them to move. "What the devil do you want me to say now?"

"Well, I don't care. Recite the alphabet if you can't think of anything else, or just carry on a conversation with me so he'll think I'm translating your words to him."

"Look, I've had enough of this. Tell the kid the

truth. I have a legal document from the British courts giving me temporary guardianship over you and your sister until we get back to London. Tell him he'll have to abide by it or face Major Coleridge's garrison at Agra."

She shook her head. "And what would stop Shashi from just having you murdered, your body mutilated and flung into the lake, then denying you ever showed up here at all?"

Her calmly uttered scenario did give Stuart some pause.

"Now, please," she continued in the wake of his silence. "Say my name clearly in English and bow very low."

"Your name? Why?"

"Just do it, Mr. Delaney."

"Angelica Blake," he said smiling and bowing but watching the girl out of the corner of his eye. He was surprised to see that she had adopted a frightened expression as she translated. Stuart dared a glance at the kid and knew right off that whatever Anjelica was saying was not to the little maharajah's liking.

"Oh, Lord, what'd you tell him this time? He's stomping his foot," he hissed an aside to Anjelica, feeling totally out of control and growing more and more alarmed as the boy threw one of his pillows at him.

"I told him that you're my husband."

"What?"

"I told him that you're the one I've been married

to since I was a little girl and that you've finally come to claim me. Don't worry, he won't be angry long because I told him that you've brought him a very rich dowry from America. He likes presents."

"I didn't bring him anything. Look at him, he looks like he's going to cry."

"Well, of course, he's sad," Anjelica replied calmly as if Stuart weren't particularly bright. "He's been planning to make me a woman and to take me for his most favored wife when he gets old enough. Don't worry, I know what I'm doing."

"Don't worry?"

"Mr. Delaney, please, I know the best way to get us out of Udaipur."

The maharajah stood up and threw a couple more pillows around, then cried a few shrill words in his own language, so upset now that his little be-jeweled hat fell off.

"He says he will consider our troth but that on the threat of death you are not to see me again until he decides whether or not I can become your bride. I guess you'd better kneel this time because he's angrier than I thought he'd be. Actually, I've never seen him throw such a tantrum. He's really a very sweet boy."

"Well, that's just wonderful. I'm glad I put my life in your hands."

"Do it, Mr. Delaney, before he really does lose his temper and has you beaten with bamboo sticks."

Stuart did it. When he looked up again, the pint-sized prince did not look even slightly appeased. The child uttered a couple of more curt sentences in Hindi, then petulantly gestured for Anjelica to move farther away from Stuart.

"He said he'll think about all this and speak again on the subject tomorrow at the tiger hunt."

"Tiger hunt? What tiger hunt?"

"I must go now. Wait here, and a servant will come and show you to your apartments. As long as you stay inside your rooms, no harm will come to you. Lock your door in case his assassins are sent to murder you in your sleep. I really don't think Shashi would do such a thing, but he's awfully upset."

Stuart could do no more than stare at her. Anjelica had no time to instruct him further as the maharajah gestured angrily at her. She rose gracefully and hurried out of sight behind the azure silks. The little potentate of Udaipur stomped out in an angry huff, and his bodyguards fell in behind their prince.

As silence descended over the immense chamber, Stuart stared at the empty throne. Good God, what had he gotten himself into?

Chapter Three

The big American was going to ruin everything if he wasn't careful, Anjelica thought furiously as she picked up a long piece of black silk. Wrapping it tightly into a turban, she grimaced with distaste. Now she was going to have to sneak into his rooms, which would be dangerous because the prince had ordered the guards to watch his every move.

But Shashi's anger couldn't compete with Stuart Delaney's. She shivered just thinking about the awful look in his clear blue eyes when he heard the lies she had to tell the prince. Of course, he didn't realize her motives or that she knew best how to handle the maharajah. She had to make him see reason or he just might pack up and leave Udaipur without her. Fierce determination narrowed her eyes. Under no circumstances could she let that happen. Delaney was her only chance to escape the palace.

The midnight hour had long since passed and she knew from experience that by now the guards would be drowsy and inattentive at their posts. She extinguished the oil lamp on the table beside the window and pushed out the lacy iron shutters.

A steady drone of crickets rose from the gardens. High above in the starry heavens, the moon sailed like a proud flagship, full and white, gleaming off the white walls of the palace and casting deep, foreboding shadows around its foundations. She waited impatiently for the bright lunar ball to disappear behind a mound of fleeting clouds. The night darkened as if a shroud had dropped over the landscape, and she swung agilely atop the broad marble sill. Though the climb was perilous, Anjelica felt no fear. For the last five years both she and her sister had had the run of the palace. Few of the restrictions suffered by the other women of the royal court applied to them. Her father had encouraged his daughters to run and play like boys and because of his leniency she was surefooted and strong of limb.

Stretching out far enough to place her toe in a crack between the stones, she slowly made her way up past the dark windows on the floor above her apartments. Within minutes she had reached the curved red tiles of the roof and hunched low as she ran quickly through the dark shadows, knowing full well that the clouds would move swiftly off the face of the moon.

The prince would have ordered old Kapir to settle the American visitor in the richly lavish scarlet chambers. By tradition all foreigners were housed far away from both the royal wing and the Court of

the Lotus where the women lived. Stuart Delaney's
rooms would be watched around the clock, but the
windows of his apartments overlooked the lake. No
one would ever expect anyone to gain entrance that
way.

She hoped Delaney had not tried to leave. He
would not be afraid because he was a brave man.
She had sensed his courage instinctively from the
first moment she had met him and had been disappointed he wasn't her English husband. He was everything that she had dreamed Nicholas Sedgwick
would be—tall, handsome, and courageous enough
to come after her when her real husband would
not.

Her mother had promised Anjelica to the son of
her best friend in England when Anjelica was only
ten. The marriage had been finalized by proxy and
against the wishes of Anjelica's father. He had insisted that she should be able to pick her own husband so she could be happy, and Anjelica knew he
spoke from experience. His own marriage had been
arranged but he had never loved her mother the
way he had loved Ramadeep.

When she was younger Anjelica didn't think
about her marital status at all, but now with her father gone, she realized that her mother had been
wise. Her roots were in England, and it was time
for her to go back there. Poor little Suzannah
couldn't even remember London and considered
herself more Hindu than British. Her mother would

have hated that even more than she had hated India.

When she reached the east wing, Anjelica avoided the guard turret and crept past the outer wall lined with narrow arrow apertures. In this part of the palace most of the rooms had stone balconies, and she used them in her descent to the scarlet rooms. Delaney's windows were opened to receive the cool night breeze off the lake, and she crouched momentarily on the tiny porch, then dropped soundlessly into the dark room. The scarlet chambers lay in complete silence, and she paused, allowing her eyes to adjust to the inky blackness.

As she took a wary step, air waved against her cheek. Before she could move, a strong arm snaked around her neck. The bicep flexed hard as a rock, cutting off her breath. She struggled helplessly against her assailant, then was jerked completely off her feet and flung bodily onto the bed. Then the man was atop her, his hands clenched lethally around her neck.

"No, stop—" she choked out somehow, fighting to breathe.

The stranglehold lessened, then stopped all together, and she sucked in a weak breath as a match was struck. Light flared, then Stuart Delaney was looming over her, gigantic, fearsome, and furious. His eyes gleamed brilliant blue in the flickering flame, and despite his rage, she thought him the most magnificent man she had ever seen.

"Good God, girl, you're lucky I didn't snap your bloody neck. Don't you know better than to sneak up on a man like that?"

Anjelica put a trembling hand to her throat and forced down a hard swallow. He lit the candle beside the bed, and her heart lurched when he glared down at her, his fists planted on his narrow hips.

"I'm sorry, but I had to find a way to talk with you."

"How the hell did you get out on the balcony?" he demanded harshly. "The drop's straight down and about three floors, at that."

His frown deepened as she struggled to her knees. She was so aware of his masculinity now that her voice sounded ragged. "It's the only way I could get past your guards."

"Then you're a little fool. One wrong step and you'd be just about as dead as you can get."

Stuart Delaney turned away. Scowling blackly, he tunneled restless fingers through wavy black hair that fell to his collar. The candlelight shone on the chiseled contours of his profile, and she admired his male beauty until he turned on her again. She tensed for another onslaught of his ire.

"Did I hurt you?" he asked, surprising her but still looking more than annoyed. "I thought you were one of the assassins you saw fit to warn me about."

He was staring down at her, no longer so angry but still forbidding. A nervous flutter erupted deep inside her body, or was it something else that caused the response to quicken deep in her loins? Whatever it was, it was embarrassing. Her face flooded with hot color, and she rushed into a hasty explanation.

"I came to tell you about the tiger hunt."

"Forget the tiger hunt. Why the hell did you tell the prince I wanted to marry you?"

"Because the maharajah knows that I am married to a man named Sedgwick. That's why he won't let me go. He didn't expect anyone would come here after me now that so much time has passed. That's why he got so upset. You see, he's in love with me."

He snorted derisively. "He's not old enough to be in love with you."

"He's already got four wives."

That pronouncement stilled Stuart's agitated pacing. "You cannot be serious."

"Royalty marries young here in India, but the marriages won't be consummated until he reaches puberty."

"No kidding."

She flushed at his sarcasm and at the way he was looking at her. Appalled, she realized she was staring at him, too, with open fascination. Most of her life she had been around men more than other women, had even studied the acts of congress between the sexes in the *Kama Sutra,* yet now she blushed and quivered and acted like a ninny when Stuart Delaney merely glanced at her. She had to get a grip on herself. After all, she was a married woman whether she had met her husband or not.

"You have to play along and marry me," she said firmly. "It's the only way Shashi will allow me to leave these walls."

Anjelica stiffened self-consciously as his eyes raked down her body, slowly, appraisingly, until goose bumps went sweeping up her arms and legs.

"I wasn't paid enough to marry you, or anyone else," he said at last.

"It won't be real, of course, you do understand that, don't you? I'm already married to Nicholas Sedgwick by English law, and besides that, it'll be a Hindu ceremony that won't be binding."

He didn't look any more convinced. She pulled out the pouch she had hidden in her tunic and tossed it onto the bed between them. "Here's a dowry you can present to him in the morning."

Stuart picked up the black velvet bag and spilled the contents into his palm.

"Good God, this emerald's worth a fortune. Where'd you get it?"

"My father was held in high esteem as the royal advisor to Shashi's father, the last Maharajah of Udaipur. He was given many gifts by those wishing him to use his influence in their behalf. I have many more precious jewels, some even larger than that one."

"You actually sound proud that your father took bribes."

"It is the accepted way in Udaipur." She didn't like his condemnation. Frowning, she took out the second gift. "This is a box of Shashi's favorite chocolates. They are made in China and come to us through the northern province of Bhutan. He rarely gets them so he'll be very pleased."

Stuart Delaney barely glanced at the small red lacquered box. "If bribes are acceptable around here, why the hell can't I just offer one to the prince?"

"The prince would never take money for me. Or for the children, either. You see, Suzannah is his best friend, and my brother Sanjay's his cousin. We'll have to think of a way to smuggle them out without him finding out."

"Your brother's a cousin to the maharajah?"

Anjelica nodded. "Papa married Shashi's oldest sister after we came here to live."

"Why did you come here?"

Even though her father had been gone for several years, it hurt Anjelica to talk about him. They had been very close. She still missed him every day. But Stuart Delaney had a right to know the answers to his questions. "About six years ago the Indian recruits in the British army rose up against the Crown. There were atrocities on both sides during the fighting, but my father blamed the British officers for ignoring Hindu culture and religion. He loved India. That's why he came to Udaipur and married Ramadeep."

"Where's she now?"

For an awful instant, Anjelica heard the terrible screams, smelled the smoke of the funeral pyre, heard the chanting of the priests. Bile rose in her throat, and she fought her revulsion at the horrible memory.

"She died in suttee."

"What's that?"

She hesitated, not wanting to tell him. "Suttee is the rite of widow-burning. Ramadeep thought it was her duty to throw herself alive into my father's funeral pyre. It is a commonplace practice here in India."

Stuart Delaney did not hide his repugnance. "That's barbaric."

"Yes, and that's another reason why you've got to get us back to England before the prince forces me to wed him." She studied his expression for any sign of relenting. "I want you to know how grateful we are to you for coming for us. We had about given up hope."

He shook his head impatiently. "Better save your gratitude until we get out of here in one piece. How do you plan to smuggle out your brother and sister?"

"I'll think of a way."

"It better be damn good if your brother's a member of the royal family."

Anjelica couldn't give him the details because she hadn't figured them out yet. "It's good. I must go now. If they find me here, they'll kill you."

"Please don't let me keep you then," he said icily.

Realizing his anger had come back, Anjelica slid off the bed and hurried to the window. She turned back just before she stepped onto the balcony.

"Tomorrow do everything I tell you without question. Shashi will be judging you on your manliness and bravery. If he doesn't find you worthy of me, he'll send you away."

"How the hell am I supposed to prove myself?"

Anjelica thought it best if he didn't know until it happened. He was upset enough. "We'll worry about that tomorrow."

"Like hell. We'll worry about it now, lady—"

She escaped out the window before he could stop her and began her precarious climb upward. When she reached the roof, Stuart was watching her from his balcony. He wouldn't like what was going to happen on the tiger hunt. She shivered to think how furious he was going to be.

Chapter Four

Not only was the Blake girl strange, she was reckless, too, that's all there was to it. Hell, how many women did he know who would scurry up the side of a wall in the dead of night like a sticky-footed lizard? Now she was making life-and-death decisions concerning him and that was one scary thought. Unfortunately, he didn't have too many other options. He had to play along with her absurd plot until he got a chance to get—with or without her and her siblings—out of Udaipur. The lovestruck prince was only a boy but he still possessed the power to lop off Stuart's head on a whim. That was plenty of reason for Stuart not to rub the kid the wrong way.

At least he had his belongings back from the inn where he had left them, delivered early that morning by two burly henchmen dressed in the red turbans and black silk uniforms of the Udaipur royal guard.

Now, he was being marched down endless deserted marble corridors between his armed nurse-

48

maids like a condemned felon on his way to the gallows. That might very well be exactly where he was going, and he was glad he still had the small caliber derringer secreted in his boot. On the other hand, it was hardly the weapon with which to confront twin scimitar-swinging Nubians or a bloodthirsty Bengal tiger. If the girl didn't get him killed as a result of her cock-and-bull stories, he still had the jungle cat to worry about.

The maharajah awaited him on a wide, covered balcony supported by a long row of carved pillars. Anjelica Blake sat beside the cushioned ivory throne on a low divan of red velvet. The carpeted terrace overlooked a vast grassy courtyard enclosed on three sides by the high palace walls. Massive red doors distinguished a structure against the far perimeter, which Stuart assumed housed the maharajah's elephants. A long stone ramp led out of the courtyard through another gigantic wooden gate set with sturdy black iron hinges. One large elephant swung slowly toward them across the grass led by a trainer. Unfortunately, the beast looked exactly like the one who had taken a violent dislike to Stuart the day before yesterday.

Anjelica had yet to look at him, and Stuart didn't know whether that was a good sign or a bad one. She still wore the same masculine attire—ridiculous mustache, diamond-studded turban, and all.

Bowing politely, he seated himself on a low leather bench and waited apprehensively for the prince to speak. The boy was dressed resplendently in a royal blue coat and matching trousers and an elaborate gold hat decorated with a purple ostrich plume. Shashi, or whatever the hell Anjelica called him, looked as irked and disgruntled as Stuart felt.

The prince first ignored Stuart's presence while making a great show of holding Anjelica's hand, then shot a threatening glare in Stuart's direction. The little tyke was enamored of the blond beauty, all right, inasmuch as a nine-year-old, pre-adolescent maharajah could be. When he finally said something to Stuart, Anjelica translated softly with downcast eyes.

"The Maharajah of Udaipur wishes a good morning to the esteemed King of Louisiana and emperor of all the redskins. He extends an invitation for your royal highness to join us in the excitement of a tiger shoot. Nod politely and get out the emerald. Bow your head and tell me you wish to present it to the maharajah. Please try not to look so sour. Don't you ever smile?"

"Not when I'm caught up in a stupid mess like this," he muttered, attempting a pleasant look that didn't come off well at all. Nonetheless, he repeated her words and got the emerald out of his coat pocket. When he started to rise, Anjelica stopped him.

"You mustn't approach the prince. Kapir, the royal vizier, will present your gift to His Highness."

The old servant with the ruby on his turban took the heavy stone from Stuart, at which time Anjelica went into a lengthy recitation the meaning of which Stuart had a feeling he was better off not knowing. The boy king gazed with only mild interest at the priceless jewel but exclaimed with delirious delight over the red box of chocolates that Stuart brought out next.

"The Maharajah of Udaipur expresses his sincere gratitude and wishes you a long, healthful life," Anjelica was translating now as the old vizier opened the box of sweets for the prince. "You see, I told you he'd be pleased with the candy."

"Is he pleased enough not to order me murdered?" Anjelica's delicate blond brows came together slightly but she kept her voice low and neutral. "We'll leave for the village of Nanpur as soon as Prafulla Veda is brought to the wall."

Stuart glanced at the big she-elephant being coaxed and prodded into position at a boarding platform in the stone balustrade. He wasn't any more eager to ride the elephant than he was to hunt the tiger. "Aren't there any decent carriages in India?"

"The elephant is the vehicle of kings, and the prince prefers the safety and comfort of the royal howdah."

Stuart thought the seating contraption perched precariously on the giant creature's back looked neither safe nor comfortable.

"Is that thing going to hold the three of us?"

"Please quit asking me so many questions or the

maharajah's going to get jealous. He already thinks
you lust after me."

Stuart clamped his teeth. That was a laugh. After
all she'd put him through? Dammit, he didn't like
women bossing him around and he didn't like
pompous little kids, either. He watched incredulously as the royal prince commenced gobbling
down chocolate candy in much the same manner as
a starving jackal. Everyone sat silently as his highness chomped and moaned ecstatically over each
piece while an emerald large enough to buy the
South a fully supplied blockade runner lay ignored
on a gold tufted pillow.

Finally, the maharajah disposed of the last morsel
and closed his eyes in a dramatic expression of
bliss. He proceeded to suck every vestige of resid-
ual candy off all ten fingers, one at a time. Afterward, he grinned magnanimously at Stuart,
revealing perfect little white teeth. He launched eagerly into a smiling, rapid-fire speech in his native
tongue.

"The Maharajah of Udaipur says he likes you a
little bit better now, but not much." Anjelica
seemed disproportionately overjoyed with the be-
grudging compliment. "You see, if you just cooperate and show great courage against the tiger, I'm
sure he'll relent and decree me a woman again."

Stuart was not impressed. "What do you mean
'against the tiger?' "

"You'll see." She rose with fluid grace as Shashi

left his throne and skipped toward the elephant landing.

Prafulla Veda was now in place, lavishly caparisoned with shimmering gold tapestry cloths that hung nearly to the ground. Long purple plumes were attached to her ornate silver headgear, and her flappy ears were heavily pierced and set with silver ornaments and a few more waving plumes.

The howdah itself was double-seated, roofed with a brocade canopy, and held in place by leather straps secured beneath the elephant's tail and girth. The driver was dressed all in gold and kept Prafulla Veda in place with sharply uttered commands and a short wooden stick with a metal jab on one end.

As Shashi's two giant Othellos stood at attention, the maharajah scampered across a crimson-carpeted plank and into the royal howdah with less than regal comportment. Anjelica followed with a provocative sway of her slender hips, which Stuart watched with appreciation. Then she curled her luscious little self gracefully on the seat opposite her princely playmate.

"You'll have to sit here with me because no one can enjoy such intimacy with the maharajah."

"Not even the King of Louisiana?"

Anjelica ignored the remark, but at the sound of Stuart's voice, Prafulla Veda swung her massive head around and watched him with one large beady eye.

This whole situation was ludicrous, Stuart thought as he stepped onto the plank. Halfway across, the elephant lurched slightly but enough to disengage the ramp. Stuart grabbed desperately for the rail of the howdah and barely managed to pull himself inside.

"What's the matter with that stupid elephant?" he demanded of Anjelica as he slumped into the seat beside her.

"She just hates you, is all. Don't touch my shoulder with yours. The prince wouldn't like that."

Stuart muttered an extremely unpleasant oath under his breath, not at all sure the flimsy contraption would support a man of his size. Inside, he found the howdah to be of similar design to a lightweight English carriage. The sides were open with silk-padded rails, and both seats were cushioned with soft velvet pillows and silken shawls. The crimson and black brocade roof provided the shade necessary to shield the occupants from the broiling Indian sun. Settling awkwardly into the small but sumptuous enclosure, he attempted to accommodate his long legs in the cramped foot space.

The prince waved a regal hand, and the driver prodded the ornery animal with his stick. The howdah lurched precariously to one side, and Stuart glanced warily down at the ground fifteen feet below.

"You'll find traveling by elephant is most enjoyable," Anjelica remarked in a surprising show of enthusiasm. "Though I would much prefer to drive Prafulla Veda as the mahout."

"Mahout?"

"The mahout is the person who guides the elephant."

Stuart turned slightly to where he could see the mahout, then rearranged his legs, his thoughts returning to the confrontation with the tiger. "All right, I'm in this thing and can't get out, so just tell me the truth. Am I supposed to fight the tiger? Is that how I get to be your husband?"

Anjelica ignored his sarcasm, endowing him with a friendly smile. "Yes, but you'll also be doing all the people of Udaipur a great service. The tiger's a man-eater who has already killed four people near the village of Nanpur. It's the most vicious, cunning Bengal ever known to roam in Udaipur."

"Why doesn't that surprise me?" Stuart asked dryly. "Isn't it a bit dangerous for the prince to come out here with a killer tiger on the loose?"

"We will be safe atop Prafulla Veda, and we will leave you with the bait goat while we ride the elephant to a safe place to wait until the tiger attacks you."

"This just keeps getting better and better," Stuart grumbled furiously, wondering just how many other ways the girl would come up with to put his life on the line before he escaped with his skin from Udaipur. He could forget about the twenty-thousand-pound reward.

Suddenly the prince began a rapid discourse in Hindi, ending the excited speech with a forefinger pointed accusingly at Stuart's head. More threats of beheading, Stuart presumed as Anjelica's gaze fol-

lowed Shashi's regard. "He wants to know if a wild
animal caused that wicked scar near your eye."

"Yeah, an animal called a Yankee. I didn't duck
fast enough during the battle of Franklin."

"What is Franklin?"

"It's a town in Tennessee near Nashville."

Her beautiful silver-gray eyes studied him con-
templatively, then she turned back to the prince
and started her translation. It didn't take Stuart
long to realize her explanation was a lot longer and
more complicated than his answer had been. He
braced himself for another preposterous story.
Whatever she had fabricated, however, the prince
obviously found to his liking. He exclaimed and
clapped his hands in delight. Even the contingent
of royal foot soldiers walking on the ground around
Prafulla Veda gazed admiringly up at him.

"What the hell did you tell him this time?" he demanded warily, half afraid to hear.

"I told him that you were sent by your exalted father, the emperor, to the high western mountains of
your country that lie across vast empty plains where
the red Indians roam looking for vicious American
animals called buffalos—"

"How the hell do you know about buffalo?"

"I used to live in the United States."

Stuart's first impulse was not to believe her. "You
did? When?"

"When I was little, about seven or eight, I guess.
Father was fascinated with the redskinned savages

and told us stories about tribes with strange names like Sioux and Crow and Comanche."

"Why'd the prince get so excited?"

"I told him you were attacked by a herd of angry grizzly bears but fought off the crazed leader with your bare hands. You were clawed across the temple in the battle."

The story was so utterly absurd that Stuart had to laugh. "That's the stupidest thing I've ever heard. For your information, grizzly bears don't travel in herds. What's more, I'd be dead right now if I got in a wrestling match with one."

"But that wouldn't sound very impressive to the prince, now would it, Mr. Delaney? If you'll remember, we're trying to convince Shashi that you're a brave man. That's why I told him you were so fierce that you could frighten bears away."

"And the kid believes something that utterly ridiculous?"

"Well, of course. He's never been outside of Udaipur, and he likes wild adventures."

"Wild is the right word."

The maharajah broke into their increasingly hostile dialogue with a speech punctuated with lots of animated gestures. His big brown eyes were shining with excitement.

"He says he knows now that you will need no assistance from his soldiers in killing the tiger. He's sure you can kill it with your bare hands, if necessary."

"Thanks, Anjelica, that's just great. Are you saying that now I'm not getting a weapon?"

Anjelica shook her head as if he were the one causing all their problems. "You are very cynical, Mr. Delaney. You'll get both a rifle and a dagger. I must warn you, though. The tiger carries a tip of a hunter's spear in his side so he's quite bloodthirsty and unpredictable."

"Just give me the damn gun. Now."

Anjelica leaned down and retrieved a long white box from where it had been stashed beneath the seat. Stuart set the beautifully inlaid ivory case on his knees, unbuckled the strap and reverently lifted the polished weapon out of its velvet bed.

"This is beautiful," he murmured, appreciating the antique musket's quality despite his annoyance with the woman at his side. "Does it work?"

"Of course. It's been handed down in my father's family for generations. My father killed six tigers with it since we came to Udaipur but I also brought along a brand-new Sharps, if you prefer."

"You're damn right I prefer. Give it to me."

"There's really no need to be rude, Mr. Delaney," Anjelica chided as she withdrew a long leather sheath. Stuart took it and quickly slid out the rifle.

"Where're the cartridges?" he demanded as he worked the breech.

"Have you killed a tiger before?" she asked as she handed him a box of ammunition.

Stuart shot her a derisive look. "Oh, yeah, lots of times. They run wild in the streets of London."

His sarcasm apparently offended her because she looked away and lapsed into brooding silence. Fine, Stuart thought, she offended him, too. He filled his pockets with shells, then loaded the rifle and held it across his lap. He felt a hell of a lot better now that he was armed and ready for whatever trap she led him into next.

For some time they rode through sun-dappled shade as the dirt road wound through the rice fields of the villages that edged the jungle. Among the mud and thatch houses, the people stopped their cooking or planting to watch Prafulla Veda's lumbering progress. When they realized the maharajah was inside the howdah, however, most fell to their knees in homage. The children ran alongside and tried to touch the royal tapestries until the soldiers forced them back.

Gradually Stuart became used to the gentle sway of the elephant's slow walk, and as they pushed their way deeper into the tangled foliage of the jungle, the prince lay his head back against the pillows and began a soft, openmouthed royal snore. Anjelica Blake ignored Stuart completely, and the ten royal guards carrying both muskets and sharp scimitars remained alert for enemies, be they animal or human.

"Why do you treat me with such contempt?" Anjelica demanded abruptly after a long peaceful silence.

Stuart observed her steadily. "Because ever since

I laid eyes on you you've been embroiling me in lies and schemes that could get me killed."

"I'm only trying to help. Besides, I suspect you were paid well enough by my husband to come here for me."

A rush of anger colored Stuart's answer. "I sure as hell wasn't paid to marry you in a sham ceremony and set myself up as bait for a man-eating tiger. I don't like women telling me what to do and that's all you've done since I got here."

His remark earned him a frown of displeasure. "I don't think you like women much."

Their eyes met and locked for an instant. "Women have their uses, but you're right, most of the time they're nothing but trouble."

Stuart could actually see the flush rise beneath the flawless skin of her face. Before she could find a suitable retort, the prince struggled upright, rubbing sleepy eyes and mumbling incoherently.

Anjelica translated through tight teeth. "He wants to know if you touched me after he dozed off."

Stuart shook his head as if the notion hadn't occurred to him. The truth was that the idea appealed to him in the most basic way, in complete contradiction to how he otherwise felt toward the vixen. Despite his derogatory remark about women, he could well understand the young maharajah's jealousy. With her long curling eyelashes, silver-blond hair, and lips designed to fit a man's mouth, Anjelica Blake was a woman who could make her suitors grovel at her feet like starving men vying for a piece of bread. Even Stuart was tempted by her allure, despite all the trouble she had caused him.

His erotic thoughts disintegrated like smoke when he was suddenly thrown forward by a jolt hard enough to put him on his knees on the floor. He grabbed the rail when the elephant threw herself violently to the other side in a powerful attempt to rid herself of the howdah and everybody in it. The mahout shouted frantically, but the elephant was trumpeting loud, terrified screeches as she left the path. Stuart lost his grip when she ruthlessly slammed sideways into the trunk of an immense rubber tree. The left rail snapped in two, and Stuart just managed to grab Anjelica as she was thrown past him.

"What's going on?" he yelled, trying to hold the prince in the seat with his other hand.

The elephant hit the tree again with even more force, then spun sideways as if dazed and disoriented. The last thud of impact loosened Stuart's hold on the prince and sent the boy shooting out the side of the howdah. Stuart lunged to grab him, and barely got a hold of his loose silk tunic.

As he jerked the boy back inside, orange and black fur flashed briefly at the corner of his eye. Anjelica screamed, but her terror was cut short by a horrific roar that curdled the blood. The leaping tiger landed on the back of the mahout who was still trying to control the spooked elephant. Long sharp claws ripped across the man's spine, and the mahout screamed as he was knocked to the ground and the cat turned back and leapt onto the elephant behind the damaged howdah.

The scent of the jungle cat set Prafulla Veda into pure panic, and she shook with great wracking shudders, trumpeting fear and danger as she tried desperately to buck the deadly predator off her back. The smashed howdah came apart, dumping them all, and Stuart fell, landing hard on his shoulder. He groaned as his arm went numb and the rifle was knocked from his hands. The elephant was stomping at everything that moved, and Stuart scrambled out of the way of her huge feet as the raging beast attacked the guards with her trunk and thrashing body. Several soldiers went down and others scattered in hysteria as the elephant crashed headlong into the jungle, raising a great shrieking of birds and monkeys.

Stuart found Anjelica on her hands and knees a few yards away, moaning and touching the blood trickling down her forehead. The prince lay facedown and unmoving within feet of where the snarling tiger was dragging the mahout's body into the bushes. Stuart crawled toward Anjelica, but when she saw the prince's danger, she went for the helpless boy.

Shashi began to moan as she reached him, and the tiger dropped his first victim, his long tail twitching as he crouched and sniffed the air. Stuart inched sideways toward the rifle, eyes glued on the tiger as the prince whimpered and sobbed. About the time Stuart got his hands on the weapon, the tiger turned his head and saw Anjelica scoop up the child. She turned to run, and the animal coiled and sprang. Stuart barely had time to lift the rifle and fire.

The bullet slammed into the tiger's flank, and the cat's roar of agony split the air, sending more jungle parrots into a squawking panic. Stuart grabbed another cartridge from his coat and shoved it into the breech. He aimed and fired again, the slug hitting the cat just below the left shoulder. The animal fell sideways, writhing and growling in the throes of death, and Stuart reloaded and fired twice more until the tiger quit twitching and lay still. Stuart dropped to his knees and tried to control his trembling hands. It had been close, too close.

Within minutes, several of the guards rushed back, shouting and prodding the dead cat with their swords. Not three yards away, Anjelica crouched at the base of a tree, rocking back and forth with the frightened little prince in her arms.

"Are you all right?" Stuart asked shakily, moving a couple of steps in her direction. He reloaded and held his weapon trained on the motionless tiger.

"I must've hit my head, I think," she mumbled, "but it's not too bad."

"Tell the kid it's okay. I killed the cat."

The sound of Stuart's voice obviously permeated the boy's daze and made him remember that he was not a crybaby, but the Maharajah of Udaipur. He shook himself loose from Anjelica's arms and made

a valiant effort to compose himself. He dried his
tears with his sleeve and spoke a few halting sentences.

"He said you can marry me since you saved his
life. He decrees you to be a great warrior and the
bravest man ever to set foot in Udaipur. Isn't that
wonderful news?" She gave him a dazzling smile.

Stuart frowned and rubbed his injured shoulder.
They were damn lucky to be alive, all of them. He
had had enough of the maharajah and dancing like
a bloody marionette on Anjelica Blake's strings. As
far as he was concerned, the only wonderful thing
about Udaipur would be getting the hell out of the
godforsaken place.

Chapter Five

"Is he really a god, Suzie? Do we gotta do puja to him?"

From their hiding place behind a pot of flaming red hibiscus, ten-year-old Suzannah Blake quickly slapped her hand over her little brother's big mouth. "Hush up, Sanjay! Do you want somebody to see us spying?"

Suzannah was assailed by a twinge of guilt when Sanjay's jade green eyes filled with hurt. After all, he was just four years old. But he was real smart for his age. Even Kapir said so.

"Shashi made a law that said he is an incarnation of Vishnu because he was so brave and killed the tiger when the fiercest soldiers ran to hide in the jungle," she whispered in a nicer voice. "Anjie says his real name is Stuart Delaney and he came here just to take us back to England. That's where Mum and Papa lived before they came to India."

"Not my mum . . . you don't wanna go back there, do you, Suzie?" Sanjay's lower lip quivered, a sure sign he was going to start bawling. "You told

65

me you didn't, and you don't want to leave Shashi,
and I don't neither."

"Anjelica says we've got to. Now shhh—"

Despite the scolding words, Sanjay was right.
Suzannah didn't want to go away, not to England or
anywhere else. She loved Udaipur, and Shashi was
the best friend she ever had, even if he was the
great king. He hadn't been the maharajah when
Suzannah's father had brought them to live in the
palace. Shashi's father had still been alive then, and
Shashi had shown her how to play tag in the hall of
great pillars and hide-and-seek among the lotus
pools. She didn't even remember the place called
London where Anjelica's husband lived.

Why did that silly old Stuart Delaney have to
show up now? Just when Anjelica was about to give
up on ever getting to meet Nicholas Sedgwick? And
why did he have to turn out to be the incarnation
of the great Vishnu and braver than anybody else in
Udaipur? Now all Shashi ever talked about was the
American god and how wonderful he was. It just
made her sick to her stomach!

Very careful that no one could see her, Suzannah
peeked around the black planter and discovered
that her older sister was nowhere to be seen. Good,
but Anjelica would come soon because time was at
hand for her first courtship ride with the god.

Sanjay tugged impatiently at her sleeve, and
Suzannah ducked down. She scowled malevolently.
"Now what do you want?"

"How are we gonna see the god from here? I

want to see him up close," her little brother insisted. "Do we have to bow down and put our forehead on the floor like we do at the temple of Brahma?"

"Yeah, we'll see him up real close and you can bow if you want to. Now quit talking so much," she ordered, impatient with his constant questions. "Okay, the coast is clear. Run fast!"

She grabbed Sanjay's hand and pulled him down the marble stairs, then ran across the grassy field to where Prafulla Veda was chained to her stake until the courtship ride started. The mahouts were feeding the other elephants with big bundles of grain and leafy branches, and Suzannah quickly lifted Prafulla Veda's trunk and stuffed her favorite treat in her mouth. It was a big leaf filled with boiled wheat and salt, and Anjelica always got up real early each morning just to make dozens of them for the big she-elephant.

Anjelica was the best mahout in the palace even if she hadn't been born to the caste. Prafulla Veda would do just about anything Anjelica commanded her to. Suzannah and Sanjay were supposed to be mahouts and have their very own elephants someday, too, but if they went back to England with the god, they probably wouldn't get to. She bet the elephants in London weren't nearly as big and powerful as Prafulla Veda. She was going to miss the elephants in the maharajah's stables dreadfully.

"Hurry up, Sanjay! Anjelica's gonna take Prafulla Veda so we've got to get ourselves hidden underneath the howdah seat before they come for her. We'll get a good long look at the god from under there."

Excited by the prospect, she patted Prafulla Veda's trunk and gave her the command to kneel. The elephant slowly complied and once the animal was down on her knees, Suzannah climbed atop her back leg, then grasped Sanjay's hand and pulled him up beside her.

It was a good thing Anjelica had got Prafulla Veda calmed down after the tiger attack. When the mahouts had first caught her and brought her back, she was still trying to stomp on everyone but Anjelica.

Suzannah grabbed the silken hangings of the courting howdah, and pulled them aside, then closed them tightly again once both Sanjay and she were inside. The howdah was all yellow and black with lots of rich silks and soft brocade cushions and silken draperies tied back with tasseled cords. It was not as grand as Shashi's imperial howdah that got torn up at the tiger shoot, but it was real nice, too. She lifted the fringed hanging that hid the space under the front seat, then ducked underneath it. Sanjay squirmed in right behind her, and once they dropped the drapery back into place, nobody could see them. She took a deep breath, pleased with herself.

"See, Sanj, I told you I could do it. Now all we have to do is peek out at the god 'cause he's gonna be sitting right over there with Anjie. But you can't say a word or they'll hear us and then we'll be in big, I mean *big*, trouble 'cause Anjelica doesn't want anything to mess up her plans to get back to that Nicholas Sedgwick man Mum married her to."

"Is he really a god come down to earth to teach us things?" Sanjay asked with wide-eyed wonder.

"Shashi thinks so, and I heard Anjelica telling her maid that he's as beautiful as Krishna. He's another incarnation of Vishnu, you know. She likes his eyes, too, 'cause they're the same color blue as the sky. I've never seen anyone else with blue eyes 'cept Mum, of course, and hers were real dark blue like the middle of the lake looks when the sun's gone down over the city and it's almost dark outside."

"Blue as the sky?" Sanjay sounded a bit skeptical.

"That's what she said, all right. Now don't say another word or somebody's gonna hear us and make us get out. Shhhh, I hear the mahouts coming to take Prafulla Veda to the boarding wall—"

Anjelica sat on the divan beside Shashi, eager to see Stuart Delaney again. Three days had passed since he had killed the tiger and saved their lives, but once the prince had declared her a woman again, she hadn't dared seek him out until the first ride of their courtship. She set her gaze on the door where he would appear, wondering what he would think of her now that she wore a flowing sari like all the other women. She wanted him to like her.

She wanted him to think she was beautiful and desirable. She certainly thought he was.

A warm blush suffused her cheeks, and she was glad no one could hear her thoughts. Stuart Delaney had been on her mind constantly since he had come to Udaipur. She had been terrible and disloyal to her husband because in bed at night, she had lain awake and relived each word Stuart had said to her. She had remembered each time he looked at her, each time he brushed up against her. He was the most beautiful man she had ever seen. He didn't seem to like her much, but she wanted him to. She wanted to see him smile at her, see how that would change his face.

When he suddenly appeared in the threshold between Shashi's bodyguards, her stomach actually quivered. He stopped in his tracks when he saw her, and she tried not to shiver as his eyes slowly took in the silvery sari she wore. Since the tiger hunt she had worked hard to make herself look beautiful so that he would like her. She had Shashi's mother line her eyes with black kohl in the way the concubines did, and she had left her hair unbound to flow down her back. The women said men liked hair done in such a fashion so they could run their hands through it. She would like Stuart Delaney to put his hands in her hair.

When Shashi saw the American he stood and motioned for him to come closer. As Stuart stopped in front of them looking so tall and manly, she swallowed hard. As usual she felt nervous in his presence.

"The maharajah said to tell you that he has decreed me a woman so that we can wed."

"I noticed." His blue eyes swept her from head to toe, but he didn't smile.

"There must be a suitable period of courtship before we can be married," she told him quickly, embarrassed by her emotional turmoil.

"How long?"

"The prince will decide that. We must continue for however long he wishes."

The prince turned to Anjelica. "Tell the American that he is the greatest warrior of all time," he said in Hindi. "Tell him I know that Vishnu has come down to earth in his body to teach me how to lead my life. I have been waiting for him to appear and guide me with wisdom since my father died and I became the Maharajah of Udaipur."

Anjelica obeyed, and Stuart's handsome face looked blank. "Who the hell's Vishnu?"

"Here in India, there are three great names for God," she explained patiently, glad he was interested in Shashi's beliefs. "They are Brahma, Vishnu, and Siva. Vishnu is the preserver of the world and the source of the universe. He has often sent his will into the mortal world through mighty heroes who are incarnations of himself. The maharajah believes you are Vishnu's latest and greatest incarnation. That's why we all now wear these vertical white marks of Vishnu upon our foreheads. He has decreed that every man, woman, and child in Udaipur must become a Vishnavite and wear similar marks in your honor."

"You've got to be kidding."

Anjelica shook her head. "No. He is very grateful that you saved us from the jaws of the tiger."

He searched her face. "If I'm a god now, why can't I take you out of here?"

"You can, but we'll have to go through the wedding ceremony first." She paused when the prince interrupted their conversation.

"What is he saying to you?" Shashi demanded in his own tongue.

"He says he is pleased that you have shown such wisdom even at your young age."

Shashi grinned with pleasure. "Tell him your first act of courtship will be a ride around the courtyard. We'll all watch and learn from him before he returns to heaven."

"He wants us to ride Prafulla Veda around the courtyard now," she told Stuart.

"Why?"

"So he can watch and see how you court me. He will soon be old enough to have congress with his wives, and he wishes to learn how to handle them from watching you."

"Congress?"

Anjelica felt the color come up to pinken her cheeks.

"Good God," Stuart muttered as he apparently realized what she meant. She rose quickly and crossed the bridge into the saffron-hung howdah. She wasn't used to wearing the long silk sari wrapped around her body. It seemed strange to have the soft folds draped about her hips and shoulder but she did feel feminine again. She wanted him to crave congress with her, she realized, and was immediately flooded with shame.

She was truly wicked to think about him in such a way. She was already married to another man. She should not have such intimate thoughts. He had only come to Udaipur to take her back to her husband. She had to try to remember that.

She strengthened her resolve as she sat down in the howdah, but as he followed with his graceful masculine stride and lounged down beside her, she forgot her good intentions. She looked at his mouth and wondered how it would feel to be kissed by him. She had never been kissed by a man, not even her father.

As Prafulla Veda began her languorous walk around the perimeter of the courtyard, the guards at the parapets bowed reverently to Stuart Delaney. High on the interior walls, Anjelica could glimpse the women of the palace watching her courtship through the ivory lattices of the Gallery of Mirrors. Now even Shashi was standing atop his carved throne to watch their progress. She wished it were her real courtship. She wished Stuart Delaney really was Nicholas Sedgwick.

"How long does this go on?" he asked after about ten minutes.

"Until Shashi gets tired of watching us." When she glanced back, the prince was waving his arm at them. "He intends to watch every move you make."

"Great. So, when do we tie the knot?"

"Several weeks at least and I've brought you more dowry to present to Shashi. Here, take this while no one can see."

When she handed over the small bag of jewels, Stuart gauged the weight in his hand. "Are you worth this much money?"

"Shashi prizes me greatly because I am his good friend and translator," she answered, annoyed that Stuart Delaney doubted she was of such high value.

Finally, at long last, she saw his smile—strong, even white teeth that made his eyes seem even bluer against his sun-darkened face.

"I daresay Nick's going to be one hell of a happy bridegroom. Too bad he can't see you in that silver sari."

Pleasure such as Anjelica had never known before throbbed through her veins. She couldn't suppress the answering smile that curved her lips.

"You have a nice smile," she told him shyly.

Stuart wasted no time spoiling her friendly overture. "I haven't had much to smile about since I came to Udaipur. Tell me how you intend to get the two kids out. I want to know what to expect this time."

"I have a good plan. You must trust my judgment."

He laughed scornfully. "Last time I trusted your judgment, I nearly got mauled by a tiger."

As they slowly proceeded past the balustraded wall where the royal party sat watching, the maharajah called out loudly for them to hurry.

"Well? What does he want this time?" Stuart demanded.

Anjelica looked at Stuart, looked at his mouth, then smiled to herself as a wicked idea occurred to her.

"You won't like it."

"That's not surprising."

"He wishes to see you kiss me."

"Why?"

"Because he is eager to learn such things. I don't like it either, but I'm afraid we have no choice."

She watched his gaze move to her mouth, and she nervously moistened her lips with the tip of her tongue. One corner of his mouth lifted in a crooked half smile.

"I guess Nick wouldn't mind a kiss or two, under the circumstances."

Anjelica's heart thudded hard and fast with mind-tingling anticipation as he raised her chin with his forefinger. She closed her eyes, every nerve on edge, and it seemed as if a whole day crawled by before he put his mouth against her lips. She began to tremble inside, her body gripped by a powerful, unfamiliar yearning that spiraled out from her core. The flame rose dangerously as his kiss deepened from the first tentative tasting to a deeper exploration that forced her mouth open.

From the balcony, Anjelica vaguely heard the maharajah calling to her in Hindi. Breathless and shaken, she opened dreamy eyes. "I think he wants you to kiss me some more."

"Then we'd better do it," Stuart muttered, sliding his arm behind her. He bent her back slightly, and Anjelica was hardly aware she was eagerly clutching the lapels of his coat.

"Ouch!"

Stuart let her go. He grimaced and rubbed his leg. "Something hit me."

Anjelica gathered her wits enough to recover from his dizzying kisses, then sat bolt upright when she saw her little sister's heart-shaped face peering out from beneath the opposite seat.

"Suzie!" She was shocked to find that they weren't alone in the howdah. "What are you doing? Is that a slingshot you're holding?"

When her smiling little brother appeared at Suzannah's side, Anjelica's humiliation was complete. They had seen her kissing the American! "Sanjay! You're as naughty as Suzie!"

"Your eyes are as pretty as the sky," Sanjay informed Stuart. "Just like Anjie said. Are you really a god?"

"Hush, Sanjay," Anjelica whispered fiercely, her face burning like fire. She glared at the children to no avail.

"You look more like Krishna to me," Sanjay was continuing with little regard for Anjelica's warning look. " 'Cept your skin's not blue like his is in the ancient paintings."

At the sound of the maharajah's voice, both children ducked out of sight.

"Shashi says the ride's over," Anjelica informed Stuart hastily as the children began to giggle beneath the seat. "I apologize for my sister and brother, Mr. Delaney. I'm afraid they're very naughty children."

"Imagine that," Stuart muttered under his breath.

"I don't think you're Vishnu! And I hate Americans who come snooping around and bothering people in Udaipur!" came Suzannah's shrill voice from her hiding place.

I'm going to kill them, Anjelica vowed, never having been so embarrassed in her life. Even worse, they had interrupted Stuart Delaney's kiss, one that had left her lips hot and throbbing, wanting more. Maybe Shashi was right after all, she thought with a sidelong look at the American, maybe Stuart Delaney was a god.

Chapter Six

After a fortnight of being worshiped and catered to by every living creature in Udaipur, Stuart decided there were worse things than being decreed a Hindu deity. The three maidens who preceded him everywhere he went with scattered rose petals was a bit much, but otherwise, his every wish had been granted. Except for the most important one—he wanted to get the devil out of India.

At the moment he was enjoying his own wedding feast, an inordinately lavish affair sans the bride. In truth, he hadn't seen Anjelica Blake since she had pressed her alluringly curvacious body up against him during the last courtship ritual—no doubt pretending he was Nicholas Sedgwick. One thing he did know for sure—Nick was a fortunate man.

Stuart had had his share of beautiful women, but even he had been stunned the first time he had seen Anjelica dressed in clinging silvery silks, her eyes and hair gleaming with the same silvery lights. If a man could forget her irritating habit of getting him into lethal binds, she was nothing less than irresistible. As unbelievable as it was, he was actually looking forward to seeing her again.

Unfortunately her two bratty siblings were a different story. At the moment they sat nearby in places of honor as members of the bride's family. He glanced casually at them, and Suzannah answered his interest with a glare that would wither a turnip. Afraid she meant to lodge some sharp-edged instrument in his skull, he glanced away. He had yet to understand why she hated his guts, but she obviously did, and almost as much as Anjelica's big stupid elephant.

When he looked at Sanjay, the boy followed Suzannah's lead but ruined the effect when he tacked on a sweet little smile at the end of his vicious stare. The evening continued with no sign of Anjelica, and Stuart suffered the constant observation of the youthful maharajah until someone tapped him on the shoulder.

"Would you like to sample a fig, Mr. Vishnu? They're most sweet and juicy."

Suzannah had materialized beside him holding a large oval basket filled with plump figs. Stuart eyed the fruit distrustfully, suspecting poison. When he hesitated, she beamed angelically. Stuart stared at her, something about her dark eyes and her smile triggering an elusive twinge of familiarity. He plumbed the murky depths of his memory but could not name who or what he was recalling.

"The best ones are down on the bottom," Suzannah informed him helpfully, bringing him back to the present with her uncharacteristic burst of goodwill.

"My, aren't you nice all of a sudden," he remarked with a raised brow. He looked down into the basket but just as he started to choose a fig, the contents of the basket shifted slightly. An ugly yellow head rose up and spread its hood, and Stuart jerked back from the snake, knocking the basket off the table. Figs flew everywhere, and Suzannah giggled with glee as a four-foot-long cobra slithered over the marble floor and disappeared beneath a silk hanging.

Stuart clamped his jaw and muttered a curse as Suzannah scampered after the snake. Little Sanjay sidled up beside Stuart, his red turban sitting askew on his head. "Suzie's snake won't hurt you, my lord. Papa cut out its fangs when he was still a little bitty baby snake."

"Well, I hate snakes, fangs or no fangs," he grumbled furiously, thinking it was time somebody taught little Suzannah Blake some manners with a few smart smacks on her backside.

"Suzie loves him," Sanjay informed him, his innocent green eyes intent on Stuart's face. "And she's the best snake charmer in all of Udaipur. She got George for a pet 'cause Papa said she couldn't get her own elephant till she was sixteen. You know what? George can't hear Suzie's flute music at all when she's charmin' him. He just follows her movements when she sways back and forth. You know, he's watchin' her real close 'cause he thinks she's gonna attack him or something. George is a real nice snake."

"Suzie named it George?"

Sanjay nodded. "Like Major George, Papa's boss at the fort in Agra. Papa said he was more a cobra than George would ever be."

Stuart had met Major George Coleridge when he had first arrived in India. The description was indeed an apt one. Sanjay was smiling at him again. He seemed to be a quiet, respectful little boy. Too bad the kid was surrounded by wild, unpredictable sisters.

Sanjay leaned closer and whispered in Stuart's ear. "I know a secret."

"What's that?"

"My sister likes you."

"I know you don't mean Suzannah."

"Nope, not her. She hates you worse than poison," Sanjay agreed with complacent honesty. "But Anjie likes you. She says you're real brave and strong and smile real pretty."

Sanjay glanced around furtively to see if anyone was listening, but the prince was now playing a board game with Suzannah. Her snake basket was on the floor beside her, but at least George was closed up under a lid. "Do you remember when Suzie and me hid in the howdah and Suzie shot you in the leg with her slingshot?" Sanjay asked in a conspirator's whisper.

"Yeah. I've still got the bruise."

"You know when Anjie told you about the prince wanting you to kiss her?"

"Yeah." Since that day he had suffered a couple of sleepless nights trying to forget just how good her mouth tasted and how she was married to another man, and Marian's cousin, at that.

"Well, guess what?" Sanjay was dragging out his revelation with a big smile and shining green eyes. "Shashi didn't say nothin' about kissing."

Stuart cocked a brow. It appeared the boy did have a secret worth listening to. "Is that a fact?"

Sanjay gave an eager nod. "He just told Anjie to hurry up and get the courting done 'cause he was tired of watching. I heard him, and so did Suzie."

Stuart wanted to laugh. Not that he'd been unaware that she had wanted to kiss him. She had melted in his arms like a pat of butter atop a hot griddle, then gripped his coat so he wouldn't pull away. Anjelica Blake was as pure as driven snow, but a seething bed of sensuality just waiting to be lain in. He had a sneaking suspicion she was using him as a dress rehearsal for her real husband and real wedding night. He was beginning to wonder just how far she intended to carry her make-believe courtship.

"Where is your sister anyway, Sanjay? Don't Hindu brides get to enjoy their own wedding feasts?"

"She'll come soon to dance for you." His next words were full of pride. "Anjie dances real good. The bells on her feet sound pretty."

Suzannah yelled to Sanjay, obviously incensed that he dared to fraternize with the enemy. Stuart propped his elbow on his knee and smiled at the pretty serving girl who brought yet another silver platter of curried rice and roasted lamb. The musicians had been playing since he had arrived in the great hall, and he found the melodies made by the stringed sitars, drums, and flutes oddly haunting. There had been no dancing among the tables of honored Udaipurians—only eating, drinking, and loud laughter.

A gong sounded from somewhere in the upper reaches of the banquet hall, and the buzz of conversation slowly dwindled. The room became still and expectant as Anjelica stepped into view at the far end of the marble hall. Shashi sat up, smiled, and clapped his hands.

As a lone sitar began to play a slow, sensual, stirring tune, Stuart's eyes riveted on Anjelica where she stood in a shimmering white sari lined in gold. As he watched, she began to sway slowly, her bare arms undulating like graceful reeds. Her feet were bare too, and though the dance wasn't particularly erotic, her languorous movements made her body so suggestive beneath the semisheer silk garment that Stuart found himself becoming aroused, so quickly and noticeably that he was appalled.

Swallowing hard, he tried to fight his burgeoning desire with no luck whatsoever. Anjelica pressed her palms together in front of her swaying pelvis then slowly, one step at a time began her provocative journey down the floor toward him, her beautiful eyes locked on him as the gold circlets of bells around her ankles jingled melodically in time to the lilting music.

By the time she had reached him and knelt subserviently at his feet, he wasn't sure he could stop himself from reaching out and jerking her bodily against his chest. He fought his own weakness, wearing a black frown of self-annoyance by the time she finally curled herself on the cushion next to him.

"So when can we get the hell out of here?" he demanded harshly.

Anjelica looked surprised and then hurt, which made him even angrier.

"Soon, but Shashi is reluctant to let us depart because he wishes to acquire knowledge from the incarnation of Vishnu."

"Does he really believe I'm a god?"

"Every Hindu knows that Vishnu has had many earthly incarnations. Krishna, Rama, and the great prophet Buddha are all such manifestations. Hindus believe in reincarnation of the spirit. It is comforting to know that if one is good and follows the right path while on earth, he will be reborn into a higher caste. When one attains the highest level of consciousness one will unite with Brahma in nirvana."

"What's nirvana?"

"That is when perfect happiness is reached by

the complete absorption of oneself into the supreme universal spirit."

Anjelica's face was very serious as she talked about gods walking the earth and people living more than one life. Perhaps old Nick wasn't so lucky after all; how would he explain this to his English family? Stuart wondered if she had truly converted to Hinduism, but he didn't ask any more questions. He didn't want to know too much about her; and sure as the devil didn't want to become too fond of her. He already wanted her about as much as he'd ever wanted any other woman. And that made him a damned fool.

She flushed slightly when he didn't encourage the conversation. She raised her chin a notch. "As your betrothed I must publicly feed you from my hand. The ritual is designed to indicate my willingness to submit to your will."

She picked up a small piece of orange and placed it into his mouth. Unfortunately, she stared at his mouth as she fed it to him. Stuart's loins reacted as she wet her soft bottom lip with the tip of her tongue. He refused her next offering.

"Shashi now thinks you look like Krishna so he'll be watching us closely to see how you handle a woman," she said softly. "May I serve you more wine?"

"No. So I'm not Vishnu anymore?"

"I just told you that Krishna is a previous incarnation of Vishnu."

"So they're really the same god?"

"That's right, but Krishna is the most romantic and handsome of all the gods. Many women are devotees of him. He is well-known for his seductions of gopis, and that is why Shashi respects your prowess with women."

"Seductions of guppies?"

"No, silly," she replied with an amused smile. "Gopi is the Hindi word for milkmaid."

"He's revered for seducing *milkmaids*?"

"Here he is considered a symbol of manliness and virility, and Shashi thinks you are very much like Krishna in those respects. He wishes to emulate your masculinity so when the time comes, he will be skillful enough to please his wives and concubines."

Stuart glanced over at the boy and found Shashi's brown eyes latched on him with a great deal of interest. He nodded at the young prince and accepted another tidbit from Anjelica's slender fingers. She smiled at him, and he was smiling back when he realized how easy it would be to seduce a young woman as innocent and eager as she was.

"Do you plan to feed Nicholas Sedgwick like this?" he asked, thinking they both needed a blunt reminder that she was a married woman.

"Is he the kind of man who will demand such servitude of his wife?" she asked, voicing her first sign of curiosity about her husband.

"Don't you know him?"

"I met him only once a long time ago when we were children, but I do have a locket I always wear with his picture inside it. Would you like to see him?"

"Not especially."

"He was a nice boy but what kind of man is he?"

Stuart shrugged. "I don't know him all that well. I know his cousin better."

"What's his cousin's name?"

"Marian."

"Is she your lover?"

Stuart was surprised by her frankness. Maybe he should tell her the truth. Maybe it would help keep their relationship from getting too complicated. "Yeah, she is. At least she was when I left London."

Her face didn't change but she eyed him somberly. "I bet you've had hundreds of lovers in your life, haven't you, Mr. Delaney?"

Stuart had to laugh. "That might be a bit of an exaggeration."

"Have you ever had a wife?"

Stuart didn't like talking about himself. He was a private person. What he did or didn't do was none of her business. "You ask too many questions."

Anjelica looked away and he admired her delicate bone structure until she spoke again. "Shashi has set our wedding day for seven days from tonight. You must be careful not to offend him in the coming week or he could change his mind."

"What about the kids?"

"He still will not give me permission to take them with us. They are both very dear to him, especially Suzannah. So I'm working on a plan to smuggle them out of the palace on our wedding night."

"What happens to me if you get caught?"

"Why are you always so suspicious?"

"Because I'm not nearly so dear to him as the rest of you are, and if he suddenly decides I'm not this god of his, he's got about three hundred soldiers on the walls he can order to murder me with their large, sharp swords."

"Have I not taken good care of you thus far? Other than the tiger attacking us, you must admit that all's gone well. And with the killing of the tiger, you won Shashi's respect much more quickly than you could have done otherwise. I've taken all that's happened as a good omen for our eventual escape from Udaipur."

Stuart felt reasonably certain that everything that had transpired since he had first seen Anjelica Blake had been the result of pure blind luck and nothing more, but he had to admit that things were on course at the moment. He turned to Anjelica and accepted a delicious morsel of lamb from her lovely fingers.

Every time Anjelica looked at Stuart, all she could think about was the way his lips had felt on hers. She was wrong to look at him in such a carnal way, disloyal to Nicholas Sedgwick and her marriage contract, but she simply could not help it. He was everything in a man that any woman would want. He was exactly the sort of husband she had always dreamed of. More than that, when he touched her, he set loose a demon in her body that lit fires she could not put out.

Even now she longed to be alone with him away from the guards and the curious courtiers. Shashi was drowsy-eyed, and Sanjay was already curled up in the cushions fast asleep. Suzannah was still wide awake and frowning at them, but then she hated the American. Now was the time for her to take Stuart to see Chandran.

"Come, we must meet with the royal astrologer."

Stuart paused, his silver wine goblet poised half-way to his mouth. "They royal what?"

"Astrologer. In India a man and woman must have their horoscopes read to find out if they are compatible for a long and prosperous marriage."

"It sounds to me like this guy Vishnu is compatible to just about any female."

Anjelica smiled. "That's true. Perhaps the reading will determine if I am a worthy bride for you."

His face sobered. "Don't you mean a worthy bride for Nicholas?"

"Of course," she agreed hastily, chagrined that he might have glimpsed her fascination with him. "But everyone here thinks you are he. In any event, perhaps you will learn much about yourself."

Rising, she reached her hand down to him. He ignored it and pushed himself to his feet without her help. The friendly moment that had passed between them earlier was gone. By mentioning Nicholas Sedgwick's name, he had erected a barrier that would discourage their growing intimacy. Perhaps that was the best thing because she no longer could think about her unknown husband without Stuart's handsome face chasing away her intention to be a good wife.

Bowing deeply before the maharajah, she waited for Shashi to sleepily acknowledge their departure. Stuart followed her example, and Suzannah stuck out her tongue at him. Anjelica gave her sister a chastening frown, then led Stuart out of the banquet hall. She would have to give Suzannah a good scolding if her rude behavior continued.

The corridors were deserted except for the guards, and Anjelica led them quickly through the west dome, eager to know what her guru, Chandran, would divine from the stars about Stuart Delaney. From the beginning the American had seemed a strange, hard man who was careful not to reveal himself in conversation. Somehow she knew he harbored many secrets inside himself, hidden so deeply that no one would ever know them.

"I'm surprised we're allowed alone with each other like this," he remarked suddenly, his low-pitched words echoing hollowly toward the high ceiling.

"Normally we wouldn't be," she whispered as they climbed up a narrow staircase that led to the fourth floor of the west wing. "If we were of Indian blood, our parents would have handled all the details of the marital contract. We wouldn't have seen or spoken to each other until after we were husband and wife. It's the Hindu way of protecting the innocence of women."

"At least the English let the girl meet her husband."

"Yet she has little choice in the matter," she reminded him. "I didn't. I was married to Nicholas before I even knew Mama was contemplating such an alliance."

She had accepted her lot as her duty and responsibility to her family—that was, at least until she met Stuart Delaney. A moment later they reached the recessed alcove that led to the garret where Chandran held his readings. "Remember you must answer Chandran's questions with total honesty. He must give us his blessing or we cannot wed."

The winding stone stairway could only accommodate one person at a time and was so narrow of breadth that Stuart had to turn his wide shoulders sideways in order to follow her. He was so big and tall that when they stepped inside the small chamber at the top of the stairs, he seemed to overwhelm the room. The strong pungent aroma of incense filled her nostrils, and she bowed respectfully to the tiny man who sat cross-legged in the center of the floor with dozens of white candles burning inside jewel-colored votives all around him.

The learned astrologer wore nothing but a white dhoti tucked up to girdle his skeletal physique. His beard hung long enough to touch the floor, its bushy gray depths grizzled with streaks of white. His hair was a darker gray and draped over his shoulders. He was very old now but he was the wisest man Anjelica had ever known. He lifted his palsied hand in an invitation for them to sit across from him on either side of a three-legged brass brazier.

Stuart obediently lounged down and watched silently as the ancient astrologer turned to him. Chandran stared unblinkingly into his face, long and hard, his eyes not dull and faded with age but as clear and black as obsidian coins. After a thorough examination of every inch of Stuart's features, the guru turned an equally focused scrutiny upon Anjelica. She returned his gaze seriously, long having awaited an opportunity to know what the future might hold for her. Now she was equally curious about Stuart Delaney's destiny.

"You are very nervous, my little White Orchid," Chandran murmured in Hindi.

Anjelica smiled at Chandran's use of the Indian name he had given to her when she had first arrived in Udaipur with her father. He had likened her delicate ivory skin to the palest orchids in the palace gardens. Since then her skin had been browned by the sun but never once had he called her by her English name.

"I am eager to learn about the man I have brought to you," she answered in a low, reverent tone.

Chandran looked deep into her eyes. "Is this the man you wish to wed?"

Anjelica hesitated, then nodded. It was true, she

realized with sinking heart. She wanted Stuart Delaney to take Nicholas's place.

"I must have the date and place of this man's birth."

"In order to compare our Navamsa Charts, Chandran needs to know your birthday," Anjelica said to Stuart.

"The fifth of February, eighteen hundred and thirty-nine."

"You are twenty-five years of age?" He was younger than she had thought, only five years older than she.

"That's right."

"Were you born in the United State?"

Stuart nodded. "The city of Newport in the state of Rhode Island."

Anjelica translated the information and Chandran scratched several notations on a piece of parchment that lay on the floor beside him. He ignored them both as he wrote more figures atop a star chart he took from a copper stand.

"What's going on?" Stuart asked as the silence drew out and Chandran seemed to have fallen asleep.

"He is casting your horoscope and will tell me if you are compatible to me. You will find it most insightful into your character."

"I doubt that. I don't believe in this kind of hocus-pocus."

Anjelica was surprised by his open criticism. "Are you saying that you discount the art of astrology?

The study of the stars divines events with much success."

Stuart didn't mince his words. "The moon and stars don't govern our actions. Men govern their own destinies, good or bad. And they have only themselves to answer for the evil they do."

"Surely you believe in a higher power to which men must answer."

He gave a careless shrug. "What do you care what I believe in?"

"Perhaps Chandran will make you appreciate your ascendant combinations and alignment of planets so that you can live through the positive power of the highest aspect of yourself. When that happens you will achieve true inner peace."

"Yeah, right."

"You are a very cynical man."

"That's right, and with good reason."

Anjelica lapsed into silence, wondering what could have made him so very bitter about life.

After some time, Chandran finished his reading, and Anjelica leaned forward as he began to speak in a monotonous drone of Hindi. She hung on every word, anxious to acquire any kind of insight into Stuart Delaney's psyche. When Chandran finally stopped and closed his eyes, she looked at Stuart.

"Do you wish to know what he has divined about you?"

"Not particularly."

Anjelica decided to tell him anyway. "He says that you are an Aquarian. Therefore you are far more rational than emotional. He says you are an idealist and value your freedom. That you are intellectually uncompromising and are unusually fixed and rigid in your ideas. He says you are emotionally isolated and suppress your feelings about others even when you care for them. You can be cold, detached, and insensitive, which makes it difficult for those who love you to continue to do so."

Stuart frowned. "It doesn't sound like I'm worth a plugged nickel, does it?"

"He told me about your good points as well."

"Well, by all means, let's hear them."

"He says you are honest and noble. He says that you are loyal to your values and fight for the causes you believe in."

"But more importantly, am I a suitable husband for you?"

"Chandran says we are a good match but that it won't be easy for you to love me because you are impersonal and like to keep women at a distance."

"Then I guess it's a good thing you're already married to Nick instead of me, isn't it?"

Anjelica didn't answer as Chandran began to speak again. She listened, gazing down at her lap until the astrologer finished nearly a quarter of an hour later.

"So now do I get to hear all your faults?" he asked with a mocking grin.

"I am a Leo, which is the sign of the heart. He said that I am a good mate for you because I hear with my heart instead of my mind. He said that you are cut off from your heart and it has caused a sickness in your soul, which is not only painful for you but hurts others in your life as well."

She stopped then, her heart reacting to her own words. He was right. None of it mattered anyway. Nicholas was the one she would live with for the rest of her life.

Humiliating tears sprang up and burned against her lids. She stood and paused only long enough to bow respectfully to her guru. She ran down the steps, leaving Stuart to find his own way back to his chambers. Chandran had told her they were a perfect match, but they weren't. They could never be anything to each other because she was already married to someone else. Until now, Anjelica had been flirting with Stuart like a game, not thinking seriously about the fact that a future with him was utterly impossible. She did hear with her heart, and her heart told her that Stuart Delaney was the man who should be her husband.

Chapter Seven

S even boring days later Stuart wondered just
how long a Hindu marriage ceremony went on.
It seemed he had been wedding Anjelica for weeks,
and now he wasn't sure she was even going through
with it. He hadn't seen her since she had gotten angry and left him to fend for himself with the old
soothsayer.

Stuart had been a bit hard on her but the time
had come to face reality and nip in the bud any attraction they shared. He had come to the conclu-
sion that she was beginning to look upon their
sham marriage as the real thing, and he could not
let that happen. Married women were strictly taboo
in his life. He had certainly learned that the hard
way a long time ago.

Guilt crusted over with age came back in all its
pain and regret. Camillia's haunting face appeared
inside his mind like a vengeful wraith, and he
forced it down as he always did. He concentrated
on his current problems instead and found himself
growing angry with the weeks he had spent waiting

for Anjelica's plan to bear fruit. He was beginning to wonder if twenty thousand pounds was enough money to recompense the aggravation to which she had subjected him.

Earlier that day he had been led to a chamber where a brass hip bath filled with yellow-tinted water and yellow rose petals awaited him. He had bathed and dressed in a yellow satin tunic and tight trousers favored by the maharajah and his retainers. To his chagrin, a small metallic gold turban had also been provided which he had yet to place on his head.

After he had finished dressing Kapir had come for him, and Stuart had followed eagerly, thinking that surely the ceremony was now at hand. He was led to the hall where he now sat, a magnificent room walled entirely in gold-framed mirrors where he found Shashi, the Blake children, and the rest of the Udaipur court listening to a woman in a blue sari pluck a sitar while another man accompanied her with a small drum. Everyone bowed and smiled and touched the white vertical stripes of Vishnu on their foreheads.

He sat up hopefully as Anjelica Blake suddenly swept into the room with her lithe grace, this time wearing a pale yellow sari sheer enough to make his throat go dry. *She's married, dammit,* he chastised himself as she bowed gracefully to the maharajah. To Stuart's shock she shot him a beautiful smile that did not look the least bit angry, then she departed again for parts unknown.

Well, did that mean they were married now? he wondered as he reclined back against the floor cushions and picked up a bunch of purple grapes. Several gorgeous dancing girls in skimpy attire twirled and tinkled the bells on their ankles. They looked good to him, but unfortunately not as good as Anjelica did. He sighed and glanced around at the merrymakers who were mostly men enjoying food, drink, and the female servants. One thing he had found out during his stay was that the denizens of Udaipur knew how to have a rip-roaring good time.

Suzannah and Sanjay seemed to be enjoying themselves as well. They sat near their pal and maharajah, but no one paid much mind to Stuart's lonely spot beneath the nuptial canopy. He sure hoped Anjelica's plot included leaving the place immediately after the wedding. In any case, she would have to do some serious maneuvering to get them out unseen when the bride and groom were the focal point of the whole proceeding.

An hour passed, then two, and Stuart was beginning to feel himself achieve a Zen-like disinterest in Anjelica Blake's person. But then it barreled back full-fledged along with a rush of pure lust when she appeared again. This time her slender limbs were wrapped in a flowing crimson sari edged in rows of pearls. The folds of her red veil hid her face and hair, and as she sank elegantly on a plush Oriental carpet in the middle of the hall, Stuart was encouraged to join her by loud shouts and whistles from the assemblage of well-wishers.

Anticipating the coming escape from Udaipur, he did so with pleasure and sat cross-legged beside Anjelica while a red-robed Hindu priest lit a stick of incense and put it into a small black iron firebox on the floor between them. The priest began a low, rhythmic mantra.

"You look handsome in your bridegroom's coat." Anjelica's whisper drifted from deep within her flowing veils of silk.

Stuart searched the opaque surface of her veil. "How can you see me?"

"With this," she whispered, inching her hand where he could see a gold ring affixed with a tiny mirror. The backs of her fingers were decorated with elaborate floral designs. "This is how the bride usually sees her husband's face for the first time."

"What if she doesn't like what she sees?"

"Then she would hope that he is a kind and generous man instead of a handsome one."

Stuart tried to see her face in the ring. "How much longer before we can leave here?"

"Soon. Tonight," she promised, tucking her hands back into the silken scarlet folds.

Stuart watched the priest pick up the incense and wave it around. "Tell me the plan," he demanded in a low tone.

"Don't worry."

"Well, I am," he answered, then nodded courteously at the maharajah who was eyeballing him without mercy. The constant surveillance had become a bit tiresome over the past few weeks, and he was glad when the muttering priest finally shut up and took Stuart's right hand. He bound his wrist to Anjelica's slender one with a narrow scarlet ribbon. Stuart looked up in surprise when the room erupted in joyous cries of celebration. Lively music started in earnest, and a flood of servants entered the rooms carrying more platters of food.

"I take it the deed's done," he murmured in a relieved breath.

"Yes. We'll be escorted to the wedding chamber soon."

Stuart settled back, feeling better than he had in a very long time. He was tired of the sham, of being trapped in Udaipur, and most of all, of being tempted unmercifully by Anjelica Blake's feminine allure.

"It's time for us to go," Anjelica whispered at length. "You can lift my veil and take my hand now. The prince and his wives will accompany us."

Stuart obliged, lifting the silk and revealing her face. She looked lovely, her blond hair pulled away from her face to display the large pearl medallion hanging at the center of her forehead. Tiny red and white flowers had been painted in a decorative line just above her eyebrows from temple to temple. He stared at the tattoos in dismay.

Anjelica relieved his fears at once. "Don't look so horrified. Shashi's wives used henna to decorate my body. The dye will last only for a few weeks."

"Good." Stuart smiled to himself, imagining Nick's expression if his wife had shown up in England tattooed like a Comanche warrior.

With a show of care he took Anjelica's hand, and as they proceeded through the wedding guests, everyone bowed and called out cheerful greetings. Once they were in the hall, a good-sized contingent of people followed them. After twenty minutes, Stuart decided he would be traversing endless marble corridors in his worst nightmares for the rest of his life.

At last they reached an arched, brass-studded red door. The company behind them quieted and stood back so the newlyweds could precede them into yet another chamber reminiscent of the palace of Versailles. The round bed that sat in the middle of the black marble floor was the size of a small room itself. Layer upon layer of sheer scarlet draperies hung from the ceiling, strategically parted to reveal a black satin bedspread piled with dozens of red cushions.

"You are expected to take me to the bed," Anjelica told him in English. Stuart glanced warily at the crowd taking up places on low divans lining the distant wall as he led her up four carpeted steps to the raised dais. Anjelica swept aside the sheers and climbed into the massive bed. She sat cross-legged awaiting him as he looked back at the silent audience.

"What are they waiting for?" Stuart asked with growing unease. "I thought the ceremony was over."

"They are required to witness the consummation."

Stuart froze where he was, then decided he must have misunderstood her. "What did you say?"

"They have to watch us consum—"

"I heard you, dammit. Are you out of your mind?"

Anjelica frowned. "Why are you so upset?"

"Why am I so upset? Why the hell do you *think* I'm so upset?" he ground out, crawling in beside her. He turned to glare at the people, just in time to see Shashi climb up into a large carved chair about ten yards from the bed. "What's he doing?"

"The maharajah thinks you're a great and virile man, the incarnation of Vishnu—"

"I don't give a damn what he thinks. Tell them all to get out."

Anjelica had the audacity to laugh. "What are you so worried about? We're not really going to do anything anyway, are we? Shashi thinks you're the best lover on earth, so he wishes to emulate you. The drapes will disguise what we're really doing. He won't know the difference if we just pretend to be joining our bodies in marital congress."

"This has to be the most ridiculous, absurd, stupid thing I've ever heard of."

"Things are different here in Udaipur."

"Damn right."

Anjelica shrugged. "He's sleepy because it's way past his bedtime. He'll get bored and doze off soon. When Kapir puts him to bed, everyone else will leave, too."

At a polite request from Shashi, Anjelica nodded and brought out a tapestry-covered book hidden among the bed hangings. "He wants me to give you this tome. It is often studied by new bridegrooms."

Stuart opened the book and stared at a beautifully detailed portrait of a man and woman locked in sexual intercourse. He slapped the book shut and raised stunned eyes. "Good God, what is this?"

"It is the great *Kama Sutra,* which teaches the laws of pleasure," she answered with a look of pure innocence. "It lists sixty-four kinds of congress between a man and a woman. It is said that a man skilled in the sixty-four arts is looked upon with love by his own wife, by the wives of others, and by courtesans."

Stuart leafed through the pages again and found what she said to be true. One erotic position after another was illustrated on the gilt-edged pages in startling detail.

"It was written by the great sage Mallinaga Vatsyayana many centuries ago," Anjelica was telling him as she leaned over to see which picture he was examining. "That position is called drawing the bow, and that one on the next page is called the lotus-like position," she informed him with no apparent embarrassment whatsoever. "I've memorized every word of the *Kama Sutra* as all young women should do before they go to their husband."

Stuart was incredulous. "You've studied this book?"

"Yes, so that I can please my husband. I believe

that it is the duty of the wife as well as the husband, although most men don't wish their wives to know so many ways of congress."

Stuart stared at a picture where an Indian maharajah was making love to his wife while shooting an arrow at a wild stag. "This is a new one on me."

They both looked up when Shashi called out again.

"Now what?"

"He said to hurry up and get started because he's getting bored."

"This is ludicrous," Stuart objected, but he couldn't help but laugh at the pure absurdity of the situation.

"You are as beautiful as Krishna when you smile," Anjelica murmured, her kohl-lined silver eyes glowing softly in the dim candlelight. The expression in her gaze was so warm, so inviting, he found himself leaning toward her, wanting to kiss her about as much as he had ever wanted anything.

"You're going to have to kiss me or something," she prompted. "Everyone's waiting for us to begin. Most men begin quickly so the witnesses will leave. I've often participated in the nuptial audience."

Stuart still hesitated, afraid that if he started making love to her, he wouldn't be able to stop, gawking audience or not. She sat there waiting, encouraging him with her angelic smile and soft lips.

"You should probably start by taking off my sari," she suggested. "Don't worry. No one will know that

I have on a shift beneath it. They won't leave until we disrobe."

This is definitely a mistake, Stuart thought as he took hold of the edge of the red cloth covering her hair. When he tugged it loose the soft sari fell away revealing silky pale blond tresses that spread over her shoulders like a wavy satin cape. A big mistake, he warned himself again, but she seemed to want it as much as he did.

Never taking his eyes off her face, he lifted the sari off her shoulders and let it fall behind her on the bed. His gaze lowered hungrily to her body. She wore a shift, all right, one that was made of lacy fabric that enhanced more than concealed her womanly charms.

"Kiss me. Please."

Her breathless whisper made Stuart forget his misgivings, forget Nicholas Sedgwick's claim to her, forget any good sense he might have had. He took her by the arms and lowered her back against the cushions. She was breathing hard, her nipples taut and straining the fabric of her shift, her eyes half closed, her lips moist and slightly parted. God, she was the most desirable woman he had ever seen. He hesitated again, but only for a moment, then he lay on his side close beside her. Her arms came up around his neck and drew his head down until their mouths touched. That was all it took to start the flame racing through his blood.

In that moment he could think of nothing but her skin that felt like warm velvet and smelled of exotic sandalwood. Her mouth opened with a sigh, and he let himself kiss her as if she were his lover, rolling atop her, tangling his hands in her long hair. She moaned with pleasure, and he heard himself groan as the kiss deepened. A spattering of applause broke them apart. Both were panting hard and looking at each other with pure, raw need. She wanted more, and so did he, God help him.

Shashi cried out something, and Anjelica slid her fingers into the hair at Stuart's temples and pulled his face down on hers. "He's leaving now but perhaps we shouldn't stop just yet."

"Yeah," he murmured, attacking her lips and watching from the corner of his eye the people filing out. As soon as the door closed, he turned and pulled her atop him. Anjelica straddled him, her hair flowing down over his face until he swept it up in his fist and held it away.

Anjelica was fumbling at his tunic, sliding her hands inside and over his chest. He took her mouth again, holding her head between his hands.

"They're gone now," he got out somehow, damn close to losing all control. Anjelica already had. She writhed against him, her sari half off and twisted around her waist, her legs long, bare, and silky. He could have her if he wanted her, right now. That thought brought him back to his senses as nothing else could.

Stuart came up on his knees and pushed her away. Not trusting himself to look at her, he climbed off the bed and strode a few steps to the center of the room. Running his hands through his hair, he clenched his jaw, disbelieving he could have been so stupid. He turned back to see Anjelica on her knees on the bed. Her hair was tousled, her lips swollen by his kisses.

Not trusting himself to look at her too long, he moved to the window overlooking the lake and let the night breeze cool his face. Good God, he had nearly ravished her, and he hadn't even gotten her out of the palace yet. How the hell was he going to make it all the way to England without the same thing happening again?

Several minutes later Anjelica came up behind him and shoved a bundle into his hands.

"I thought you'd want these to travel in," she said softly as if nothing improper had just happened between them. She stepped upon the window seat, obviously not as affected as he by the intimacies they had just shared. He wasn't sure he liked that or not.

Stuart looked down and found that he held a pair of his own English trousers and a white cotton shirt. As she unlatched one of the windows, he quickly stripped off his bridegroom's tunic and donned the familiar clothing.

"What are you doing?" he demanded, hurriedly tucking his shirt into his waistband.

"It's time for us to go." She wrapped her flowing hair up into a black turban. She had already donned the black tunic and pants she had worn the last time she had slithered up and down the palace walls. He hoped that didn't mean that a death-defying leap was included in her escape plans.

"I take it we're going out the window." He stepped up on the sill beside her. She was knotting a rope around one of the narrow stone pillars framing the window.

"It's the only way I could think of to get the children out without being seen. I'll go first, then you follow."

Stuart frowned as she turned and backed out the window. He looked down at the dark lake far below. "Tell me that's not your elephant I see down there."

Poised over the drop, Anjelica actually smiled. "Suzie and Sanjay brought her down to the lake while everyone was still celebrating the wedding. The festivities will go on all night and all day tomorrow. They will take it as a good omen if we don't emerge from the bedchamber."

"We're three stories high. That rope's not nearly long enough to get us down that far."

"Prafulla Veda will help us the rest of the way down with her trunk. Come on, you're wasting time."

"Wait a minute, I don't trust that elephant!"

"Don't be silly," she muttered as she swung out and started to make her way down the sheer vertical wall.

In the faint light he could just make out when the elephant raised her trunk. Anjelica slid down it like some damn monkey. Once she was standing on

Prafulla Veda's head, she motioned for him to follow.

"God, will this nightmare never end?" he grumbled to himself, then swung out into the night and began the harrowing descent.

Chapter Eight

From the mahout position on Prafulla Veda's neck, Suzannah gazed up the palace wall where the big American was making his way down to them. She still didn't see why Anjelica thought he had to come along. He hadn't made the plans or helped in the least. And Suzannah didn't like her sister liking him so much.

"Did you have any trouble getting Prafulla Veda out of the stables?" Anjelica whispered as she climbed into the howdah and checked through their bags of belongings.

"Huh-uh. The mahouts were drunk from that beer you gave them."

"Good."

While Anjelica was checking on Sanjay, Stuart Delaney reached the end of the rope. Suzannah smiled maliciously to herself and gave Prafulla Veda the command to raise her trunk. Stuart hesitated, and Suzannah encouraged him in her best honey-coated voice.

"Don't worry. She won't drop you."

"Yeah," he muttered as he gingerly stepped atop the elephant's forehead, fingers still clinging to the rope.

"Back," Suzannah ordered in Hindi, then grinned with glee as the elephant lurched violently and left Stuart's feet hanging in midair. She heard him curse, then hit the water with one gigantic splash. Suzannah laughed, pleased with herself until Anjelica reprimanded her.

"Suzie! Why did you do that?"

"It was an accident," Suzannah insisted penitently as Stuart resurfaced, coughing and sputtering in anger.

"Do you want the guards to hear us and set out an alarm?" Anjelica hissed furiously. "If they do, they won't let you leave with me. Is that what you want?"

"Yes. I don't wanna go back to England."

"Well, you're going. Now behave yourself and get into the howdah with Sanjay before I really lose my temper!"

Suzannah obeyed with a sullen face.

"You shouldn't have dumped the great Vishnu in the lake." Sanjay sounded frightened.

"He's not Vishnu or he wouldn't have fallen in," Suzannah returned with an uncaring shrug, then leaned forward and listened when she heard Anjelica speaking to the man in the water.

"Would you quit splashing around so much before the guards hear you?"

"That damn elephant's trying to kill me," came his furious growl from the water.

"Don't be silly. If she had wanted to kill you, she would have thrown you up against the wall. Mahouts are killed that way all the time. Just hold still so she can lift you up to the howdah."

Now his voice sounded as if it were coming from between gritted teeth. "I'll get up by myself."

"You can't. Just tread water and she'll get her trunk around your waist and pull you up to the howdah."

"No, I said—" His words were cut off when Anjelica gave the command anyway. With a snort and angry swing of her head, Prafulla Veda snaked her long trunk into the water and around Stuart's waist. She jerked him out of the water and high into the air.

"Grab the side of the howdah when she lets go," Anjelica told him. "And hurry up before someone hears us."

Suzannah laughed as Prafulla Veda shoved him headfirst into the floor of the howdah between Sanjay and her.

"Why the hell does this elephant hate me?" Stuart grumbled as he got to his feet. "You'd think I beat it over the head with a club."

Suzannah smiled, enjoying his plight. But to her annoyance Sanjay attempted to make him feel better.

"She's just jealous because Anjie likes you," her little brother said politely.

"If you're really Vishnu or Lord Krishna," Suzannah pointed out at once, "why don't you just order your army of monkeys to come rescue us like you did when you were King Rama and had to rescue your wife Sita from the evil Ravana? Why does Anjelica always have to do everything, if you're really a god like everyone says?"

"What the devil are you talking about?" Stuart muttered impatiently as he wrung out his shirt. Anjelica was in position on Prafulla Veda's neck and was prodding her to move toward the shore.

"Wanna piece of candy?" Sanjay offered to Stuart. "It's got dates and honey in it."

Suzannah wished her brother would quit being so nice to the American.

"Hush!" Anjelica hissed over her shoulder as Prafulla Veda moved into deeper water.

"I want to know where we're going," Stuart demanded of their sister.

Anjelica acted like she didn't hear him, and as the quiet night closed all around them, Suzannah turned to look back at the palace. High on the west wing, the windows of the mirrored hall were still glowing with light. She would never see it again, she thought. Her throat clogged up and felt thick like she had a lump of bread caught in it. She wouldn't see Shashi anymore, wouldn't play with him ever again. And it was all Stuart Delaney's fault. She hated him more than Prafulla Veda did.

"How did you two get out of the palace without being seen?" Stuart asked Sanjay.

Suzannah spoke up quickly. "Anjie put a sleeping potion in the mahouts' beer. Too bad she didn't put it in yours, too."

"I'd probably be better off," he snapped in return.

While Suzannah was trying to think up some mean retort to that, Sanjay cuddled up close to Stuart as if he was his best friend.

"Is England as pretty as it is here in Udaipur? We don't have those long sticks of ice that hang off rooftops that Anjie likes so much, but we have lots of flowers and pretty places to look at."

"Yeah, I guess England's all right. It's a lot colder so you'll see plenty of icicles. Snow, too."

"I hate icicles and snow," Suzannah interjected venomously. "I hate everything about England."

Stuart ignored her and continued his conversation with her little brother. "Do you know where we're going?"

"To the temple of Ganesh," Sanjay answered, proud of his knowledge, but Suzannah cut him off.

"Ganesh is the god with the head of an elephant so Prafulla Veda is sacred in his temple. You better quit saying nasty things about Prafulla Veda or Ganesh might get mad and cast an evil spell on you."

"I think somebody already has. I never should've come here in the first place."

"Anjelica's great rishi lives there," Sanjay volunteered. "He will help us. He is very kind."

"Rishi?"

"That's a holy man," Suzannah informed him

Linda Ladd

with haughty disdain. "Don't you know anything? I thought gods knew stuff."

"The rishi's not really bald," Sanjay added, ruining all Suzannah's attempts to put the American in his place. "He shaves his head. Shashi wanted me to be a priest, too, but Anjelica said I couldn't because we have to go back to England. Can I be a priest there if I want to?"

"Probably not," Suzannah said, angry all over again. "There's probably not even anything fun to do there. That's why I brought George along."

"You've got that cobra with you?" Stuart's tone was sharp.

"Suzie, I told you to be quiet!" came Anjelica's stern voice.

Suzannah knew Anjelica meant it this time. She pulled Sanjay back over beside her.

"C'mon, Sanjay, let's take a nap and not talk to him anymore."

Sanjay obediently snuggled up into the cushions beside her, and Suzannah gave one last glare at Stuart Delaney before she closed her eyes. She was tired, too, but tomorrow she would think of more things to do to the American to let him know that none of them liked him one little bit.

Stuart leaned back and dried his hair with a silk shawl, glad Anjelica had stopped Suzannah's constant abuse. He stared into the night as black as ink and hoped Anjelica knew her way through a part of the jungle where tigers weren't apt to roam. He sure the devil wasn't up to killing another tiger for her. Somehow he had a feeling that the ingenious, silver-eyed beauty knew exactly where she was going. Whether she did or not, however, he was going along. So far, so good. She had gotten all four of them out of the palace without one scimitar wound.

Once Anjelica urged the beast onto the land and into the dense jungle foliage, he quit worrying and let the desultory sway of the elephant lull him into a shallow doze. When he awoke later and sat bolt upright, the first glow of dawn was melting the night into gray mists. Directly in front of them, surrounded by lush vegetation, a stone temple rose with the ornate arched roof of Hindu architecture, the ground fog making the edifice appear to float on a nebulous cloud.

A bell echoed hollowly as Prafulla Veda lumbered slowly toward the great vine-covered structure. As they neared, both children roused and Suzannah began to fuss about some of Sanjay's candy being stuck in her hair.

By the time Anjelica brought them to a halt at the base of a long flight of stone steps, three Hindu priests dressed in yellow robes had appeared to meet them. All knelt and paid homage to Prafulla Veda, presenting her with oranges and a huge garland of yellow flowers which they hung reverently over her trunk. She promptly ate it.

From her place atop Prafulla Veda's neck Anjelica waited patiently until they were finished with their prayers. When the old man standing at the forefront placed his palms together in front of his face and bent very low from the waist, Anjelica spoke at length to him in Hindi. Afterward the Hindu priest looked mightily concerned. Stuart shook his head, sick and tired of not understanding anything anyone said. He would be glad to get back to civilization where he could take charge.

For the first time in weeks he thought of Marian Foxworthy and wondered what she'd think when he returned to London with Anjelica Blake. He wondered what her cousin, Nicholas, would think when he found out that Stuart had married his beautiful bride in a Hindu ceremony, then took certain liberties with her in the wedding bed. Nicholas hadn't been eager to get Anjelica back to England, but then he hadn't seen her grown-up yet, either. He would be more than appreciative once he saw how lovely she was, not to mention the fact that she knew the *Kama Sutra* by heart.

"Suzie, bring Sanjay and let Ishan take you to the bed chambers so you can go back to sleep."

Anjelica commanded the elephant to kneel, and Suzannah grumpily herded her little brother out of the howdah and into the care of the waiting priests. As the children were led down a side passage into the depths of the temple, Stuart slid down Prafulla Veda's side before the animal could hurl him against the stone wall.

Luckily the obnoxious beast was busy lifting her mistress onto the ground as gently as if she were a piece of precious Chinese porcelain. Anjelica still looked fresh and desirable despite the long trek through the jungle. He remembered how sweet she had smelled when she had welcomed him so eagerly against her silken flesh. He quickly banished such thoughts from his mind.

"You are not allowed access to the temple since you are not a Hindu, but the rishi has invited us to break the night fast with rice and tea in one of the outside chambers," Anjelica informed him softly as she patted Prafulla Veda's trunk. "I realize you are tired but it would be rude to refuse such hospitality."

"What about you? Aren't you tired?"

"I'll sleep later. Come, he'll show us the way."

The holy man led them up the steps and into a vast, domed chamber. The walls were painted with detailed murals portraying Hindu mythology. Many pictured Ganesh, the elephant-headed god that Suzannah had mentioned. Other statues of strange deities set in niches along the walls and rows of candles glittered in stands all around them.

Without speaking the barefoot priest moved slowly through the damp, cool light of dawn, then through a beaded curtain. Small and windowless, the room smelled of incense and strongly brewed tea. A low glass-topped rattan table was set with a small teapot and four cups, but there were no other furnishings except for a couple of pallets covered with blankets. The priest bent in a low bow and spoke softly to Anjelica before disappearing through the beads again.

"He invites us to make ourselves comfortable while he attends to Prafulla Veda. You see, here in the temple of Ganesh, it is considered a sacred duty and honor to care for a weary elephant." She sat back on her heels and presented him with a smile. "I told you that if you were patient, I would lead us to safety."

"And you did it." He sat down cross-legged opposite her. "But I'll feel better once we're aboard ship and out to sea."

Anjelica nodded and tugged loose the length of silk, releasing shiny blond ringlets down her back. Stuart watched admiringly as she slipped her fingers through the long silky tresses. He wondered if Nicholas Sedgwick would have enough sense to appreciate her. One thing was for certain, Stuart wasn't having any trouble doing so.

"We'll travel due south to the seaport of Bombay. English ships arrive and disembark there often, and I know the city well."

"Good. How long will it take us to get there?"

"A week perhaps, if the rains don't delay us."

Stuart watched her lift the tiny copper teapot and pour the steaming brew into two white porcelain cups adorned with golden elephants.

"It will take us much longer once we are on foot."

"We're not taking Prafulla Veda?"

"She'll go with us until I release her to the wild.

There's a river not far from here where the elephant herds stop on their migration north. We can follow it south toward Bombay. That's the stream where my father and I captured Prafulla Veda when she was a baby so that's where I'll free her. She'll be happier in the jungle. She hates working for man and taking orders."

"She obeys you."

"I trained her from the beginning. She trusts me."

Anjelica's voice roughened with emotion, and he realized that it was as hard for her to leave Udaipur as it was for Suzannah.

"I thought you were anxious to get back to England."

Anjelica looked down but not before he saw the glisten of tears. "I've lived in India for ten years. It's a wonderful place and I love it. But I promised Mother I'd take Suzannah home. And I must honor my commitment to Nicholas."

Her last words came out hard. Their eyes met and held. He knew she was remembering what had happened between them on the bed so he changed the subject.

"How'd you know about this temple?"

"My father brought all of us here to study."

Glad for a neutral topic, he asked, "What did you study?"

"There are two great Indian epics passed down for centuries called the *Mahabharata* and *Rama-*

yana. After Father converted to Hinduism, he wanted us to understand why."

"Did you convert, too?"

"Yes. I have always felt a deep serenity when I am inside these walls."

"It is peaceful," he said, realizing how deep the quiet was.

She seemed pleased by his remark. "I'm glad you feel it, too."

"Suzannah said this is a temple to Ganesh. What kind of god is he?"

"He's the god of good luck and fortune. He's the one with the body of a man and the head of an elephant. That's why they're treating Prafulla Veda with such kindness and respect."

Stuart realized this was the first time they'd had any kind of real conversation together. He found himself wanting to know more about her. "Do you really believe in all these gods?"

"Actually Ganesh and all the other gods and goddesses are just manifestations of one all-powerful god called Brahma. It is little different from Christianity in that respect. Hindus prefer to put a name and a face on each aspect of him so that they can worship a certain god for each of their wants and needs."

"I'm sorry you have to leave here," he said, impulsively responding to the pain so evident in her face.

Anjelica looked sadly at him. "Was it hard for you

to leave your home and family and go live in England?"

An image of the velvety green lawns of Twin Pines Plantation rose up in Stuart's memory. He wondered if the Yankees had burned the lovely old mansion to the ground as he had seen them do to so many others. "America had a war that tore the country in half and destroyed my family. I doubt if I'll ever return there."

"But how can your family be destroyed?" Anjelica asked gently. "That's one thing a person has forever."

"Not my family. I haven't seen my sister since before the war started."

"How long did the war last?"

"Five years."

Anjelica looked appalled. "That must've been awful for you."

Stuart shrugged, not liking to dredge up old wounds. He especially didn't like talking about the past. When he did, he remembered Camillia.

"We will be your family," Anjelica murmured softly, placing her hand lightly on his knee. "Suzie, Sanjay, and I would be honored to have you as a brother."

Stuart was absurdly touched by her sweetness, so much so that a lump rose in his throat. Embarrassed by the uncharacteristic rush of emotion, he frowned. "Why would you say something like that? You hardly even know me."

"I know that you came for me when Nicholas Sedgwick would not."

Oh, God help him, how easy it would be to fall in love with a woman like Anjelica. She was so innocent and so good. And so married and so out of reach.

"You don't know me at all," he repeated stubbornly. What would she think if she knew the awful things he had done in his past? He didn't want her to know anything about him. For all the wisdom and ingenuity she had shown getting them out of the palace, she had led a sheltered life in the wilds of India. She had yet to see war and despair, loneliness or betrayal. He hoped she never would.

She sighed heavily. "Poor Shashi. He will feel very betrayed. He will cry, then he will have a terrible temper tantrum and send his royal guards rushing off to fetch us back. He thinks of us as his family, you know. I'm glad he has Kapir and Chandran to advise him. They are both very loyal."

Again, Anjelica's face revealed her sorrow at leaving Udaipur. She rose and looked down at him. "I must do puja for Shashi and ask Ganesh to watch over him. You may sleep here on the pallet. I will wake you when it's time to go."

She pulled back the curtains and was gone, leaving only the quiet clicking of the beads in her wake. He lay down on the gray-quilted pallet on his back and stared up at the ceiling. Somewhere nearby he could hear the priest chanting a low, soothing mantra. Eventually the rhythmic drone lulled him into dreams filled with elephant-headed gods and warm silver eyes that seemed able to look into the blackness of his soul where he had buried the terrible sins of his past.

Chapter Nine

Several hours later Anjelica padded silently through the worn-stone corridors of the temple. She had done puja to Ganesh and spent an hour in meditation, trying to come to terms with her confused feelings. She had prayed for peace of mind and the strength to honor her commitment to Nicholas Sedgwick. She felt better in her heart and had made a fierce vow to fight her carnal weakness for the American.

From that day onward she would treat him as a respected friend, a brother, and never again consider him as a potential lover. Many of the intimacies they had shared had been prompted by her own machinations. She now knew that she had been wrong to encourage such physical contact and would never allow any more tender moments to happen between them. It would be hard since she had never met her husband, and of course Stuart Delaney was so overwhelmingly masculine. She stopped walking abruptly when she came unexpectedly upon the object of her dilemma.

Stuart stood at the courtyard well where he performed his morning ablutions. His back was to her as he splashed water over his face and chest. He was naked from the waist up. Bands of sinewy muscles rippled and flexed with each movement, and she admired his lean physique as he rubbed a towel over the muscular contours of his chest. When he turned and caught sight of her, the towel stilled in his hands.

"You have a beautiful body," she said truthfully.

First he looked shocked, then he laughed. "Do you always come right out like that with your opinions of men?"

Anjelica nodded. "Shouldn't I?"

"I wouldn't compliment gentlemen quite so openly once we get back to England."

"Why?"

"English ladies are more mysterious with their affections. They feign disinterest so the man will pursue them."

"Isn't that dishonest?"

"Yes. But honesty's one virtue sadly lacking in the drawing rooms of London."

"Then London doesn't sound like a pleasant place to live."

He shrugged a shoulder and finished drying his hair.

"You have warned me so many times about the people of England. Aren't you happy living there?"

"Yeah, but then I'm not a beautiful, innocent young girl."

"Do you really think I'm beautiful?" she asked, knowing full well that she shouldn't care or even voice such a question.

His blue eyes observed her in that magnetic, absorbing way of his. "I think you'll put all the London beauties to shame."

Her heart melted, and she steeled herself against her extreme attraction to him. "Maybe your friend named Marian will teach me how to behave like an English lady."

To her surprise, Stuart laughed. "I think you could teach her a couple of lessons in that department."

"Your Marian isn't a lady?"

"Sometimes she is, and she's not *my* Marian."

Anjelica watched him pick up a clean shirt and thrust his arm into the sleeve. He was as strong and every bit as beautiful as Krishna. Chandran had said they were perfectly matched to each other. They were certainly suited in the carnal way. When she had lain in his arms, his mouth on hers, she had felt weak and disembodied as if she had become a part of his body with no will of her own. *Stop,* she cried fiercely to herself, *just stop thinking such wicked thoughts!*

She forced herself to be brusque. "Prafulla Veda and the children are ready to travel."

"Is Prafulla Veda in a better mood today? Or is she still out to help Suzannah make my life miserable?"

His aura of resignation caused Anjelica to smile.

"You must treat her like a favored child, and she will learn to like you. Perhaps today the two of you will become friends. We will do puja to Ganesh before we leave here so that he will encourage Prafulla Veda to stop her abuse of you."

"Do puja?"

"That's the Hindu ritual of purification, sacrifice, and prayer. It is always done before the dangers of a long journey."

As she led him outside where the children waited with Prafulla Veda, she decided it would behoove her to pray again more diligently not to long for Stuart Delaney's lips upon hers. She would look at Nicholas Sedgwick's portrait every time she thought of how warm and hard Stuart Delaney's body had felt against hers.

Deciding it wouldn't hurt to look at her husband's image, she retrieved the silver chain from where it hung inside her shirt and clicked open her mother's old locket. She gazed at the age-worn miniature of the young boy. She wondered how Nicholas looked now, if he was as tall and handsome as Stuart Delaney. Furious with herself, she quickly shook off such disloyal thoughts.

"Come, Suzie, Sanjay. We must pray to Ganesh." She knelt in front of the stone statue of the benevolent god with the head of an elephant. The children joined her and put their palms together. She was aware that Stuart Delaney stood somewhere behind them.

"Protect us from harm as we begin our journey,"

she intoned in Hindi. "Forgive us our mistakes and entreat the mighty Prafulla Veda to treat our worthy American friend with more respect." Inwardly she added, *And help me dwell only on Nicholas Sedgwick and be as devoted and dutiful a wife to him as Sita was to Lord Rama.*

"Are we really going to leave the howdah here, Anjie?" Suzannah was at her most petulant this morning. "The mahout pad is too uncomfortable to ride on."

"The howdah belongs to Shashi. We would be no better than thieves if we took it farther than the temple. You have ridden on Prafulla Veda many times without the comfort of a howdah. Besides, I intend to teach Mr. Delaney how to ride as mahout so that Prafulla Veda will not try to harm him."

"Prafulla Veda will never let him drive her," Suzannah predicted with devious pleasure as she gave the kneeling command to the elephant. When Prafulla Veda obeyed, she mounted up her rear leg and onto her back with Sanjay following right behind her.

Stuart Delaney braced his fists on his hips and looked up at the little girl. "I'm not sure Suzannah and I can survive each other long enough to make it back to England."

"She just hates leaving Shashi so she takes it out on you. She'll do better now because I told her this morning that she could come back to Udaipur someday if she dislikes England so very much. She swore to come back and marry Shashi as soon as she's old enough, but I suspect that'll change before long."

Anjelica sat down on the ground and began wrapping a length of soft white cotton around her bare foot. "You must remove your boots and wrap your feet so that you can drive Prafulla Veda. That's the only way she will learn to respect you."

"I'll believe that when I see it," he returned but he took the cloth she handed him, sat down and carefully wound it around his instep.

"There is a rope around the elephant's neck with which we guide her movements," she told him, rising and pointing to the appropriate strap. "See, there's where it runs around her girth and beneath her tail. All our supplies have been strapped on with the weight distributed equally so we won't injure her spine. Elephants can carry great loads for many miles, you know."

"Right, so where are the reins?"

Both children giggled, and Anjelica smiled. "There are no reins. You use your feet to guide her. That's why we wrapped them."

Calling a sharp command, Anjelica patted Prafulla Veda's trunk, then allowed her to lift her to her forehead. "Stand still and she will give you a boost."

"No, thanks. She'd be more likely to stomp me into the ground. I'll go up the back like the kids did."

He did so with surprising agility for a man so large, and she guided him to the mahout's position on Prafulla Veda's neck. "Hold this rope in your hands and stick your toes under the one behind her ears."

Stuart sat down and pushed his feet into the proper position, but the minute he got them situated correctly, Prafulla Veda lifted her head backward until the cord tightened causing excruciating pain across his feet.

"Good God, she's trying to cut my toes off," he groaned through gritted teeth.

"She doesn't want you to drive her but she'll come around. Behave yourself, Prafulla Veda!" she ordered in Hindi.

Stuart sighed in relief when the elephant swung her trunk downward, relieving the pressure on his feet. "Isn't this technique a bit hard on the feet?"

"You'll get used to the pressure. Flex your toes and dig in your heels when you want her to stop. Here's the stick to make her go left and right. Just pat her head gently on the side you wish to go. She is very well trained. She responds to nearly thirty commands."

"I don't know about this," he said, frowning.

"I'll sit right behind you, in case she becomes obstinate. Don't insult her, or she'll throw back her head again and make you sorry."

"Nice elephant," he said with clenched jaw.

Anjelica called the command to move forward, and Prafulla Veda began a slow walk away from the temple steps. She quickly adapted her body to the rocking, rolling rhythm of the ride. It felt good to be in the jungle atop Prafulla Veda's back. It felt good sitting behind Stuart Delaney and holding onto his broad shoulders while she listened to his deep voice.

"Sway forward and back with the roll of Prafulla Veda's gait," she told Stuart, who seemed to be fighting the elephant's graceful movements. "You see, if you move with her, it's a most soothing ride. Elephants are very surefooted you know, and in fact the ancient writings implore women to emulate the walk of an elephant because it is considered most sensual."

"I'm beginning to see what they mean," he said, as he relaxed back against her, the exaggerated undulations of the great animal forcing Anjelica's thighs close against the outside of his legs. Once again she was in an intimate position with him, one that did not help her remember her bond with another man. Quickly, she pulled out her betrothal locket. She sighed heavily, gazing once again upon her husband. No longer did Nicholas Sedgwick seem quite so pleasant to gaze upon. Not with the incarnation of the god of love, Lord Krishna himself, sitting so close between her legs.

Chapter Ten

As they struck off through the towering trees, Stuart decided that he would rather have his toes amputated by a dull knife than to be caught between a tight strap and the neck of a vindictive elephant who hated his guts. Anjelica was insistent that he continue, however, and true to her promise, by midafternoon he had begun to get the hang of driving the temperamental beast.

He actually found himself enjoying the ride as Anjelica pointed out the ruins of ancient, vine-tangled temples and villages along the narrow jungle road they traversed so slowly. Everything seemed to slow down and become one with the methodical rocking motion of the elephant. The more Anjelica told him about the warm, sultry land that she loved, the more he could hear her reluctance to leave.

"You are doing quite well. Better than I thought you would," Anjelica complimented him as they passed the outskirts of a tiny village composed of crude huts and cattle pens made from thorn bushes.

"It does make you feel rather princely to control such a giant," he answered, patting Prafulla Veda's head to make her veer right.

"I thought you didn't like poor Prafulla Veda."

"I don't. I'm just trying to humor her."

She laughed, and he smiled at the happy sound. He liked her smile. Hell, he liked everything about her except for the fact that she was married to Marian's cousin. His fascination with her was growing worse instead of better. And sometimes she looked at him as if she wanted to devour him, immediately after which she would jerk out Nicholas's locket and gaze guiltily at her poor husband. She was too inexperienced even to know how to hide her yearning. Yet another thing she would have to learn from the grand dames of English society who were so skillful in the art of deceit.

"Ganesh! Ganesh! Ganesh!"

Stuart looked up at the joyful cries and found men and women slogging from their work in a water-covered rice field. Children had gathered at the side of the road to meet the elephant and its passengers with offerings of fruit and bowls of rice.

Prafulla Veda stopped short, taking a proffered orange with her trunk and popping it into her mouth. As the children cheered and bowed with their palms together, she wound her trunk around a second orange and made short work of it, too.

"It's their way of showing respect," Anjelica explained. "Ganesh is the god of good fortune, and they want him to bless their harvest."

She called something down in Hindi, and the children responded with a great deal of shouting and gesturing.

"What was that all about?" he asked as he prodded Prafulla Veda's ear and she rocked on, leaving the villagers to wave and trot alongside.

"I asked them where we could camp tonight, and they said there is a river just over the hill with clear, clean water. There's a protected cove there where we will be safe."

"Good." He was more than ready to extricate his feet from the torture device.

When they reached the stream a short time later, Anjelica ordered Prafulla Veda to kneel. The children slid down her trunk with happy shouts, then ran toward the river. Stuart slid off the side with more care, determined to be nowhere near the evil appendage that Prafulla Veda used to threaten him. He groaned as he landed on numb feet and found all feeling in his toes deadened by the constricted blood supply. He limped a couple of steps, wincing. Anjelica called to him from where she was busy unharnessing her wicked pachyderm.

"Go down and soak your feet in the river if you wish. I can unstrap her myself."

Stuart tried not to hobble as the sensation began to return to his toes along with the equally painful feeling of being pricked by hundreds of sharp pins. He sat down on a half-submerged log and plunged his throbbing feet into the swift-running water. He sighed audibly as the cold water soothed the burning at once, then wriggled his toes to see if they still worked.

The children were splashing and diving like frisky otters. Suzannah threw a shiny stone and plunged after it, apparently forgetting her depression about leaving India, at least for the moment. Anjelica seemed to think they would adjust to life in England, but Stuart wasn't so sure. It would be difficult for them to walk into a new, alien culture with such set and rigid mores. He had a bad feeling they would hate every minute of their life there, and it probably would be even more difficult for Anjelica.

Stuart swung his gaze back to watch as she led her elephant into the shallows. She walked straight down through the rippling water with no regard for the fact that she was fully clothed. His interest doubled in intensity as the wet silk of her tunic plastered against her breasts and hips, revealing every curve and hollow of her slender body and the fact that she wore nothing at all underneath.

Look away, for God's sake, he chided himself, but his riveted eyes did not waver as she coaxed and cajoled the animal to kneel as if it were a trained spaniel instead of a twenty-ton creature. God in heaven, but she was incredible, he thought, rising slowly without even realizing he had done so.

"This is Prafulla Veda's reward for working so hard for us today," she called with a smile as Stuart waded out to where she stood waist deep in the river. "I wash and massage every inch of her body because it gives her such pleasure."

I sure as hell would walk all day with a load on my back for such a reward, Stuart mused, then realized he was lusting after her like some monk who hadn't touched a woman in a decade. The analogy wasn't far from the truth. His forced celibacy since leaving London wasn't helping his problem keeping her at bay.

"Come help me," Anjelica invited with a sweet smile. "She'll like you better if you do. See, you take a coconut husk like this one and rub her skin very vigorously, but don't touch her spine because she's too sensitive there." As she demonstrated the task she stretched as far as she could over the elephant's back, her clinging clothes as transparent as Stuart's desire for her.

Stuart hastened to wade a few steps deeper into the stream, counting on the cold water to calm his blood a bit. The girl had no idea what she did to him. And they had a long journey yet ahead, with months together in the close proximity of an ocean-bound vessel. It was a good thing that the two children would be along for the ride.

"We'll let her enjoy herself for as long as she wants, then she'll be ready to eat her supper." Anjelica vigorously scrubbed the wrinkled gray skin. "Isn't that right, my lovely Prafulla Veda?"

The huge elephant wriggled with ecstasy just like a pampered pup, and Stuart set to work washing the animal's shoulder. Prafulla Veda watched him suspiciously, and he fastidiously avoided her pesky trunk and the deadly weapons that were her feet.

After a time Anjelica left her elephant wallowing blissfully in the shallows and swam with graceful strokes to a low rocky bluff where the water was shaded. The children were picking some kind of berries off a bramble of bushes about twenty yards upstream.

All the while telling himself he should not, Stuart followed Anjelica. She was treading water, her white-blond hair wet and slicked down over her back, but the bath had done little to erase the delicate wedding flowers painted so painstakingly across her forehead.

"When did you say the paint will wear off?" he asked as he stopped a few feet away from her.

"Not for several weeks, I'm afraid."

Stuart stared at her young face—tanned, tattooed, and still beautiful beyond compare. He sobered, glad no one in London would see her looking so exotic and enticing. She would already be the fodder of gossipmongers with her strange upbringing and Hindu faith.

"Why are you looking at me like that?" she asked seriously. "Do you find the flowers ugly?"

"Nothing could make you ugly."

His remark pleased her and that pleased him, and he knew he should get the hell out of the water and away from her before it was too late. Somehow he couldn't quite make his arms propel him back to shore.

"Do you really think I'm pretty or have you been saying that just to be nice?"

"I think you're beautiful."

"I think you are, too."

He smiled as she came close enough that he could see eyes that glowed pure silver now that twilight was darkening the river. Her face was so serious that he tried to lighten the moment.

"You'd better not get too much closer or your jealous elephant will swim out here and drown me."

"Can I hold on to you? I can't touch bottom here," she said, reaching out and grasping his shoulders before he could reply.

He put his hands around her waist and found bare skin beneath the floating top. All he had to do was slide his fingers a fraction of an inch upward and he would touch her naked breasts.

Her eyes were a darker hue now, filled with sexual longing, which she probably didn't even understand. He fought his inclination to give in to his desire for one long, excruciatingly intense moment, then he brought her body in hard against his own, wrapping his arms around her back and shutting his eyes with the pure pleasure of holding her so tightly. She put her arms around his neck and sighed, fitting inside his embrace as if she were a lost part of himself.

"We shouldn't be doing this, you know," she half moaned, her lips cold and soft against his ear. "It's wrong and will only bring us trouble."

"Yeah, I know," he muttered, his mouth finding the side of her throat.

Her chest began to heave as his mouth found her temple, then inched downward along her cheek.

"Oh, Stuart, we must stop this!"

"I know, I know," he mumbled but she was opening her mouth under his now and he could think of nothing but the feel of her, the sweet scent of her skin.

"No, we can't!" Anjelica pushed against his chest, and he released her. She looked at him with stark agony in her eyes, then struck off for shore with long, hard strokes.

Stuart stood chest deep in the water and watched her wade out near where the elephant lay relaxing on her side. Anjelica stopped and looked back at him. Every nerve and fiber in his body quivered with the desire to follow her wherever she went, to force her to her knees, then onto her back, to make her lie beneath him and cry out with pleasure. Cursing, he turned and swam slowly across the river. He was such a fool, such an utter idiot. When would he ever learn?

It was past dark when he finally sloshed out of the water. His body had cooled off, and he had come back to his senses. Anjelica affected him in extraordinary ways. He had rarely wanted a woman the way he wanted her. He had rarely met a woman he couldn't have. Unfortunately, Anjelica was just that.

Prafulla Veda was tethered by a chain to a tree

too big for her to uproot with her trunk and throw around. As he passed she turned her massive head and gave him a familiar, hostile look out of one teensy little eye. She shook her trunk and made an uncouth gargling sound.

Stuart grimaced, then climbed the hill overlooking the river where the children were throwing rocks down into the water. Anjelica was squatted before a tiny cookpot set over a campfire, busily preparing their evening meal. She didn't look at him.

"Do you want me to gather up some firewood?"

"The kids have already done that. The rice is almost ready."

He sat down on the ground and tried not to look at her until the children ran up and demanded he show them how far a god could skip a rock. Glad for the diversion he followed them, pleased when even Suzannah seemed impressed with his prowess.

After a tense meal with not one word spoken between them, Anjelica was prudent enough to put both Suzannah and Sanjay and the fire between herself and Stuart. He knew she was trying to do the honorable thing but it didn't stop him from lying on his side and staring across the flames at her. She did the same, and they watched each other in a mutually charged, lustful silence for the better part of an hour before she spoke.

"I am married to another man. You must help me remember my duty."

Her words were uttered so quietly he could barely hear them, but he certainly couldn't miss the steely quality in her voice. She rolled over with her back to him. He stared at the fire glinting off her silvery hair, and envied Nicholas Sedgwick with a passion that frightened him.

Chapter Eleven

Anjelica sat on her heels on a high rock that overlooked the calm river. She could hear Suzannah and Sanjay laughing and splashing as they bathed Prafulla Veda one last time. She sighed, gazing down the stream toward the east. She had meant every word she said to Stuart Delaney when they had camped upriver several days ago. They must not act again upon their feelings.

Already she had distanced herself from the man. She had used her inner strength to escape the hold he had on her. She had spent the days of travel meditating long and hard. She knew now that the dishonor was hers alone. She had been the one who had encouraged him to touch her, over and over. She should never have told him that Shashi ordered him to kiss her that very first time. She had wanted to know what it would feel like to be kissed by a man like him, but how could she have known that his lips on hers would awaken desires that could be quenched by no other man? Even now she missed the heady sensations he could arouse within her. She was weak! Weak and wicked!

For the last few days he had always been close enough to touch. Every time he looked at her, his azure eyes made her skin tingle. Why did Nicholas Sedgwick have to send such a man after her?

"Nice view."

She hadn't heard Stuart approach. Even the timbre of his voice caressed her flesh like the gentle stroke of his fingers. He had thrown her body into a perpetual state of awareness. She yearned for him. She feared she was obsessed with him. His very nearness was agony for her.

"What are you doing up here by yourself?"

Anjelica tensed all over as he lounged down a few feet away. Her physical response to his proximity rocked through her. She felt drawn to him as inexorably as if he had a rope around her neck and was pulling her to him. She wondered if he felt guilty about what had happened. She regretted her actions, but down deep was glad she knew how it felt to have her body burn and shiver as if caught in the throes of fever. She hoped Nicholas Sedgwick affected her the same way. But what if he didn't? What if she despised him?

"Is this where you're going to release Prafulla Veda?"

She nodded. "The herds stop here to water. Just downriver is where my father and I caught her."

"This must be hard for you."

"She'll be happy again when she walks free. She doesn't like men."

"Yeah, I figured that out."

Anjelica smiled a little, remembering how many pushes and shoves Stuart had endured from the trunk of her beloved elephant. "I'll try to be happy for her."

His blue eyes lingered on hers, and the awful longing began again. She immediately stood and moved a few steps away, when suddenly a large bull elephant burst through the undergrowth a good distance downstream. The great male raised his trunk and sniffed the air, then trumpeted an impressive mating call. Prafulla Veda swung around and hoisted her trunk from side to side.

"Suzie! Sanjay! Come up here and let her go to him—" Anjelica's voice choked, and she fought back the moisture filling her eyes. She would not cry. Her faithful friend had served her well. Now she deserved her freedom.

"Go, Prafulla Veda," she cried when the she-elephant paused and flapped her ears in agitation.

The male trumpeted more forcefully, and swung his head violently from side to side. Slowly, with a graceful swing of her hips, Prafulla Veda moved off through the shallows toward the male. Half a dozen more elephants moved out of the jungle cover and into view, and Anjelica turned away.

"She'll go with them now," Anjelica sighed. She couldn't watch her old friend join the herd. "There's a trading village not far from here. We can make it there before nightfall. No one will pay attention to us if we're afoot and dressed as untouchables."

"Dressed as what?"

"Untouchables are the lowest born of India. They perform the most menial of tasks so most contact between them and other castes is forbidden. Even the maharajah's guard will avoid untouchables."

"Doesn't sound like anyone gives these people much of a chance."

Anjelica heard the disapproval in his remark. She glanced at him in surprise. "Do your wealthy friends in London associate with the poor? Papa said it is even worse there for those who live in the slums."

"That's right, except that in England and America the lower class can rise above their station. Here they're just supposed to accept their lot and not complain about it."

"They believe they'll be rewarded in the next life if they perform their duty well. In India, patience is a highly honored virtue."

"That's one I don't have. How do untouchables dress?"

"Like any peasant. But we'll have to act as beggars so people won't recognize you as an Englishman. Suzie, Sanjay, roll around on the ground and get your clothes dirty."

"Truly, Anjie? Can we?" Suzannah asked in disbelief.

"Yes. Make yourselves as unrecognizable as you

can and don't forget to rub off the white marks of Vishnu."

"The rishi says it's wrong to change castes," Sanjay cried fearfully. "The gods'll get angry and punish us."

"We're not changing castes, we're just pretending so the guards won't find us and take you away from me. You don't want that, do you?"

Sanjay shook his head and looked like he was about to cry until Suzannah threw a handful of dirt at him. He retaliated and the two children proceeded to roll around gleefully in the dust, but Stuart Delaney didn't look as enthusiastic.

"You've got to hide the fact that you're a white man," Anjelica said. "Perhaps you could stuff your shirt with rags and pretend you're a hunchback so you won't look so tall."

"I'll be damned if I will."

Anjelica shrugged as she scooped up a palmful of dirt and rubbed it over her face. "Traveling will be more dangerous without Prafulla Veda, both from robbers and the maharajah's guards. Haven't I gotten us this far safe and sound? Won't you trust my judgment and cooperate?"

Scowling, Stuart knelt down and picked up a clod of dirt. "I liked it a hell of a lot better when I was a god."

Anjelica watched the two children giggle as they helped tear holes in each other's clothes. She was glad they were having fun. Maybe if she could

make the coming journey into an adventure it
wouldn't be so hard for them to leave India.

By late that evening Stuart realized that Anjelica
had been right again. There had been no sign of
pursuit by the maharajah's soldiers, and as Anjelica
had predicted, any travelers they had encountered
during the long walk had avoided them like the
plague. India was a strange place with strange customs, and he'd had a gut full of it. He couldn't wait
to reach the ship and get back to his own life.

Leaning forward he fed a couple of sticks into
the fire, wondering why it was taking Anjelica and
the kids so long. They had walked to the nearest
village to buy food. He hadn't liked them going
there by themselves, but Anjelica had pointed out
that his size alone made him an object of interest
among the shorter-statured men of India. He had
washed off his beggar disguise and built up the fire,
but now he was beginning to get worried. He was
debating the idea of going after them when the
snap of a twig brought all his senses alert.

Stuart gripped the revolver he wore strapped beneath his pauper robe as a man materialized from
among the trees. He was an Indian, small and
swarthy-skinned, but Stuart was relieved he didn't
wear the black uniform of the Udaipur guard. He
was bareheaded, dressed in a dark brown tunic and
travel-stained trousers. As Stuart stood up and eyed
him warily, the stranger held up both hands, palms
outward in a gesture of goodwill. When he began to

speak in rapid Hindi, Stuart grimaced to himself. Dammit, where was Anjelica? He didn't have a clue as to what the man was saying.

The Hindu traveler pressed his palms together and bowed courteously. Stuart's finger tensed on the trigger when the stranger suddenly reached into the loose folds of his coat. He relaxed again as the man brought out a gunnysack. The little man made a production of laying out a bottle of wine and several loaves of bread on the ground between them, then gestured at the fire then at Stuart then back at the food. His actions were an obvious invitation for Stuart to share his meal. Stuart was highly tempted. They had run out of food the night before. Other than a few wild berries he had found growing alongside the road, he hadn't eaten anything all day.

The man was small and appeared harmless. Stuart was twice his size and armed; he would have no trouble subduing him, if necessary. Nodding, he motioned for the Indian to join him. The man grinned, revealing sharp yellowish teeth as he sat down cross-legged on the other side of the fire. He kept smiling and bowing his head in a friendly manner as he broke the loaf and handed half to Stuart. The dark bread seemed fresh enough, without weevils or mold, which was better than some he had been given since leaving the palace of Udaipur. Stuart tore off a hunk, leaving enough for Anjelica and the children if they came back empty-handed.

The man kept up a friendly sounding conversation in his own tongue, to which Stuart nodded though he had no idea what he was discussing. He took a bite of bread, found it palatable but he kept a close eye on his new friend. The little fellow seemed amiable, and harmless enough, but he had found out the hard way that in India nothing was ever as it seemed.

After perhaps a half hour of listening to the talkative little man, Stuart was highly relieved to see Anjelica make her way into the firelight.

"Where have you been so long? I've been worried. Where's Sanjay and Suzannah?" he added, looking behind her.

"Who is this man?" she asked, ignoring his questions. She smiled at the stranger who remained seated as she approached the fire.

"I guess he's a traveler. He just showed up and offered to share his supper with me. There's enough for all of us. Where are the kids?"

Anjelica smiled and spoke in rapid Hindi to the man. When he rose to his knees and offered her a hunk of bread, she took it and politely returned his bow. The man settled back, grinning and nodding.

"Who is he? What'd he say?"

"He's on a religious pilgrimage to the temples of Calcutta. He says he's pleased to share his food with us. Smile at him and say something to keep his attention on you."

"Why? What are you doing?"

"I told him I was your wife and I was going to

Linda Ladd

fetch more wood to build up the fire. Please, just do what I ask you."

"This is really good bread, my friend," Stuart said cheerfully to the smiling man. He held up the crust and nodding enthusiastically. "Did you make it yourself or is there a bake shop near here?"

The man held up his own morsel and smacked his lips, then took a hearty swig from his cup as Anjelica seemed to wander aimlessly around in the shadows just behind him. She finally bent and picked up a large piece of wood for the fire. As she came closer, she lifted it high over her head, almost as if she were going to club the stranger, he thought, then froze where he sat as she suddenly swung the chunk of wood hard against the back of the man's skull. The impact produced the most sickening thud, and the Indian went over sideways and lay still, a piece of bread still clutched in one hand.

"Good God," Stuart said, shooting to his feet. "Why did you do that?"

"He's a thuggee," she told him calmly as she searched through the man's clothing. "He was going to murder you."

"Murder me? You've got to be kidding. Why?"

"Here, this proves it," she cried triumphantly, jerking a yellow cord from the man's tunic. "Suzie, you can bring Sanjay out now."

Stuart looked past her and saw the children run out from the darkness of the trees. "What's going on? What's a thuggee?"

"I shouldn't have left you alone. You're too naive about Indian ways. Thuggees are the disciples of Siva who prey on innocent travelers. You see, Siva is the destroyer of the world and you were to be this man's blood sacrifice to her."

Stuart stared at the yellow cord she was dangling from her fingers.

"It's a ritual murder, you see," Anjelica was explaining patiently. "He would have asked permission to sleep by the fire, then the moment you fell asleep he would have strangled you with this cord. Usually thuggees travel in groups so that several can hold down their victim while one performs the actual murder. You are lucky I came back when I did."

"Good God." Stuart stared out into the darkness. "Do you think he has accomplices out there?"

"No, he's traveling alone or they would've killed you already. But we'd better move on and find a safer place to stay the night."

"I've never seen a real thuggee before," Suzannah was saying as she bent over to examine the unconscious man with the same curiosity of a student studying a butterfly specimen. "He looks just like anybody else, doesn't he? But he isn't. Thuggees have no mercy on their victims. They like to cut open their bodies and take out their internal organs and do lots of other real horrible things to them."

"Let's get the hell out of here before his friends show up," Stuart suggested uncomfortably.

"He won't wake up for a long time," Anjelica predicted as she gathered up their meager belongings. "We'll have plenty of time to get away."

Stuart looked down at the unconscious murderer. Suddenly, Bombay seemed very far away. He had a feeling he wouldn't rest easy again until he was aboard an English ship headed out to sea.

Chapter Twelve

Stuart had been astounded to find the bustling city of Bombay teeming with a population of nearly a million people. He pushed his way through a maze of peddler pushcarts, two-wheeled rickshaws drawn by natives in brief dhotis, and sari-draped women carrying jugs of water atop their heads. As Anjelica had said, foreign ships by the dozens lay at anchor in the harbor, and Stuart was able to buy them passage on the *Jesse Porter* bound for England on the night tide. As far as Stuart was concerned, even that wasn't soon enough.

When he finally made his way almost to the end of Netaji Subhash Road, he could see the Walkesshwar Temple where he had left Anjelica and the children to say good-bye to their gods. Ironically, the old temple was built in honor of Rama, one of Vishnu's other incarnations. As he neared it he saw that the godly place seemed to be doing a brisk business.

Pilgrims beseeching favors hovered around every entrance of the ancient stone structure. Holding candles of incense, wreaths of colorful amaranth flowers, and the clarified butter called ghee—he had learned that devout Hindus liked to fling it on statues of their vast pantheon of gods—they knelt, meditated, and bought favors from robed Hindu priests. It was an exotic life that James Blake had embraced. Though not particularly to Stuart's liking, India was a bizarre, beautiful, fascinating place. No wonder Blake's children were having trouble leaving it all behind.

Stuart found a place to wait on a low wall in the shade of a huge banana tree. He braced his elbow on his knee and watched the people. He felt better than he had in days now that the clean, salty tang of the ocean filled his nostrils and he had tickets of passage in his inside coat pocket.

Before they had reached the outskirts of the sprawling city, they had washed at a stream and he had been able to don his European clothes. He found himself restless to be gone before something else happened to delay them. Searching the brightly colored bazaar tents, he found Anjelica at once, looking as lovely as ever in a sari of purple silk that nearly matched the shade of a morning glory vine climbing the temple walls in gorgeous profusion not far from her.

As usual he found himself watching her every movement. She bent and gave a yellow flower to a small child. Deep down he felt some warm, tender emotion taking hold of his heart. He clamped his jaw, furious at himself for letting it happen. He didn't want to be fond of her. He had been a fool to agree to come in the first place, but how could he have known what Anjelica would be like? No woman had captivated him so, not since Camillia. After the war, after so many seasons in London, he had thought himself immune to any kind of tenderness, much less love.

And her constant encouragement didn't help his resolve to remember she was married. Her silver eyes burned for him. He could almost feel the heat coming off her skin when they stood closer than they should. How many times in the last ten days of their journey had he lain awake and stared at the stars, tasting her mouth, remembering the silken texture of her flesh? Every time he caught the essence of sandalwood he wanted her. Every time he looked at her, he wanted her.

Now the afternoon sun glinted against her fair hair, turning it to gold, and he wanted to touch it, slide his fingers freely into the soft, curling tresses and hold her still while he kissed her till she swooned.

"Damn her," he muttered without much emotion. It was hopeless. He forced his gaze away and looked for her brother and sister.

Just down the road Suzannah had taken up business. Like any ten-year-old entrepreneur, she sat cross-legged on the ground among the milling worshipers, her oval willow basket settled before her. George the snake was swaying obediently to the notes of her flute, and a dozen or so devotees of the goddess Siva were on their knees in reverent awe while Sanjay happily skipped from person to person gathering up coins and other offerings from the generous disciples.

A different kind of affection stole across his heart as he watched them, an alien feeling that immediately astonished him. He was not a sentimental man. In fact, he couldn't tolerate most children, and Suzannah was just about the worst kid he had ever had the misfortune to meet. For all her pesky ways of making his life miserable, he had a sinking feeling that he just might miss her and Sanjay once he delivered them back to London and out of his life.

Again, he doubted how well they would adjust to life in England. Suzannah loved India too much. She would find London a cold, drab place after the warmth and lush green of the Udaipur jungles. Growing up as the pampered best friend of a maharajah in his magnificent palace would be a life hard to surpass anywhere else. Poor little Sanjay with only half English blood would fare even worse.

"Why are you frowning? Couldn't you get us passage?"

Anjelica's concerned words infiltrated his thoughts. Almost warily, he turned to face her. Lord help him, she had to be the most gorgeous woman on the face of the earth. She smiled, and he fought down the desire that rose like a skyrocket inside him. He should never have touched her, he should never have kissed her, and he sure as hell shouldn't have lain with her so intimately in his arms in the wedding bed.

"I said many prayers for you." Her warm smile turned her face into that of an angel, and his self-control weakened further when she took a garland of bright yellow marigolds from around her neck and carefully placed them over his head. "Krishna will be sure to protect you because you embodied him here on earth with great honor and dignity."

"I need all the help I can get," he replied, trying to resist her and failing miserably. He reached out and cupped the elegant curve of her cheek, and their eyes clung together in the way their bodies could not.

"I have prayed for strength to resist you," she whispered very low. "Because every time you touch me I waver in my devotion to Nicholas Sedgwick."

"How can you be devoted to someone you've never even met?"

She looked genuinely shocked. "Because I'm promised to him."

"You don't love him."

"Few wives love their husbands until they understand the inner workings of his heart."

"And some wives hate their husband's guts."

"Hate blackens one's soul. I won't hate him even if he is an unworthy man."

Stuart absorbed her low words, searched her clear, untroubled gaze. He envied the inner peace she gained from her droning sessions of meditation and her belief in the predestination of fate. He, on the other hand, had never been one to accept his lot easily. He had always taken what he wanted. Camillia's face floated out of nowhere as darkly miserable as Anjelica's was calm and serene. He had desperately wronged her all those years ago, wronged his own brother, and himself. Anjelica despised hatred but she would hate him if she knew the things he had done, the things he was capable of. If she was purity and innocence, he was the opposite.

"You're right, of course," he said with a brisk nod of dismissal. "Now get the kids and let's go. We've wasted enough time. I want to get the hell out of here."

The sharpness of his tone had been nothing more than a manifestation of his own guilt, totally undeserved by Anjelica. For an instant she looked hurt, then she turned and called for the children. For once they both jumped up and ran to join them. He vowed to keep his distance from all three of them on the voyage home. He would turn them over to Nick the minute they stepped ashore in London. They would go their way, and he would go his, and they would all be better off.

"Look at all the money George got for us, Anjie," Suzannah chimed out happily, jingling the small pouch full of coins. "I'm gonna take George to the temples of Siva in London, and we'll have lots of money there, too!"

Anjelica gentled her voice. "I don't think they have temples to Siva, sweetie. England is a Christian land with big, beautiful churches with lovely stained-glass windows of every color, and bells on tall towers that ring to bring people to worship."

"They *do* have snake charmers in their big churches, don't they?" Suzannah asked in alarm.

A vision rose up in Stuart's head of the stern and pompous Reverend Ludlum at his high podium in the prestigious Anglican church of London, thundering hell and brimstone, an Indian cobra dangling around his neck. He laughed, and all three of his companions gave him quizzical looks.

"Is that true, Stuart? No one's gonna worship George where we're going?" Suzannah seemed so distraught that Stuart wished he could tell her otherwise.

"Afraid not, kid. Most Englishmen only worship money and social standing."

Suzannah and Sanjay gave him a blank look, but Anjelica was quick to reassure them.

"Don't worry, Suzie. You can do puja to Siva, if you want to. We will praise Jesus Christ in His church, and we will have a shrine to all our Hindu gods at home."

Suzannah seemed pacified, even smiled a bit as she took the coins Sanjay had retrieved from his pockets and stuck them in her drawstring bag.

"How much longer do you plan to put this off?" Stuart asked in annoyance.

The way Anjelica looked at him made him ashamed of his impatience.

"It's difficult to leave the land one has grown up

in. Why can't you understand and feel compassion for us? Surely you felt some regret when your terrible war forced you to leave America."

On that long-ago day, Stuart had felt only relief at being delivered from the anguish of watching the South overrun by the hordes of burning, looting Yankee victors. "Sorry. I just don't want to take a chance of losing our passage to someone else."

"We're ready. Just show us the way." Anjelica took Sanjay's hand and walked toward the busy street that led west toward the docks. Stuart slung their bag of possessions over one shoulder and followed, afraid to hope that they would really get to set sail before the sun went down.

Once they had left the busy wharves and walked out on the long, wood-planked dock where the English ship was being readied to sail, Anjelica looked at the schooner that would take them away from India forever. She had mentally prepared herself many times for the actual departure. She had prayed for strength in the temple that very day, but her eyes ached with grief. She realized then just how much she loved India. She well understood Suzannah's heartbreak even though she knew they were doing the best thing for all of them.

Stuart had hurried them along relentlessly, gotten them immediate passage. He was eager to get aboard and settled in their cabin. He was as anxious to leave as they were to stay. Even now he was restlessly pacing back and forth a few yards away. Suddenly he stopped.

"They're checking the baggage as the passengers embark. There's no way Suzannah can take that cobra on board."

"But I'll keep him hidden in his basket!" Suzannah cried with shrill horror.

"They'll look in the basket," he told her impatiently. "You've got to let him go the way Anjelica did Prafulla Veda. Nobody'll hurt him with all these Siva worshipers around here."

"No, no, no!" The little girl's scream suddenly ended as she burst into loud tears.

Anjelica bit her lip, not knowing what to do. "She loves George so. Can't we hide him somehow?"

Stuart shook his head. "No. They'll check everything we carry aboard. Look up there and see for yourself."

Anjelica focused on the deck near the gangplank where several sailors were going through the baskets, trunks, and boxes being carried aboard.

"I'm not going then! I'm gonna stay here and marry Shashi the way he wants me to! I like him, and I want to be one of his wives! Go on, go off to that stupid old England and leave me here! I hate it! I hate churches with stained-glass windows and big loud bells!"

Suzannah's outburst crescendoed into near hysteria, making passersby turn and stare at them.

"Hush now, darling. Maybe we can think of a way George can go. They aren't checking the passengers. Perhaps one of us can hide him inside our clothes."

"No, he's too big," Sanjay noted in his usual calm way. "They'll see him."

Anjelica looked at the children's tight tunics and her own soft, flowing sari. It was true. The cobra would be noticeable. Her eyes moved to Stuart Delaney's loose white shirt and white cotton frockcoat. The children followed her speculative gaze. It didn't take Stuart long to catch their drift.

"Not a chance," he said in no uncertain terms.

"But your shirt is loose there where it's tucked in around your waist, and your coat would hide any bulges."

"No, I said. I hate snakes, especially that cobra."

Suzannah ran to Stuart and pulled out the side of his coat. "Look, Anjie, you're right, there's plenty of room for George. He can wrap himself around Stuart's waist a couple of times and nobody would know."

"Well, *I'd* know, that's for damn sure!" Stuart ground out furiously. "I'm not going to do it, and that's final."

Suzannah sank to the ground in a crumpled heap of unbridled despair. She dropped her face into her hands and began a loud, violent sobbing. Tenderhearted Sanjay burst into a fit of sympathetic weeping. Anjelica's eyes brimmed with condemnation.

"It's very little to ask, you know, and it means so much to the children."

"Little to ask? Are you crazy?"

"But, Stuart, she's had to leave behind everything else she cares about. I promised her from the beginning that she could take George if she swore to keep him in his basket. That's the only way I could get her to agree to leave Udaipur and come with us."

Stuart muttered a string of oaths so unpleasant that Anjelica blushed and looked away. He paced several steps from them and ran his fingers through his long hair.

"You're the only one who can hide him," she ventured cautiously a few moments later. "I'd do it if I could. And you know George has been defanged. He can't really hurt anybody. He's really very sweet for such a big snake."

Stuart shook his head angrily. Suzannah was lying on her belly in the dirt, sobbing heartbrokenly as she clutched George's basket in the circle of her arms.

"Go without me, let me be an orphan with nobody to love me," she was blubbering over and over.

"No, no, Suzie, I'd never leave you behind." Anjelica was on her knees attempting to comfort the distraught child. "None of us want to go without you—"

"Oh, all right, for God's sake," Stuart said tightly, "but I'm telling you one thing, Suzannah, you better not ever give me any more trouble, not about anything, do you understand? I've had it up to here with your constant whining and complaining."

Anjelica's heart softened toward Stuart. Suzannah raised her small, tear-stained face, a tremulous smile curving her lips.

"Oh, thank you, thank you, Mr. Delaney, Lord Krishna, thank you so much. I'm sorry for all those terrible names I've been calling you, I'm sorry for scaring you with George and making Prafulla Veda dump you in the lake, and hitting you with my slingshot, and telling everybody you weren't really a god—"

"Okay, okay, I get the idea," Stuart muttered sourly as he unbuttoned his shirt.

"I'll get him all settled in, and I'll tell him to lie real still and not to slither around too much," Suzannah chirped happily, her tears forgotten as she carefully lifted the writhing cobra out of the basket.

Stuart's face looked absolutely revolted as she began to uncoil the reptile and carefully push it inside his shirt and around the lean muscles of his waist.

"Oh God, do I ever hate snakes. Make him lie still, will you?"

"Think of something else, Stuart," Anjelica suggested with a smile. "Your fear of snakes is all in your mind, you know."

"Like hell. My fear of snakes is slithering up my back," he replied harshly through clamped teeth. "C'mon, let's get this over with before the damn thing finds a way down my pants."

Stuart struck off at a rapid pace toward the gangplank, and sweet warm feelings of gratitude began to glow deep inside of Anjelica. He was the man who had come to India to get them. He had faced danger and hardship for them. Now, he had even won Suzannah's heart. Oh, God help her, she was falling hopelessly in love with him. Despite all her prayers and efforts to resist him, she cared more deeply for him than she had ever felt about anyone in her life. How could she ever say good-bye to him and watch him walk out of her life forever?

Chapter Thirteen

Anjelica looked across the cramped cabin at Stuart where he stretched out across the opposite bunk, his long, lean frame looking ridiculously oversized in its narrow confines. Although she realized they had been incredibly lucky to have attained such expedient passage at all, they had been forced to share accommodations in one small cabin. During the long weeks at sea it would be difficult for her to be so close to him.

Sanjay stirred drowsily where he had snuggled in close against her side. Smiling, she rubbed his back in circles the way he had liked her to do since he was a small baby. Suzannah sat on the floor playing with George, and Anjelica smiled to herself when she remembered the way Stuart had pulled open his shirt and violently jerked the wiggling snake out of his clothes the minute he had reached their cabin. He had not enjoyed the ruse but he had certainly earned Suzannah's affection.

Suzannah emitted a huge yawn, then rubbed sleepy eyes with her balled fist. Anjelica watched

her carefully place George into his basket, then settle the lid securely on top. As the little girl stood
up, Angelica made room for her on their bunk but
instead Suzannah climbed in beside Stuart. Without a word, she cuddled against his side.

Stuart looked stunned and Anjelica realized he
was rather uncomfortable with Suzannah's new-
found affection. Their eyes met, and she was
pleased when he tentatively draped his arm around
her little sister. The feud between them had been
bitter during their tenure in Udaipur, but now
Suzannah was completely devoted. Within minutes,
the tired little girl was sleeping peacefully.

Stuart shook his head. "I can't figure this kid
out."

Anjelica only smiled.

They lapsed into silence again, but she knew he
watched her, could see the glint of his blue eyes
even in the semi-darkness of the cabin. She wondered if he knew how she felt about him. Her feelings had grown deeper since that afternoon, so
much more intense and disturbing that she was almost frightened.

"My feelings for you have changed," she said.

"How?" he asked quietly.

"I'm not sure. I don't understand them."

"Take my advice and forget them. That's what I'm
going to do."

Anjelica frowned. "Do you really care about me
or is it just the desire for congress you want from
me?"

Stuart said nothing. She wondered if his silence meant he did not know or that he was uncomfortable saying the words. He was not a man of many words or one to express his inner feelings. Why? she mused, why was he so closed and cold? She suddenly wanted to know everything about his past.

"You've never said much about your family," she prompted gently. She really shouldn't be interested. She should be asking him more questions about Nicholas Sedgwick's family.

He lifted a shoulder in a small shrug and closed his eyes as if to discourage her.

"You have a sister, I know, but do you have any brothers?"

"No."

"What about your parents? Are they still living?"

"No."

"When did they die?"

"My father died when I was little. I barely remember him. Mother died a few years back. My sister was with her but I was still with my unit in Tennessee."

"What is Tennessee?"

"It's a state down south."

"Is that near New Orleans?"

He nodded. "Fairly close, I guess. Why?"

"Maybe I'm just curious to know how you developed into such a fine man."

To her surprise, he became annoyed. "Don't kid yourself. I have more faults than you'd be interested in hearing about."

"I haven't noticed many," she said truthfully. "Except that you get angry and upset when I ask about your past."

"I don't get angry and upset," he said in an angry, upset tone.

She smiled when he seemed to realize that she was right. "Were you close to your mother?"

"No."

"What was she like?"

"She was beautiful and petite, like my sister Cassandra is, and like you are."

"Do you think I'll ever get to meet your sister?"

"I don't know if I'll ever see her again."

Anjelica frowned. "Doesn't that bother you?"

"I don't think about it much. I'm trying to start a new life in England just like you are."

Anjelica no longer enjoyed fantasizing about a life with her husband. She wished Stuart wouldn't bring it up. She didn't want to think about arriving in England and perhaps never seeing Stuart again. Her heart twisted painfully.

"Are you going to stay in London with us for a while after we arrive?"

"I'm your legal guardian, so I guess I'll have to. At least until you move in with Nick."

Absurdly the destiny for which she had anticipated and prepared herself for so many years suddenly seemed terribly threatening. "Sometimes I can't believe I'm married to a man I've never met."

"It is a bit feudal."

"Not in India."

"You aren't in India anymore."

For the first time she could ever remember since her mother had died, she doubted her duty. Not only did she doubt it, she wanted to forget all about it, forget her honor and her promises. All she wanted was to walk across the cabin and let Stuart Delaney hold her tight against him the way he was holding her little sister. She wanted him to tell her he loved her.

Frightened that she was in danger of doing that very thing, she turned her head away from him. She lay down beside Sanjay and stared at the planked wall, fighting tears that burned so deep she felt the ache would never go away.

After a time, she heard Stuart move off the bunk. He snuffed the candle hanging in the ceiling lamp. The cabin was plunged into darkness, and she heard him quietly let himself out the door. She lay still, listening to the quiet surge of the sea as the ship plunged through ocean waves that would take her to the husband she had never met.

Nearly a fortnight later Suzannah stood watching her sister where she stood at the starboard bow. Quickly, she glanced back to the stern where Stuart Delaney leaned against the rail. He was watching Anjelica the way he always did, and Anjelica was pretending not to watch him, the way she always did. What was the matter with them, anyway? They were acting downright dumb.

"I've decided that Anjelica should be married to

Stuart and not that old Sedgwick husband she's got."

At her unexpected proclamation, Sanjay turned big, shocked eyes on her. "You do? Why?"

"Because I like him now, and I want him to live with us."

Sanjay sent an incredulous gaze toward the back of the ship. "Me, too, but will Anjie's new husband let him live with us?"

Suzannah snorted. "Well, 'course not. He'll want Anjelica all to himself, if he's got any sense about him. But I'll bet he's not nearly as handsome as Stuart is or smart, either. And he sure didn't come all the way down to Udaipur to get her for himself, now did he? He sent Stuart 'cause he's braver and better."

"But he's already her husband," Sanjay reminded her.

"Maybe he'll die or get killed before we get back and then she'd be a widow," she decided callously, much to Sanjay's consternation.

"Oh, the gods will punish you for sayin' stuff like that. You better take it back in a big hurry."

"Well, I guess I don't wish he was dead, but we gotta help Stuart get Anjelica instead of Nicholas Sedgwick. He wants her for his wife, you know."

"He does? How'd you know that?"

" 'Cause I pretended to be asleep that first night on board so I'd get to hear what they said. She said straight out that her feelings were all mixed up about Nicholas and I heard her crying after he left.

And after that he hasn't come back to the cabin to sleep, not once, and that's why."

Sanjay's expression remained solemn. "She has to stay married to him. Your mum said so. And you always say your mum was nice and everybody always did what she asked them to."

The thought of her mother made Suzannah's throat get all thick and made it hard to swallow. She still missed her lots, but sometimes she couldn't remember just exactly what her face looked like unless she opened up her gold locket and looked at the little painting of her.

"But Mum never did meet Stuart Delaney, either," she insisted stubbornly. "Or she would've liked him best, too, just like all the ladies on this ship do. Just look up there. That woman with the red hair is always trying to start up talking with him."

With a frown of displeasure she watched the pretty young woman with the flaming hair smile up at Stuart Delaney's face like he'd told her a real funny joke. Well, that was sure going to have to stop, she decided, if Anjelica was to get him. She took Sanjay's hand and pulled him down the deck.

"Come on, Sanj, let's get Stuart to take us down to help us catch George. He's been loose in the cabin all morning so we can put him back in his basket. And if that red-haired woman keeps hanging around, I'll put George under her skirt and see how much she likes Stuart then!"

Chapter Fourteen

England, Anjelica mused wistfully as she looked out over the myriad of church spires and garroted rooftops lining the River Thames. As the steam schooner glided to berth through the murky gray waters, she recalled vividly the pleasure with which her mother had remembered the great edifices of the fabled city of London.

Even after Mary Blake had been stricken with tuberculosis and lay so desperately weak, her suffering exascerbated by the sweltering climate of India, she had reminisced over the delicious scents of fresh bread wafting from the pushcart venders of Charing Cross and the flutter of pigeons taking flight from the roof of the magnificent dome and pillars of Saint Paul's Cathedral.

Now all the grandeur and history of the British capital spread out before them. Anjelica had realized Mary Blake's wishes. Her children were back where they belonged. Anjelica gazed out over the old city, so famous for its royal pomp and circumstance. Here tradition was rich and ancient, perhaps revered even more than that of the Hindu cultures of India.

Surprisingly, Anjelica felt as if she were coming home after enduring a long, forced absence. Her sentimentality about the country of her birth shocked her; she had expected to feel as much a foreigner to her family's heritage as Suzannah and Sanjay did.

The children stood beside her at the rail. Though they were putting up a brave front, she knew they were both frightened about the future. Anjelica intended to help them accept the new English customs, so alien from everything they had known in Udaipur, and she would start that very moment.

"Look, my dears." Anjelica pointed at a massive stand of buildings lining the west bank of the river. "There are the Houses of Parliament. Remember, I told you that the English have both a House of Lords and a House of Commons who make the laws."

"Their old government buildings aren't nearly as grand as Shashi's palace, if you ask me." Suzannah curled her lips into a haughty snarl. "They don't even have an elephant gate!"

Anjelica shook her head. Her work was cut out for her if she was to convince Suzannah there was anything of value on the isle of Britain. Nothing could compare to Udaipur in her eyes, but at least Sanjay seemed a bit more receptive to learning about England.

"Is that big clock over there the one Stuart calls

Ben?" The small boy had to stand on his tiptoes to see the structure better. He used his cupped palm to shield his eyes from the early morning sun.

"That's right, sweetie. Everyone calls it Big Ben. And there are hundreds of churches everywhere in the city, and their bells will peal together. It's a wonderful sound. I can remember hearing them ring when I was as little as you, and Mama took me riding through Hyde Park in Grandpapa's fine carriage."

"Why have you been so mean to poor Stuart since we got on the ship in Bombay?" Suzannah demanded unexpectedly. She peered at Anjelica with a hostile frown. It wasn't the first time Suzannah had pointed out her estrangement from Stuart. Anjelica sighed.

"I haven't been mean to Stuart."

"Yes, you have, and you know it, too! You hardly never say anything to him."

"*Ever* say anything," Anjelica corrected absently, not wanting to argue with Suzannah.

"See, now even you admit it. When he walks up to you on the deck, you just hurry off by yourself. Then you cry at night in the bunk and keep us all awake, and that's because you like him so much. You've gone and fallen in love with him, haven't you? That's the truth, isn't it?" Suzannah awaited Anjelica's response with her hands planted on her hips.

Anjelica gasped and glanced around, hoping no one had overheard her sister's outrageous remarks.

"Suzannah!" she hissed under her breath, "Don't you dare say such things out loud where people can hear you. I'm already married to Nicholas Sedgwick. You know that very well. I'll be joining him shortly so please don't make things any harder. Stuart's been a good friend to us but now we'll have to move on, as I'm sure he'll do himself."

Suzannah raised her chin defiantly, but she did lower her voice. "I still think you and Stuart make a pretty couple. He *is* the one who killed the tiger for you and came after us, you know, and he's the best man around anywheres. And you know that, too!"

Aware of just how stubborn her sister could be, Anjelica immediately changed the subject to something more neutral. She fixed her attention on her little brother. "Look, Sanj, down there in the distance around the bend, you'll soon see the Tower of London. It's a great English fortress. It's very old, and sometimes the king uses it as a prison."

"Will they put us in there?" Sanjay asked, wide-eyed.

Anjelica put her arm around him. "Of course not, sweetheart. It's for the king's enemies."

Sanjay looked relieved. "Are there lots of soldiers in there, too? Are they all dressed up in red like the ones who marched around with their guns in the Red Fort at Agra?"

Sanjay's voice was worried, and she realized that he was more afraid than she had thought. Shashi had always been afraid that the British would attack his princedom, and he had no doubt communicated his concern to Sanjay. Sanjay would soon see he had nothing to worry about in England.

"Yes, but they're here to protect us, not to harm us." She smiled encouragingly, and her brother looked back at the buildings lining the river. Sanjay was very intelligent, and amazingly mature for his age. He would no doubt become a scholar someday, perhaps even study in the great university at Oxford. If he had remained in India, she felt sure he would have become a great rishi. Guilt gouged into her breast for taking him away from all he had known. Had she done the wrong thing? But how could she have ever left him behind? He was her brother. And she felt more like a mother to both children.

"Do you think you'll like it here in England after you get used to things, Sanjay?" she asked gently.

For a moment, the little boy was thoughtful. When he finally looked up at her, his wavy black hair blew around in the brisk harbor wind. "I guess so, but I'm sure gonna miss riding up in Prafulla Veda's howdah, and washing all the other elephants down in Pichola Lake, you know, the way we always did when the sun was getting ready to set?"

Unfortunately, Anjelica knew exactly what he meant. "Me, too, but Prafulla Veda's free now. That's what she wanted, you know. I'm sure you'll find lots of interesting things to do here that'll be just as much fun as washing the elephants."

"You didn't really answer my question, Anjie."

Suzannah was not about to give up on Stuart. She tugged sharply on Anjelica's yellow sari in order to emphasize her point. Then she adopted the black scowl that was becoming all too familiar. "Are you gonna just forget all about Stuart now that he's brought us back, even after the way you kissed him on his mouth and got in the marriage bed in front of the nuptial audience—"

This time Anjelica effectively squelched her sister's humiliating litany with the palm of her hand. She certainly did not want to be reminded of her sins in the arms of Stuart Delaney. She remembered his every touch much too vividly anyway. She couldn't let herself dwell on him, not now when she was on the verge of meeting her husband. "Now you hush, Suzie, and I mean it! Do you hear me? Not another word about Stuart and me. It's a secret that Nicholas Sedgwick must never know about. Do you understand? You could get us all in very big trouble talking like that."

"Talking like what?"

At the sound of Stuart's deep voice, Anjelica's entire body drew up to defend herself against his overwhelming effect on her. With an emotion akin to fear clutching her heartstrings, she turned slowly around and faced him. He stood very close, too close, his hand resting on the rail. His handsome features were stark and cold with the awful taciturn expression he had worn since the night they had left Bombay.

Throughout the long, tedious weeks of the voyage, he had avoided her, always appearing angry and short-tempered if they did happen to meet. He had single-mindedly spurned any friendly overture she had attempted until she had stopped trying. He had been doing exactly what she had asked him to do. He was helping her keep her troth to Nicholas. They could never be anything to each other, not even friends, she feared. The realization hurt almost more than she could bear.

At the sight of Stuart, Suzannah grinned with delight and slipped her hand into Stuart's large one. Stuart's hard-frozen look dissolved when he looked down at her sister, and Anjelica was embarrassed to find herself coveting the warm smile he bestowed on Suzannah.

"Can we come stay at your house, Stuart?" Suzannah begged, bobbing her head up and down as if that would make him agreeable.

Anjelica stared at Stuart's hand, almost able to feel his fingers sliding over her bare flesh. Just like Suzannah's small fingers, her hands had been lost inside those long, tanned fingers. Her heart sank to the pit of her stomach. He would never be able to hold her hand or touch her again. Only Nicholas Sedgwick could do so—a complete stranger who would soon take her into his bed and have congress with her.

Though she had not seen him since she was a little girl and had mentally prepared herself for the eventual marital act, the idea made her physically sick. What if he were an awful man? Repulsive or loathesome or abusive? She was gripped by the terrible feeling that any man would seem wanting after spending time in Stuart Delaney's arms.

Stuart's answer was short and to the point. "For a night or two, I suppose, but then you'll go live in the Sedgwick mansion with Anjelica's husband."

When his blue eyes cut mockingly to her face, Anjelica glanced away, unable to meet them. She bit her lip. He had obviously used the long days at sea purging himself of the desire he felt for her. He was making it perfectly clear that he intended to end any contact between them. If only she could be as cool and detached as he was. Instead, she longed incessantly for a look, a touch, a smile from him.

"You mean we aren't never gonna see you again after this night?" Suzannah's eyes went round with the horror of the idea. "Are you really gonna just dump us off at Nicholas Sedgwick's house like old stray dogs nobody wants anymore?"

Stuart looked uncomfortable at the analogy, and Anjelica waited with bated breath, terrified that Suzannah's fears were exactly what Stuart intended to do. "I suspect you and Sanjay can come over to visit, that is, if I stay here in London. I'm thinking of moving on."

"Are you gonna take us sailing on that yacht you were telling us about? Is it really tied up on the river just waiting for you to come back?" Sanjay asked excitedly.

Suzannah was more to the point. "Move on? You

can't go off and leave us here alone! What do you mean move on?"

"I may return to Virginia one of these days, but I'll see you before I go, I promise."

The children were appeased, albeit mildly, but Anjelica was hurt to be excluded. Although she knew she should not, she voiced that fear.

"Am I to take it that I'm not invited to come along with the children?" she asked, on as light a note as she could manage. She waited, desperately wanting him to say he wished her to come, too.

Stuart's eyes seemed to look through her, the same cold blue, like ice chipped from a frozen pail of water. "I think you'd be better off spending the time getting to know your husband."

His voice was detached, as if he could care less. She was glad when Sanjay took her hand and pulled her down so that he could whisper in her ear. "That's all right, Anjie. I'll tell you all about Stuart's boat, I promise."

"The crew's about got the gangplank in place," Stuart said with his new brusqueness. "I'll get you to my place but then I'll have to leave and take care of some business."

Marian Foxworthy was probably that business, Anjelica thought angrily as Stuart strode off ahead of them toward the spot where their fellow passengers were lining up for disembarkation. Their own meager baggage had been brought up beforehand, and the crew was rushing around, securing the lines and winching to shore the heavier steamer trunks and freight crates. Ship-weary people were crowding ever closer to the rail, holding bandboxes and valises, more than ready to step down on the solid soil of England.

Anjelica stood back with the children and watched Stuart take charge of the arrangements. He made his way quickly toward a line of hackney cabs awaiting fares along the edge of the wharf. He secured one at the forefront, and within a space of half an hour, they were aboard the rented coach, their meager belongings strapped to the rear luggage rack. She had made a point to choose the seat across from Stuart, exacerbating her own desire to gaze at him. She wouldn't be around him much longer, and she endeavored to memorize the chiseled contours of his face—his strong chin and high cheekbones, the way his eyes were slightly hooded under his straight black brows, the way his shaggy hair curled slightly behind his ears.

The wheels had barely begun to roll when Suzannah left her place beside Anjelica and hopped across the carriage to sit close to Stuart. Her sister had certainly done an about-face with the man. At least Stuart had decided not to cut the children loose as he had done with her. She was glad because at the moment he was Suzannah's and Sanjay's only friend in the whole of England.

"How does it feel to be back home?" She wanted to make him talk with her so she could hear his voice.

"I'm damn glad to resume my life, if that's what

you mean." He doggedly observed the storefronts along the busy street.

After that remark Anjelica remained silent, and so did Stuart. The children leaned out the window and remarked on everything they passed until the crowded cobbled streets eventually turned into narrow dirt roads that led into the outskirts of the capital. By the time the cabby stopped at their destination, Anjelica knew Stuart resided in a wooded rural tract that edged the Thames.

She leaned forward to peer up at the ivy-twined, two-story Georgian brick. At the precise moment the coach rocked to a standstill in the front drive, a dreary-visaged butler dressed in staid black coat and trousers opened the double oak doors and descended the front steps.

"Did you send word that we were arriving?" she asked, half afraid Nicholas Sedgwick might be waiting inside to meet her. She wasn't ready for that yet. She wasn't sure she ever would be. Stuart merely shook his head, then opened the door and jumped to the ground. The children nearly knocked each other down scrambling out behind him. Hesitating briefly, Stuart seemed to consider assisting her, then obviously changed his mind. He turned to the butler, and Anjelica lifted the silken folds of her sari and stepped down by herself.

"Mr. Delaney, sir, please allow me to be the first to welcome you home after such a lengthy absence. I do hope you had a pleasant and rewarding journey."

"Yeah," was Stuart's less than enthusiastic reply, to which he added, "I've brought along some overnight guests, but they'll be leaving promptly as soon as we can contact their kin. Please see that they're comfortable, would you?"

"Of course, sir. Is there anything you would like? The entire staff is assembled and ready for service. Would the young people here like a spot of supper, perhaps?"

The elderly manservant looked at Anjelica with an improper degree of curiosity and she could see the contempt thinly veiled in his dark eyes as he took in her softly draped garment of India.

Somewhere, though, in the lacy cobwebs of her dimmest recollections he reminded her of her Grandfather Blake who had let her play with his long white beard when she was a child. Far too much time had passed for her to clearly remember his face, but she did recall that he always smelled of tobacco and port wine.

Stuart led the way up the steps to the front door and the children hastened after him, eagerly questioning him about his boat. As he answered that it was moored on the river behind the house, Anjelica followed silently, more than aware that she was being deliberately ignored.

No one waited for her at the doorway, and she stepped inside the house and found the interior cozy and comfortable with rich and gleaming cherry wainscoting in the narrow front hall. As the butler hurried after the two children romping wildly toward the rear of the house, she glanced into the formal dining parlor to the right of the front door. A lovely brass chandelier hung above the cherrywood table, and twelve brocaded chairs encircled the walls. The other side of the foyer opened into a dark-paneled library, and it was into that room that Stuart had walked without a backward glance in her direction.

His uncharacteristic rudeness would almost have been amusing if it hadn't hurt her feelings so much. She watched him proceed to a large rectangular mahogany desk, then she glanced around the room. A large stack of unanswered correspondence lay on a library table beside the door. When she picked up the top letter, she saw the stiff white parchment envelope carried Marian Foxworthy's name embossed in gold. A good portion of the remaining letters did as well.

"It appears you've missed quite a few social engagements," she remarked, replacing the letter in the silver tray.

Stuart looked up as if he had already forgotten she was there. She wondered if he was really so immune to her and envied him if he was. "Then I'll just have to make up for lost time now that I'm back." He returned to where he had been leafing through the papers atop his desk.

"Why are you treating me like this?" she entreated softly when he continued to ignore her.

"Like what?" His voice was guarded.

She took a step toward him.

"I want us to be friends, if nothing else. I know it's my fault things went so far between us while we were in Udaipur. I'll take all the blame. I just don't want to lose you completely—"

Stuart threw the letter he held to the desktop, and she stiffened at the dangerous look on his face. "Look, Anjelica, don't you get it? I don't want to be your friend. I don't want to be anything to you." He stopped speaking, and the lean muscle of his cheek flexed tight. "After tonight you'll go your way, and I'll go mine. That's the way we both want it, now isn't it?"

Stunned by his harshness, Anjelica stood silently as he rounded the desk and walked past her and out the door.

"Willie'll be here, if you need anything," he said over his shoulder. "I'll be staying the night at Marian's. I'll have her arrange for Nicholas to pick you and the kids up in the morning just as early as he can."

Then he was gone, probably forever, without even a good-bye. Anjelica stared at the empty doorway for a long, awful moment, then sank down on a straight-back chair beside her. She was never going to see him again, she knew it. A rush of tears burned her eyelids, but she fought her grief back by grinding her teeth together until her jaw ached.

She wouldn't cry over him like some little foolish maiden whose feelings were hurt. She would go on without him. She would meet Nicholas and learn to love him. Her life would be wonderful just the way her mother had always promised it would be. She didn't need Stuart Delaney any more than he needed her, she thought fiercely, but she knew it wasn't true. She would never forget him, not as long as she lived.

Chapter Fifteen

Stuart slapped his riding gloves impatiently against his thigh as the groom finished saddling his horse. He swung into the saddle, pulled the reins sharply, then kicked the gelding into a brisk trot back down the road to London. He was damn sick and tired of the whole bloody mess. And he was angry—at Marian for sending him to India in the first place, at Anjelica for turning out to be so beautiful and desirable, but more than anything he was furious with himself for falling in love with her. He was the worst kind of fool to have lost himself to her innocent charms.

For days upon days, for weeks he had endured a never-ending, miserable voyage from hell, trying not to think about Anjelica, not to want her, not to miss her or look at her or touch her. Damn her! Damn everybody and everything!

Now she wanted to be his goddamn friend, as if they ever could be anything less than lovers. He supposed she wanted him to come over and take tea with her and watch Nicholas hold her hand and kiss her mouth. Damned if he'd ever do that. He intended to get the hell out of England as soon as he collected his pay from Stonegate and Havenstern. Maybe he would go to France for a while, or Scotland, eventually he might even want to return to Virginia. Anywhere would do, as long as he was a thousand miles away from Anjelica Blake.

The roiling rage that had been building up inside him for weeks had not dissipated by the time he reached the offices of Stonegate and Havenstern on King's Cross Road. Before he left London he had spent three days there in their velvet-hung establishment being briefed about his mission to India. Now it was finished, and he wanted his money. He had damn well earned every penny, mentally and physically.

A diminutive male secretary sat in the antechamber working behind a polished mahogany desk. He was dressed meticulously in a primly cut brown and black pin-striped suit and black string bow tie, his white cuffs protected by a black sleeve protector. He glanced up from his lined blue ledger book when Stuart entered, frowning as if highly annoyed by the interruption. He peered over his tiny round wire-rimmed glasses, then slicked back a lock of pale blond hair into the oiled part down the middle of his head. He looked Stuart up and down as if he found his shaggy black hair less than acceptable.

"Tell Stonegate that Stuart Delaney's back."

The man looked highly offended. "If you're referring to Mr. Stonegate, our senior partner here at the firm, sir, I'll see if he's available to receive you."

"He damn well better receive me. I've spent the last three months tracking down his bloody client for him."

"Indeed?" The slender young man arched a suspicious eyebrow. "Please be seated, sir, and I'll announce your arrival to Mr. Stonegate."

Stuart didn't sit down. He paced back and forth in front of the window that overlooked the busy thoroughfare below where carriages and wagons continually rattled past. He wanted the whole episode over and done with, once and for all. He wanted Anjelica out of his life.

"Mr. Stonegate will see you now."

Following the sissified secretary down a narrow corridor lined with glass-doored offices, Stuart was finally shown into the well-appointed one of Mr. Thomas Stonegate himself. The esteemed lawyer stood at once and came around the desk. He extended his arm for a handshake, and Stuart clasped his fingers in a firm grip, then seated himself in the leather upholstered chair positioned at the front of the large Chippendale desk.

"So you're back. It took longer than we anticipated, I believe," Stonegate remarked, relaxing back into his swivel chair. "Did you find the Blake girls?"

"Yeah, along with a brother no one knew about."

"A brother, you say? How extraordinary."

"Blake's dead now but he had time to remarry after his first wife died."

"I see. Did you have any trouble getting them out?"

Stuart wanted to laugh, but he wasn't in the mood. "I got them here, didn't I?"

Stonegate observed him over his steepled fingers. "Are they all right? In good health, I mean?"

Stuart nodded. "Yeah. You can notify Nicholas Sedgwick that he can pick up his wife at my house first thing tomorrow. I won't be staying there myself so there's no need for him to start yelling about impropriety."

The portly lawyer sat forward and lit a cigar he had taken from a flat box made of fine cut glass. "Would you care for a smoke? They're Cuban, the very best I might add."

"I'm in a hurry. I'm here to collect my fee and be on my way."

"Are you sure nothing's wrong? Are the two girls all right?"

Stuart was beginning to get annoyed. He was seething just under the surface and had been for some time, and Stonegate was inches from setting him off. "Dammit, I've been gone three bloody long months. I'd say I've waited long enough."

Stonegate took his time puffing his cheroot until it caught. He nodded slowly. "You've earned your commission, Mr. Delaney, that's for sure. I'm really quite pleased you've been so successful. Frankly I was afraid you wouldn't find hide nor hair of James Blake, much less his girls. They've been gone for years."

"They were waiting to be found. Now let's get down to business. Like I said, I've got things to do."

As the white-haired senior law partner began to shift in his swivel chair, Stuart got an uneasy feeling in his gut. The sensation intensified as the older man cleared his throat and retrieved a tan file folder from his desk drawer.

"Well, Mr. Delaney, I can certainly write you out a bank draft for half the amount right now."

Stuart watched him withdraw a bound blue book. His eyes narrowed. "Half the amount?"

"That's right. I'm afraid there's a condition to getting the other half."

Stuart sat forward, his brows furrowing into a straight line. "What the bloody devil's going on? We had a deal. I carried out my part. Now I want my due."

"And you'll get it, of course. There'll just be a short delay. You see, one of the parties interested in finding the Blakes lives in America. She wishes to come here herself and meet the two girls."

"So? What's that got to do with my money?"

"She insisted that you keep them with you until such time as she can arrive. Anjelica Blake will need a place to stay for a time until she actually moves in with her husband. Their parents wrote in a clause giving her a short time to get to know Sedgwick before they actually consummate the marriage. By that time, my American client will have reached England and can take care of the details, including the release of your bank draft."

"Wait a damn minute. I didn't agree to nursemaid the girl after I got her back here."

"She really doesn't have anywhere else to go, Mr. Delaney. It'll only be for a matter of weeks, at the most. That'll give your grandmother time to arrive."

Stuart looked blankly at him, thinking he must have misunderstood what Stonegate had said. "What do you mean, *my* grandmother?"

"I mean our American client is your grandmother, Sarah Delaney of Newport, Rhode Island. She contacted us just after your Civil War ended and hired us to find Mary Blake's daughters. In fact, she was the one who insisted that you had the best qualifications to go after them."

Completely nonplussed, Stuart could only stare at him in silence. "Why would she do that? How the devil did she even know that I was here in England?" He scowled, then his eyes narrowed as he began to realize to what extent he had been manipulated. "I think you'd better tell me exactly what's going on, Stonegate."

"I suspect you'll have to discuss that with Mrs. Delaney as soon as she arrives in London. From what I could divine, however, your grandmother considers herself an old and dear friend to the mother of these girls."

"What are you talking about? How could they be old friends?"

"As I said, you'll have to ask her when she arrives here in London."

"I don't want the girl at my house." And that was

the understatement of the year, Stuart thought angrily.

"I'm afraid you have little choice if you want to receive payment from Mrs. Delaney. She wants them to stay with you until she arrives. I suspect that when your grandmother arrives, she intends to take the girls under her wing. Until then I'm afraid she's entrusted them into your care."

Stuart had to grit his teeth to restrain his desire to grab the elderly lawyer by the throat. Without a word, he rose and stalked out of the room. Whether the truth came from Marian, Sarah Delaney, or Anjelica herself, somebody was going to tell him just what the hell was going on.

For a long time after Stuart left, Anjelica sat in the same chair in Stuart's office wrapped in melancholy. When staid Willie appeared in the threshold announcing a visitor, anxiety burst like a balloon in her breast. What if the caller was her unknown husband? She was both relieved and upset to learn that it was not Nicholas Sedgwick who was waiting for admittance, but a certain Mrs. Marian Foxworthy.

With some reluctance she asked Willie to show the lady in, then wished she had at least taken a moment to comb her hair and put on a fresh costume. Her sari was wrinkled and drooping from the long carriage ride. A moment later a tall, statuesque brunette appeared in the doorway, looking strikingly lovely in a lemon yellow taffeta dress and matching black beribboned bonnet.

Anjelica's heart sank to her knees. So this was Stuart's beautiful, cultured English lover. Marian Foxworthy was everything Anjelica was not. No wonder Stuart had been able to put her aside so quickly when he had such a woman waiting here for him.

"I'm so sorry to disturb you," said the slender woman as she moved gracefully into the room. "I'm Marian Foxworthy. I understand that Stuart's not available at the moment?"

Anjelica stood, very aware how inappropriate she looked in the Indian sari and even more ashamed that she felt so overshadowed by the other woman's fine English bearing. "He left a short time ago." She hesitated. "I was under the impression that he intended to visit you, Mrs. Foxworthy."

Marian looked relieved. "I'm so glad. I've been coming out here every day in the hopes of finding him home. We expected him nearly a month ago, and we've heard no word at all. I've been terribly worried."

Realization seemed to dawn in Marian's eyes. "Oh, my goodness, you must be Anjelica Blake? Stuart found you after all!" Her scarlet-painted lips curved in a delighted smile. "Did Stuart tell you that I'm Nickie's cousin? You and I are practically related."

"Yes, he mentioned something about it. I'm very

pleased to make your acquaintance, Mrs. Fox-worthy."

"Oh, no, please call me Marian. I'm just so glad you're finally here. My aunt's been quite distressed thinking that Stuart wouldn't be able to find you."

"Stuart said Nicholas would be picking me up in the morning," Anjelica said warily. "Do you know if he's learned of my arrival?"

"As a matter of fact, he isn't even in the country yet. According to Aunt Julia, he's due in any day, however. He's been working in Africa at some sort of medical facility. You do know that Nickie's become a doctor, don't you?"

Anjelica didn't know one thing about Nicholas. "No, I didn't. So I won't get to meet him for a time?" She tried to keep the sheer relief out of her voice.

"No, I suppose not, but don't worry, that'll just give us time to get acquainted first." Marian glanced around and immediately caught sight of Suzannah and Sanjay through the wide library windows. "Is that your little sister running down the lawn toward the river?"

Anjelica nodded. "Her name is Suzannah. The little boy is my brother, Sanjay."

"Brother? I didn't know you had a brother."

"Father remarried after Mama passed away."

"I see. My aunt and your mother were very close friends, you know. That's why you and Nickie were betrothed to each other. Aunt Julia misses your mother very much, even after all this time has passed."

Anjelica remained silent as the other woman smilingly removed her black lace gloves. "May I sit down and wait for Stuart? Did he mention me to you often while you were in India?"

Anjelica was surprised she would ask such a personal thing of another woman. She couldn't bring herself to admit that she knew their true relationship. "He rarely speaks about himself, but he did mention that you were a relative of Nicholas's."

Marian shook her raven curls. "Sometimes I wonder if he cares a fig about me, although he did intimate that he might let me announce our engagement once he returned."

Anjelica felt her chin go up a notch, not sure she could hide the hurt that pronouncement brought about. Would he really marry Marian? How could she stand it if he did? "How nice," she managed somehow.

Marian eyed her speculatively. "You really are a very lovely girl. I'm sure Stuart noticed that, didn't he?"

Anjelica was not used to such frank questions. She looked down in embarrassment, wondering what her new in-laws would think if they found out about the intimacies she had shared with Stuart Delaney. What would Nicholas think? Would he still want her? For a moment panic gripped her as she imagined herself shunned and cast out into the vast, foreign city of London.

"I suppose all this is very hard on you, isn't it, dear?" Marian was murmuring sympathetically. "How old were you when you left England to go to India?"

"I had just turned ten."

"The London social season can be quite overwhelming. I hope you'll let me help you perfect the proper etiquette and social graces, and such as that. I know just about everyone in the city who you'd need to meet. As Nicholas's cousin, it would be quite appropriate for us to spend a good deal of time together."

"Would you?" Anjelica was pleased to find a potential ally to help her prepare for her English husband, especially now that Stuart had made it clear he wasn't going to be around to do so. "I have to admit I'm very nervous about meeting Nicholas."

"Oh, Nickie's an absolute angel. He'll be more than thrilled when he sees you, I can assure you. I can help you with your costumes, too, if you like. I'm afraid that Indian scarf affair just won't be acceptable here, although I wish it were. It does look divinely comfortable, and you do look beautiful with it draped around your hair that way." She beamed engagingly, and Anjelica was suddenly very grateful to Marian for her offer of help. She wondered, though, if Stuart would approve of their association.

Suddenly Marian's face seemed to light up, and she clapped her hands as if an idea had occurred to her. "Why, you know what, Anjelica? I'm on my way this very minute to confer with my favorite couturiere. Why don't you come along with me? We'll order you a new wardrobe while we're there. I'm giving a ball two weeks from Saturday, and Nickie should be home by then. I know he'd want you to look your best. We'll charge everything to him, of course, and I can help you pick out the very latest styles and wonderful colors to suit your lovely blond hair. Perhaps we'll even run across Stuart somewhere in town. I've missed him dreadfully. I know I shouldn't admit such a thing, but it's true. I just have no pride when it comes to that man."

Anjelica understood that all too well, but she said nothing as she debated the merits of Marian's suggestion. She was inclined to agree with the idea. Marian seemed nice enough, and Anjelica would much prefer to meet her husband in a stylish English gown. Stuart certainly wouldn't accompany her to a dressmaker's shop. He wouldn't even speak to her. "I would like that very much, but I'm not sure I should leave the children alone here on their first day in England—"

"Nonsense. Look at them down there on Stuart's yacht. They're having a grand time exploring by the looks of it, and besides, they're hardly alone. Stuart's whole staff has been sitting idle for months. Just tell the maids to keep an eye on them, and I know that persnickety old Willie certainly won't let them get into trouble."

"Well, I don't know," Anjelica glanced down the

lawns where she could see the children playing around a long black and white boat.

"Come along with me, Anjelica, please do. Stuart won't object, I assure you. He'll be glad we've become friends. I daresay the four of us will spend a good deal of time together in the coming months."

Anjelica was certain that would not happen. Marian had no idea how complicated their relationships would be. "All right, if you're sure it won't take long, but you must let me tell the children where I'm going."

It turned out Suzannah and Sanjay were completely content in playing on the decks of Stuart's boat where it was moored to the boathouse dock. They promised to behave, and a short time later, Anjelica rode inside Marian's shiny black carriage toward the heart of London. The dressmaker's establishment was on Bishopsgate, in a deceptively modest-looking building that proved otherwise when they entered its lavish interior.

Decorated in coordinating shades of green and gold, rich lengths of silk, satin, and other fine fabrics lay draped over velvet chairs and lounging couches. Gold-framed viewing mirrors hung on the walls, and several customers were being fitted in small draped alcoves hung with flowing satin curtains. Great baskets of lilies, roses, and tall gladiolus were everywhere, perfuming the air with their sweet fragrances.

"Mildred, darling. I've brought you a new customer. This is my cousin's betrothed wife, Anjelica

Blake. Isn't she the loveliest little thing? I'm sure you'll have no trouble fitting her as petite as she is. You'll be happy to hear that she must have a whole wardrobe of your latest fashions. She's been abroad for some time and she'll be coming out this season. As you can see, she's used to wearing foreign apparel."

Mildred Lansing was a woman of thirty or so with russet brown hair pinned in twisted plaits atop her head. She wore thick spectacles with black rims, and a long white apron sewn with dozens of deep pockets across the front. She gazed at Anjelica over the tops of her glasses.

"How do you do, Miss Blake. Won't you sit down and allow me to present some of my latest designs?"

Anjelica obeyed, and for the next hour, examined every sort of gown imaginable, lovely taffetas for afternoon teas and evening soirees; others made from the softest white lawn and delicate dotted swiss for day dresses and receiving morning callers. Then the magnificent costumes worn for balls and operas were brought out, their beauty nearly taking her breath away.

Every accessory was presented for her selection as well—daintily plumed hats and sheer hosieries, lace-edged silk chemises with embroidered ribbon straps, ornate lace fans sewn with seed pearls, satin pumps with silk bows. So much was included in each outfit, in fact, that the silk sari of India seemed laughably simple by comparison.

Marian clucked and complimented and donned a gown or two herself as Anjelica sat in a velvet chair and watched the proceedings with some awe.

"Come now, Anjelica," Marian insisted after a time, "you really must try on some dresses, too. Mildred will measure you and start your own wardrobe but you must choose something to take home with you today. It'll be my wedding present to you and Nickie."

Anjelica let the seamstress guide her in the exhausting round of trying on day silks and satins, muslins and chintzes. As the afternoon lengthened, she donned a white lace evening gown with a gigantic hooped skirt that Anjelica swore could never fit into the confines of a carriage. She envisioned herself wearing such a garment in India, in an elephant's howdah perhaps, then shook her head in amusement. She froze in the process of buttoning on a pair of long white elbow gloves when she heard Marian exclaim in delight.

"Stuart, darling! I'm so glad to see you!"

Anjelica peeked furtively through the curtains of the dressing booth, just as Marian flung herself bodily into Stuart's arms. He held her a moment, smiling until he caught sight of Anjelica's reflection in the mirror. He stared straight at her with a look that scraped across her heart like a shard of glass.

"You shouldn't have whisked my guest off like this," he murmured to Marian but his eyes never left Anjelica's face. "I was worried when the children told me she'd been gone so long."

"Sorry, darling, but I couldn't bear to have Nickie's poor bride running around in Indian garb when I was headed straight for Mildred's dress shop. She needed someone to show her around here in England, and you know how impulsive I am. Darling, come sit down. Anjelica's trying on a gown right now to wear to my next party. Now that you're here, you can help us decide what young Nickie will like on her."

"How the hell would I know what he likes?"

"You're a man, and all men look at women the same way. Oh, darling, I'm so happy to see you. I've been so lonely without you." She lowered her voice. "You'll come to me tonight, won't you? As a reward for my good deed with Anjelica?"

Anjelica dropped the curtain, wishing she had not come with Marian. The fun had gone out of the afternoon replaced by images of Stuart making love to Marian, holding her as he had once come so close to doing with Anjelica in the nuptial chamber. Her insides quivered with the most terrible ache of jealousy as Stuart lounged down on the settee and draped his arm around Marian's shoulders.

"Come out and show me your dress, Anjelica," he said mockingly. "I've always wondered how you'd look in fine English clothing."

Anjelica drew in a deep, cleansing breath. She wished she were back in Udaipur decreed a man again. The life of a woman was turning out to be much too painful. When she stepped through the curtains, Marian clapped her hands with pleasure, but Stuart merely stared at her, his blue eyes slowly taking in every inch of her bare shoulders and arms. He didn't look away until Marian turned to him.

"The dress is lovely, Marian," he said tightly. "I predict that Nicholas will be more than pleased."

"It's perfect for the ball I'm having Saturday after next. You'll escort me, won't you, my love?"

"Of course."

His gaze found Anjelica's eyes again, challenging her not to care. She felt her spirits spiral downward into the darkest pit of despair. She turned and reentered the dressing room. She would meet Nicholas soon. He would be as nice as his cousin was, and she would forget all about Stuart Delaney.

"Pardon me, Miss, but Mr. Delaney asks that you put on the lavender silk dress with the black satin bow in the back. He wishes to see you in that color. Miss Mildred sent me to help you with the hooks and buttons."

The young assistant began to unfasten the long row of tiny pearl buttons, and Anjelica frowned, not sure she liked other people helping her to dress. The sari had no buttons or hooks or fastenings at all. It was easy to put on and to take off.

The gown was exquisite, however, and when she was dressed and stepped outside, Stuart sat alone in the waiting alcove. He had his right boot propped across his knee and was casually smoking a cheroot. Despite his relaxed mien, she sensed he was still angry. She looked around.

"Where's Marian? She didn't leave, did she?"

"I sent her home to get ready for this evening. I'm taking her to the theater tonight."

Anjelica's pride rose to shield her hurt. "I'm tired. Could you take me home? Suzie and Sanjay will be worried."

"My carriage is right outside."

Once they had settled inside, he leaned back and smiled at her. She wondered why he was pretending he wasn't angry anymore, when she knew he was.

"You're going to be staying with me longer than I thought."

Surprised by his unexpected remark, Anjelica looked quickly at him. "Really? Marian told me Nicholas wasn't home yet so I assumed you'd make us go to the Sedgwick mansion to live."

"No, you're staying with me until my grandmother gets here and pays me for bringing you back. Why didn't you tell me she was a friend of your mother's?"

"What are you talking about? I don't even know your grandmother."

"Apparently she knows you."

"That's strange."

Stuart kept staring at her as if he didn't believe her, but at least he wasn't acting as angry as before. And she was going to get to stay with him a little while longer. She was ashamed at how much that news delighted her.

"I told Mildred to give top priority to your wardrobe. You'll need it when Nick starts squiring you around town."

Anjelica looked away, not wanting to talk about Nicholas, but Stuart seemed determined to carry on a conversation.

"How did you like Marian?" he asked, leaning forward to flick his cigar from the coach window.

She met his eyes. "I thought she was very nice. Are you going to marry her?"

"Does that matter to you?"

"It matters to her. She thinks you might be ready to settle down with a wife now that you're back."

"I might be."

Anjelica bit her lip. "Why are you doing this to me? Why are you making everything so difficult? You know I have no choice about Nicholas."

"Because you're making a big mistake. You know it. I know it. And it won't take Nick long to know it, either. Ask him for an annulment. Free yourself while you still can."

When she refused to answer, Stuart lapsed into silence himself. Anjelica struggled desperately because she was so tempted to do what he said. She fought the desire to throw herself into his arms and tell him how much she loved him. She wished she had never left India, had never met Stuart Delaney. If he hadn't come for her, she wouldn't be suffering the terrible agony inside her, the unhappiness she was not sure she could bear much longer.

Chapter Sixteen

"My dear, dear Anjelica. I cannot tell you how pleased I am that Mr. Delaney has delivered you back to us, safe and sound."

Julia Sedgwick beamed such a genuine look of gratitude in Stuart's direction that Stuart was compelled to return an uncomfortable nod to Nicholas's plump mother. The truth was that he would rather drill a hole in his head than have Anjelica anywhere near the Sedgwick mansion. He dreaded her first meeting with her stranger-husband. Like one big happy family, they all sat together in the elaborate, doily-decorated parlor taking afternoon tea atop a shiny cherry-wood table and waiting for Nicholas Sedgwick to grace them with his presence.

Anjelica was still mad, hurt, or whatever her confused emotions were telling her to feel at the moment. During the week that had passed since the ride home from Mildred Lansing's dress shop, she had been pointedly avoiding Stuart. According to Marian, Nicholas had finally landed back in England the previous day, hence the strained tea party now in progress. He wondered if the lad had gotten cold feet or would eventually deign to appear. Stuart was prone to hope that he had been overrun by a runaway carriage.

For the last week while enduring Anjelica's angry silence, he had time to examine his conscience and accept the truth. Even Marian had seen the writing on the wall and cooled their affair. She had accused him of being in love with Anjelica, and she was right. What's more, he was ashamed of his behavior the day they had returned from England. He had been frustrated past his limits and had acted the part of an insufferable boor. Anjelica had every right to be angry, even to hate him.

Now that he had admitted that he wanted her for himself, he was determined to have her, one way or another. He had been given the unexpected gift of a few weeks' time in which to seduce Anjelica into spurning Nicholas on her own. Unfortunately, she was still holding strong to her misguided duty to the Sedgwicks.

For the last few evenings Stuart had left Anjelica at home alone with the children, hoping she was imagining him in Marian's arms while in truth he was mingling among his old acquaintances in the gaming rooms of various gentlemen's clubs of the city. He had tried his valiant best to dig up dirt on Nicholas Sedgwick—hopefully enough to entice Anjelica to seek an immediate annulment before they took the final vows.

To his chagrin he had heard nothing remotely

scandalous about the gentleman, which made Sedgwick either dead or incredibly boring. Stuart was beginning to prefer the first. He had never met Marian's cousin but surely the man possessed some of her passion for life and propensity to enjoy herself. When he refocused his attention on his two female companions, Julia was cooing like an affectionate turtle dove and patting Anjelica's arm.

"Your mother and I were such devoted friends, just inseparable as girls. You know that's why we were so pleased to unite our families through your marriage to Nicholas. You do look so very much like her, except those big gray eyes of yours are your father's all over again. We were all just heartbroken when he took Mary away to that godforsaken place."

Stuart observed Anjelica hopefully for any sign of disapproval over Julia's disparaging remarks about India. Disappointingly, she didn't seem offended.

"Mother always spoke fondly of you, too, Mrs. Sedgwick. I remember her saying how happy you were and how you were always smiling and laughing."

Julia Sedgwick proved the truth of that statement by leaning back her head and emitting a shrill, tittering laugh that came close to sending a chill down Stuart's spine. The old woman would irritate a host of saints with her never-ending prattle, and Stuart's mood was not the best anyway. The strain of handing Anjelica over to another man was getting to him, especially when he knew she wanted him as much as he desired her, if that were possible.

"Oh, my, but we did have some good times, Mary, Sarah, and I," Julia said in a sudden fit of weepy nostalgia. She dabbed at misty eyes. "That was long before any of us girls were wed, of course, and certainly well before you and Nicholas came along." Shaking her head over her wistful memories, she suddenly addressed Stuart. "Isn't it strange, Mr. Delaney, how all three of our families are so irretrievably entwined?"

Stuart had no clue to what she meant. "I guess I don't understand you, Mrs. Sedgwick. I have no family here in England."

"But I'm talking about your Grandmother Delaney, of course. Sarah's a distant cousin of ours. She attended the same London finishing school as Anjelica's mother and I did. That's when we became so close."

"My grandmother is a good friend of yours?" Stuart repeated, Thomas Stonegate's revelations beginning to make more sense now. He hadn't seen or heard from his father's mother since he had visited her house when he was sixteen, and that was the summer he'd fallen for Camillia—a time he never wanted to remember. He thrust his first love out of his mind, curious about Sarah's interest in finding Anjelica. He started to ask a few pertinent questions of Julia Sedgwick but she was now peering worriedly toward the French doors of mirrored glass that led into the front foyer. She nervously adjusted her lace shawl over her shoulders.

"Oh, dear me, I do hope that's Nicholas's horse I hear out on the driveway. I cannot imagine why he's tardy for such a momentous occasion as meeting you, Anjelica, dear. I do declare that he was beside himself yesterday when Marian told him Mr. Delaney had found you."

Again she glowed approvingly at Stuart, and again Stuart wished he was still in Udaipur being worshiped as a god.

The low murmur of a male voice could now be heard in the hall. Stuart noted without much pleasure how eagerly Anjelica watched the threshold for the first sight of her husband. Stuart watched the portal with just as much interest, hoping to see a troll with a hunched back drag a misshapen leg through the opened doors.

Instead a tall, well-formed young man strode into view. Stuart scrutinized his appearance, annoyed that he was relatively handsome with blond hair and light brown eyes but pleased he was hardly presentable with droplets of mud spattered over his blue trousers and gray frockcoat. Mud was also caked on the soles of his brown knee boots leaving a visible residue in the form of footprints all the way across his mother's expensive gold and white carpet.

"Please forgive me for coming in late like this," were the first words out of Nicholas Sedgwick's mouth. "I happened upon an overturned carriage in Lambert's Lane and felt I must stop and render assistance to the poor ladies trapped inside. One was with child and I felt compelled to see her safely home to her husband."

That's just great, a bloody do-gooder, Stuart thought sourly to himself as Anjelica's betrothed kept his eyes glued on his bride. Anjelica was smiling as if she very much liked what she saw. Stuart's frown intensified.

"Nickie is always so gallant," his mother informed Anjelica with a proud nod as the handsome youth smiled indulgently at her. "He's a doctor, you know."

Stuart stiffened with irritation as Nicholas proceeded to examine every inch of Anjelica's beautiful face. When his gaze dipped briefly to the curve of her bosom, Stuart set his jaw. Luckily Nicholas was gentleman enough not to linger on the finer points of her figure.

"Miss Blake, do you think you can ever forgive me for showing up here so dirty and disheveled? I have truly been counting the minutes since Marian told me you were finally back in England."

Stuart watched Anjelica blush prettily. "There's no need to apologize. I think it was most admirable of you to stop and help those unfortunate ladies at the accident. I hope no one was hurt."

"No. I made sure of that before I left them."

When Nicholas and Anjelica shared a smile, Stuart shifted in his chair. Dammit, she liked him. Surely the man had a fault or two. If he did, Stuart would sure as hell find it and point it out to her.

"This is Mr. Stuart Delaney, Nicholas, dear," said

his mother, obviously enraptured by the proceedings thus far. "He's the one who brought our lovely little Anjelica home from India. We all owe him a great deal."

Not to mention the rest of the twenty thousand pounds he had been promised, Stuart thought as Nicholas Sedgwick turned a pair of light hazel-brown eyes upon his face for the first time. He graciously extended his hand to Stuart. "I owe you more than I can ever say, Mr. Delaney. My bride is far more beautiful than I could have hoped for."

Reluctantly Stuart took his rival's hand. Nicholas had a strong, decisive grip, and Stuart resisted the impulse to squeeze hard enough to force the smaller man to his knees. "Too bad you didn't go after her yourself. We had quite an interesting time of it down in the jungles of Udaipur. It's a very romantic place."

Anjelica shot him a startled look, then cast down her eyes. Nicholas did not seem to sense her inner turmoil. "I would have certainly enjoyed that," he replied with a broad grin. "Especially now that I've seen her." Anjelica's betrothed slid his eyes over her person again in a way that caused Stuart to grind his teeth. "I would have gone with you, of course, except that I've been out of the country for over a year. The work was so important I felt I couldn't leave. You see, some of my colleagues from Saint Thomas's Hospital and I have been treating the poor souls in a leper colony on an island just off the coast of Africa. We're working desperately to develop a cure, or at least a medicine that will arrest the disease in its early stages."

Anjelica seemed impressed with his humanitarianism. "I think that's very commendable. I seem to remember now that you wished to become a doctor even back when we were little children."

Nicholas smiled expansively as he chose to seat himself upon the velvet loveseat very close to Anjelica. "And I remember the day you skinned your knee on the stable yard cobblestones when your parents brought you over to Sloandrake for a visit. That's our country estate in Kent. It's very close to Blake House, if you'll recall. The wound was a wicked gash, I remember that clearly. I bandaged it up for you. Did I do a good job or did I leave you with a scar?" He cast his eyes suggestively over her gown-covered legs.

You'll never know one way or the other, if I have my way about it, Stuart swore inwardly.

Anjelica laughed and apparently recollected the long-gone occasion with some fondness. "I remember now. You were very kind to me that day. I'm glad you've pursued your dream. Father always told us that the practice of medicine is the most rewarding of all the professions."

Nicholas liked her compliments almost as much as Stuart didn't like them. Stuart decided it was time to put in his two cents' worth.

"I do hope you're not contemplating the idea of whisking Anjelica off to a leper colony on your honeymoon, Sedgwick."

Everyone looked at him as if astounded by his remark, and Nicholas was suddenly eager to reassure his fears. "Oh, no, sir, I would never endanger my wife's health in such a way, not even in the interest of scientific advancement. Now that Anjelica has been restored to me, I assure you I'll never leave her side. I've waited much too long to have her with me. Mother's been telling me it's time to settle down and have a family, and now I know she's right."

Anjelica lowered her eyes and gazed shyly at the fragile teacup she held atop her lap. Nicholas took advantage of the moment and stared unblinkingly at her. Stuart stared unblinkingly at him.

Mrs. Sedgwick filled up the unsettling moment of silence with her shrill voice. "Mr. Delaney's an American, Nicholas, dear. His family owns a plantation in Virginia, but he's been in London since the war ended. He's been an invaluable help to your cousin Marian in her business affairs."

"Yes, I know." Nicholas eyed Stuart appraisingly. "Marian has told me all about you."

Julia's blue eyes twinkled with a knowing look that was somewhat magnified by her thick spectacles. "My niece is really quite taken with you, Mr. Delaney. She missed you desperately while you were away."

Stuart wasn't sure how to respond to that. Nicholas save him the problem of coming up with a noncommittal reply.

"I say, Mr. Delaney, would you, by any chance, have a sister by the name of Cassandra Delaney?"

Shocked and immediately uncomfortable with the subject of his family, Stuart nodded slightly. "I do."

"Well, isn't that an interesting coincidence? About five years back, I met her when we were both studying tropical medicines at the University of London in Bloomsbury. I remember her vividly. She's really quite a brilliant young woman."

"Cassie's always been the scholar in the family."

"Your sister has lived here in London?" Anjelica didn't hide her surprise. "You never mentioned that."

"I didn't know it."

"Your American war between the states was certainly a tragedy of monumental proportions." Mrs. Sedgwick clucked her tongue sympathetically. She shook her fashionably coiffured silvery hair. "But do let us discuss happier things. According to the marriage contract, there's another ceremony necessary in which to finalize your vows. I'm sure you'll both wish to expedite this last step."

"I really think we should make it as soon as possible." Nicholas grinned warmly at Anjelica. "We've waited long enough already. I'd say we should wed within the month, if Anjelica has no objection."

Stuart objected for her. "Sorry, my friend, but I have to disagree. I think it would be for the best if Anjelica and the children have the time to adjust to

life here in England before taking on the responsi-
bilities of marriage."

"But, Mr. Delaney, we'll make every attempt to
make them feel at home here at Sedgwick Hall—"

"No, he's exactly right," Nicholas said, inter-
rupting his mother's anxious appeal. "I do want
Anjelica to be comfortable when she comes to us,
but please realize my eagerness to make her my
wife."

More than you know, Stuart thought, aware that
Nicholas was smart enough not to annoy Anjelica's
legal guardian.

"How long did you have in mind, Mr. Delaney?
Mother believes if we keep the wedding small and
intimate the planning of the affair would not take
overly long."

"I was thinking a year or so might be more appropriate," Stuart suggested to the consternation of all
present.

Anjelica was clearly stunned, and Nicholas
looked appalled. "Don't you think that's a bit exces-
sive under the circumstances? Anjelica and I have
waited so long already."

"I happen to think it in her best interest to get to
know you better."

"Now, Mr. Delaney, I realize you mean well, but
don't you think you should reconsider?" Mrs.
Sedgwick set down her cup with a rattle. "These
poor children are obviously eager to be wed, and
the contract only specifies a short time."

"I'll agree to wait as long as Anjelica thinks necessary," Nicholas said firmly, then turned to Anjelica. "Mr. Delaney is right, of course. You'll need time to adjust to England. I only want you to be happy in my home."

Anjelica had sat silently as the conversation flowed around her. She looked at Nicholas. "I've prepared myself for this wedding all my life but I'm worried about my brother and sister. They didn't want to leave India, and London is very strange to them. I'm the only family they have left."

"Then they must come live with us after we are wed," Nicholas said with so much enthusiasm that Stuart deemed it a ruse to gain Anjelica's affection. "I like little children ever so much. As a matter of fact, I donate my services as a physician twice a week at the Presbyterian orphanage in Southwark."

Who the hell is this guy? Stuart thought incredulously, *Sedgwick the Saint?* Could he really be as perfect as he was pretending to be?

"Would you grant me leave to show Miss Blake my mother's rose garden?" Nicholas asked Stuart in much too polite a manner for Stuart to gracefully refuse. Stuart had to nod.

The young man stood, crooked an inviting elbow and smiled down at Anjelica. "Shall we, my dear?"

Anjelica rose with a demure rustle of pink satin, apparently having adapted herself admirably to the art of wearing corsets and stays and all manner of feminine English garments. As they made their way out the open doors into the shady garden, Stuart steeled his willpower not to get up and dog the couple's every footstep. Instead he was left to sit and suffer Julia Sedgwick's high-pitched tittering giggles as she related tales of Nicholas's youthful years, every bit as angelic and inspired as his adulthood appeared to be.

"Mr. Delaney is very protective of you, isn't he?" Nicholas Sedgwick remarked to Anjelica as they strolled down a shell-covered garden path that led into a small latticed gazebo.

Anjelica knew very well the reason why, but she certainly couldn't tell Nicholas the truth. He seemed like a very nice young man, but she wondered what he would think of her if he knew the things she and Stuart had done in Udaipur, especially their Hindu marriage and the near consummation afterward. Her blood stirred and ran warmer through her veins, despite the weeks that had passed since Stuart had nearly ravished her that night. Guilt leapt through her, and she tried desperately to hide her agitation.

"He went to a lot of trouble to get us here. I guess he just wants to make sure I'll be happy with you." The explanation sounded weak, even to her, but Nicholas didn't seem to notice.

"I can make you happy, Anjelica, if you'll just give me the chance. I have to admit that I've always rather resented the way our mothers arranged this marriage of ours when we were too little to object. But now that we've met I suspect I should send Mother a dozen red roses in thanks."

"That's very sweet."

"I could've looked the world over, you know, and never found a more beautiful bride."

Anjelica was increasingly uncomfortable with his effusive compliments. She got the feeling he wasn't used to giving them, either. "I'm not sure I can be the kind of wife you have a right to expect. I've not had the upbringing that other English girls receive from their schooling here in London. Things are very different in India. I lived outside the British compound for the last five years, did you know that?"

"No, but it sounds intriguing. I understand that India is quite an exotic place. You'll have to teach me all about its customs."

His interest seemed genuine enough, and Anjelica was touched by his sensitivity. "I'm pleased you're willing to hear about my life in Udaipur. I already miss it a great deal." She hesitated, afraid of how he would react to Sanjay's heritage. "I feel it's only fair for you to know that my brother is half-caste. His mother was an Indian princess."

Though she watched him closely, Nicholas's amber eyes revealed no disgust. "So I'll have a child of royal blood residing in my house. I hardly see how I could find that objectionable."

Anjelica wondered if Nicholas could really be so unprejudiced. Few of the English men and women she had known did not look down upon the native Hindus and their beliefs. Except for her father, of course, and he had been an exceptional man.

Though shocked to the core by Stuart's sudden determination to delay the wedding, secretly she was pleased. She wanted to see how Nicholas treated Suzannah and Sanjay before she was forced to proceed with the final ceremony.

"Tell me about India, Anjelica. I've heard about the elephants and the jungle tigers."

Anjelica nodded, a touch of pain twisting her heart. Where was Prafulla Veda? How was Shashi faring now so long after they had left him on his own? She began to tell Nicholas about Prafulla Veda and the maharajah's palace, glad to speak of such things but every tale she told seemed to bring back more vividly her time spent there in Stuart's company. Her heart grew heavier and heavier until it felt like a huge stone lodged at the center of her breast. Nicholas Sedgwick seemed to be a more than suitable husband for her. Now she had no excuse to refuse to fulfill her duty.

Chapter Seventeen

"Is he here yet, Suzie?"

"No, but he's coming today for sure. That's why we're hiding underneath this table."

Sanjay sat calmly beside Suzannah, obviously not nearly as upset as Suzannah was over the way her sister was acting. Anjelica had to marry Stuart; not that silly old Englishman. Stuart didn't like the idea, either. He had been in an awful bad mood ever since Anjelica had gone to meet with her almost-husband.

Perplexed by the seriousness of the problem, she watched absently as her brother scooped out a handful of cherries from the pie tin they had snatched when Stuart's cook left it cooling unattended on the kitchen windowsill.

With great care she lifted up the edge of the gold velvet tablecloth. Just as she peered out into the parlor, the door to the foyer opened. She saw Stuart and another man come into the room. When they seated themselves on the brown couch right beside the tea table, she cautiously lowered the fringe so they wouldn't see her.

"Anjelica isn't ready," Stuart said in the coldest, unfriendliest voice Suzannah had ever heard. He didn't like Anjelica's husband, not one bit, she decided, pleased to the bone, because usually he was pretty polite to most people.

"That's quite all right, Mr. Delaney. I have all the time in the world."

"That's a long time."

"The remark was merely a figure of speech, sir."

The man named Nicholas seemed nervous. From her vantage point, she could only see his feet, and he kept crossing and uncrossing his legs while Stuart stood up with his legs braced apart.

"I've given some thought to the matter, and I really don't want you pressuring Miss Blake about moving in with your family. I know her better, *much* better"—Stuart emphasized the word outrageously—"than you do. She needs a period of adjustment, and I intend to make sure she gets all the time she needs."

Nicholas hurriedly reassured him. "Mr. Delaney, sir, I'm willing to wait years to have her if I must. Just so she's eventually mine."

Stuart didn't answer anything to that. Curious about his silence, Suzannah hazarded a peek and found a real awful-looking frown on his face. It got even worse when Nicholas said some more things about Anjelica.

"You see, I've fallen desperately in love with her,

even after just these few meetings. She's beautiful and sweet and somehow so charmingly innocent. I'm entirely enchanted with her."

"Enchanted?"

"I must be because I think of nothing else, night or day. I've even lost interest in my medical slides of virulent viruses."

"That's damn flattering."

Suzannah grinned at the way Stuart said that, like he really thought it was real stupid.

Nicholas uncrossed his legs and sat up on the edge of the sofa.

"I mean it, truly I do. She's absolutely perfect in every way."

"Don't delude yourself, Mr. Sedgwick. Anjelica is far from perfect. She has plenty of faults. Trust me, I've seen them all."

"Did you hear that?" Sanjay whispered, pursing his lips with displeasure. "I thought Stuart liked Anjie."

"He does, silly," she whispered back hastily. "He's just saying that to get Nicholas not to want to have her as a wife."

Suzannah resumed her eavesdropping just as Nicholas answered Stuart's unkind remarks about her older sister.

"I find that hard to fathom, sir, but be it the case, I shall be happy to overlook them. I, myself, harbor certain frailties of character, as do we all."

"Then perhaps you should tell me just what these frailties of yours are, Mr. Sedgwick," Stuart demanded at once, and sounding angry, too. "I do have a duty to protect my ward from entering an unsuitable alliance."

Nicholas got all upset and began to stutter a bit. "I—I didn't mean to—to imply that I'm some kind of rake or roué, sir. You must know that I entertain only the most honorable intentions concerning my wife."

Suzannah grinned. Stuart sure was good at making the other man squirm around in his chair. He was crossing his legs again. Maybe he'd just get so uncomfortable that he'd walk out and leave even before Anjelica could get all the way downstairs. Then they could all go boating together on the river the way she and Sanjay wanted to. Her attention was diverted back to Sanjay when her brother slurped cherry juice out of the pie plate so loud that she thought for sure the two gentlemen must have heard. She quickly grabbed the plate out of his hands and gave him her fiercest scowl. It must have been good because he looked scared.

"I guess I'll tell her you're here," Stuart said tightly as if he didn't like saying it at all.

After the door shut behind him, everything got real quiet again. After a minute or two, Nicholas stood up and walked over to the window. Suzannah placed her finger on her lips so Sanjay wouldn't say anything, then frowned at the way her brother was dripping cherry juice all down his face and staining his clean white shirt.

"I don't like that Nicholas any more than Stuart

does," she whispered so low she could barely hear herself. "We gotta make Anjelica see that he's not nearly as good a husband as Stuart would be. She's gotta back out of getting hitched, and she will, if we run Nicholas off from here."

"How we gonna do that, Suzie? Anjelica thinks she's his wife already."

"I sneaked down the hall last night and listened at her door. And you know what? She was crying real hard, and you know why? 'Cause she likes Stuart so much she can't stand not being married to him. I know she does. She's always looking like a gloomy gus especially when he's going around with that fancy lady named Marian. She just don't know how to get out of all these lawyer papers and things like that."

Suzannah contemplated the problem with a serious face as Sanjay shoveled some more cherries and sugared crust into his mouth. He'd decided right off that cherry pie was his favorite food now that they lived in London and ate all kinds of English dishes without curry or rice or anything like that in them.

"What are we gonna do, Suzie?" Sanjay mumbled, his mouth so full she could barely understand him.

"I'm gonna think up something so bloody awful that he'll go running back 'cross town to that big mansion of his like a tiger running from soldiers beating the bushes," she vowed with vicious enjoyment.

"You said a curse word. You're gonna get in trouble."

"Not if you don't tell on me."

"I won't," Sanjay promised. His face sobered. "Won't Anjelica get mad if we do something rude to him? She always fusses at us a long time when we don't use all these new English kind of manners."

Suzannah's face twisted with a grimace of dismay. Sanjay was right. Anjelica wouldn't like them thinking up mean things to do to Nicholas Sedgwick. Venturing another surreptitious peek, she saw he was still way across the room staring out at Stuart's garden. She had to think of a way to get him to leave right now and never come back, no matter how perfect he thought their sister was. And right now, too, before Stuart brought Anjelica down to the parlor. Something dreadful and terrible.

When she looked at Sanjay again, he was licking cherry juice out of the bottom of the pan. He didn't usually go that far but he really did like cherries a whole bunch. She watched the red juice run out the corner of his mouth. It sort of reminded her of the time when he was two and had fallen off Prafulla Veda's trunk and hit his nose on the ground. More blood had poured out of him that day than she ever thought could come out of such a little bitty body as his was then. Anjelica had thought he was dead for sure when she saw him lying there all wet and shiny and red.

Suzannah's eyes grew round as the solution to her problem came to her in a brilliant flash of genius. Why, she knew just exactly how they could get rid of the unwanted husband once and for all.

"Sanjay," she whispered urgently, "quit slurping on that pan and listen to this. I know just how to get that Nicholas to leave forever. Hurry 'cause we got to do it before Anjie comes. Now here's what you've gotta do—"

Stuart Delaney recrossed the foyer and stopped before the parlor doors, still angry that Anjelica was being so stubborn about ending her marriage to Nicholas Sedgwick. She didn't love the blasted boy. What's more she was about to make the biggest bloody mistake of her life, and there wasn't one damn thing he could do about it, short of throwing a blanket over her head and abducting her like a medieval warlord. He raised a speculative brow. Now that was an idea worth considering.

Of all the bad luck, Nicholas had even turned out to be a decent man. London was chock-full of reprobates and villains. Why did her intended have to be a veritable saint? Now after only days enjoying Anjelica's company, he was so smitten he'd vowed to wait for her forever. Not that Stuart couldn't understand that particular motivation. He would, too. All she had to do was level her long-lashed silver-gray eyes on a man, and he'd dance like a fool to her every whim.

With more reluctance than he cared to admit, he slid open the parlor door. He stepped inside, deciding that enough time had passed to send Nicholas packing. He hadn't been stupid enough to inform Anjelica that Nicholas was waiting, and he'd be damned if he would. According to her personal maid, she was still at her toilette. His gaze swept the parlor and found Nicholas standing in the window alcove.

Before he could proceed with the idea, however, he caught sight of Suzannah crawling out from under the tea table. Shocked to find her there, he watched as she squirmed the rest of the way out. What was she up to? It didn't take the child long to show him her mischievous plan.

"You know what I did, mister?" she said to Nicholas Sedgwick in a loud and clear voice. Her hapless victim swung around in surprise. "I punched my little brother in the nose and knocked him clean out until he's just laying there under this here table with his eyes shut and everything. He may even be dead as a doornail for all I know."

"I beg your pardon?" Nicholas responded with a look of alarm. Suzannah's next pronouncement was even more astonishing.

"I hit him with my fist. See this blood stainin' up my knuckles. It all came running out of poor little Sanjay's nose."

"Good gracious, young lady, that's a beastly thing to do to your little brother," Nicholas muttered in undisguised horror. "Why'd you do such a terrible thing?"

Suzannah lifted one shoulder and gave a nonchalant toss of her brown braids. "Just 'cause I felt like it. I don't need a reason to be mean. You see, mister, I got this awful, dreadful disease that some little girls get that makes them just fly into these most terrible rages for no reason whatsoever. Everyone 'round here is always in great danger of me and afraid for their very lives. I guess you might call me a"—she drew out the revelation, for added effect, no doubt—"bloody maniac."

Stuart felt the most delicious urge to laugh bubble up inside him, but she wasn't finished with Nicholas yet.

"My big sister's a bloody maniac, too, but she hides it better'n me. I sure feel sorry for her husband someday. I know she'll probably do him in with some of those knives and guns she hides under her mattress and in her skirt pockets and lots of other places."

After that crafty speech she waited for Nicholas's reaction. Unfortunately, Stuart could tell her ridiculous story was too far-fetched for even Sedgwick to fall for.

"Then I suppose I should be afraid to be alone here with you?" Nicholas said, taking a step closer to Suzannah.

"That's right, mister, and you had better hightail it out of here quick, q-u-i-k, 'cause I especially get riled up about English people who talk real uppidy the way you do. Before you run away all scared to death, though, you can take a quick peek at him if you want."

"A peek? At whom?"

"At Sanj, of course!" Suzannah shook her head as if Nicholas were a simpleminded dolt. "He's the one I gave that mean and horrendous thrashing to, isn't he? Who else would I be talking about?"

Her tone dripped exasperation in a way Stuart well remembered from his early days in Udaipur.

"Where is he?" Nicholas was asking, obviously sport enough to play along with the hoax.

"I dragged him under this table so my sister wouldn't find his bloody carcass and have a hissy." With that, Suzannah whipped up the end of the tablecloth like a magician pulling out a rabbit, unveiling her unfortunate little victim.

Nicholas bent down to peer under the table, and Stuart moved closer to see just what she had put Sanjay up to. He saw the boy lying motionlessly under the table, his face and shirt covered with a crimson substance that did indeed look like bloodstains but which Stuart had a distinct feeling came instead from the cherry pie that had been purloined from the kitchen window earlier that morning.

"Good heavens, girl, is that really blood all over him?" Nicholas asked in consternation. When he reached down with the intention of finding out, Sanjay obviously got cold feet. He scrambled out, nearly knocking over the table in his panic.

"Let go, let go! Help! Help! Suzie, make him stop!" he yelled hysterically.

"You leave my baby brother alone!" Now Suzannah joined in the screaming as Anjelica's betrothed took a hasty step back from the melee.

Stuart laughed softly to himself, crossed his arms across his chest, and let the fun continue until he heard Anjelica's shocked voice at the foyer door.

"What in the world's going on in here?"

Both children whipped around, their faces stricken white with identical guilty looks. Nicholas looked at Anjelica as if he felt he was caught in a bad dream.

Stuart decided he had better intervene before the little imps got a healthy dose of their sister's wrath.

"Now you two know better than to come in here and roughhouse when we have guests. Come with me right this minute and let Anjelica have her visit with Mr. Sedgwick."

Both children scampered in his direction with a great deal of relief, but Anjelica stepped forward to block their flight. She stared in wordless dismay at Sanjay's stained face. "What on earth have you got all over yourself, Sanjay? Why, it smells like cherries. You took that pie this morning, didn't you?"

"Anjelica, you have a guest. I'll take care of this," Stuart interjected calmly. "You've kept Nicholas waiting too long already."

"Nicholas is here?" She found the man at the window. "Why didn't someone tell me?"

"Suzannah, Sanjay, come along with me," Stuart intoned sternly. "It's time someone taught you some manners."

"Now, Mr. Delaney, no harm was done," Nicholas called after them with his usual good nature.

"Children will be children, Stuart," Anjelica said as he marched them past her out of the room, but she followed their flight with not a little suspicion before Nicholas reminded her of his presence. Stuart did not stop until he had safely reached the sanctuary of his library and had the door secured behind them. Both youngsters were now the picture of innocence, their eyes downcast, their hands clasped behind their backs.

Suzannah finally dared a surprisingly meek look. "You're not gonna thrash us, are you, Stuart?"

"Why don't you just tell me what you're trying to do to Mr. Sedgwick."

Suzannah scuffed the toe of her white slipper on the red roses patterning the carpet. She shook her pigtails in a fashion that didn't harbor an overabundance of repentance. "Well, I'm not very sorry 'cause I don't like him. And I don't think he oughta marry up with Anjie. We were only trying to scare him off so she could marry you, and we could live here with you forever and ever." She raised wary brown eyes and awaited his reply. Sanjay hazarded a scared look from under his long black eyelashes.

Stuart placed his fists on his hips. "Well, now, I guess I just have one thing to say about what you just did." He paused for a moment, then grinned. "Better luck next time."

The worried concern on their small faces melted. They looked at each other, then broke into wide, relieved smiles.

"I'm sure glad you aren't mad," Suzannah said in

a long exhalation. "I thought we was in big trouble, t-r-u-b-l-e."

Stuart laughed softly. "All right, I'll tell you what. I agree wholeheartedly about Nicholas. What's more, I think you're on the right track about getting rid of him for good."

"Really, Stuart? Do you? I know I can do it, if I keep trying."

He nodded. "Unfortunately, Anjelica seems to think she has no other choice but to go through with this stupid marriage. So our best shot is to convince Nicholas it wouldn't be in his best interest to become a part of the family. If he releases her, then she won't feel obligated anymore, right?"

"Right!" Suzannah and Sanjay cried in unison. Their faces were wreathed in delighted smiles.

"It's up to the three of us to make him change his mind about her, right?"

"Right!" they chimed in glee.

"We'll make him sorry he ever stepped foot into our house, right?"

"Right, right!"

"Good, now let's sit down right here and map out a worthy course of action that won't get you in too much trouble. We'll make his life miserable until he gives up and retreats back to his leper colony."

Sanjay's cherry-stained face lost its elation. "Won't Anjie get mad and make us stop?"

"We'll just have to make sure she doesn't know what we're doing. Leave that part to me."

Suzannah came forward and leaned her head against his chest. "You're a genius, Stuart, j-e-n-u-s."

Stuart smiled, glad the little mischief makers were on his side for a change. He had found out the hard way that it was a hell of a lot better to be Suzannah's friend than her enemy, especially where George the snake was concerned. *George,* he considered with raised brow, now that was an idea that might wither some of Nicholas's ardor.

Chapter Eighteen

En route to Marian's ball a week later Anjelica tried her best to listen to Nicholas Sedgwick's polite small talk, but she was so acutely aware of Stuart's sullen silence on the far side of the carriage that she couldn't concentrate on his words. Despite the uncomfortable sensation of being in the company of both the man who was to be her husband and the man whom she really wanted to marry, Anjelica looked forward to her first taste of the excitement of London's grand social whirl.

"I know I've already told you, Anjelica, but you look exquisite in that white gown. Indeed you look as angelic as your name implies you are."

Anjelica smiled at the rather clumsy compliment from the shy scholar but Stuart's sniff of disdain was readily audible. He was taking his job as chaperon seriously and so was poor Nicholas who strove constantly to please Stuart at every turn.

"Thank you, Nicholas," she replied before he noticed Stuart's open contempt. "I'm truly amazed at just how complicated English dresses are. A sari is simply a length of cloth wound around the body."

"Yes, Nick, old boy, you really should see Anjelica in a silk sari. A crimson one, I should think, when she's dancing and making the gold bracelets on her ankles jingle in time to the sitars."

Anjelica stiffened, knowing full well Stuart's remarks were designed to shock Nicholas's sense of propriety as well as to bring back that night in Udaipur and all the tingling desires that went along with the memory. His plan worked admirably. A fiery longing shot through her blood, and she grew hot then cold then angry that Stuart could do such things to her.

"I would have loved to have witnessed such a dance," Nicholas answered, amazingly liberal-minded and completely innocent of all the underlying innuendo. "Did you bring any Indian garments back with you?"

Anjelica nodded. "Yes, several of my favorites."

"Wonderful. I'll look forward to my own private showing."

"Afraid not, Nick," Stuart interjected at once.

"I certainly didn't mean to suggest anything improper," Nick said apologetically.

Anjelica was becoming irked with Stuart's condescending manner toward the other man. Nicholas was trying his best to be agreeable and Stuart was making it as difficult as possible.

"I'm sure you didn't," Anjelica said kindly. "If you ask me, I think Mr. Delaney is taking his position of guardian a bit too seriously. Only days ago he told me he couldn't wait to get rid of me and now he's acting like my father. I'll remind you, Mr. Delaney, that I got along quite well for years in India without you to watch over me like a hawk."

"Did you now?" Stuart's words were silky smooth. "I should think there was a time or two when you might have been better off with a chaperon as assiduous as I looking over your shoulder."

Again, Anjelica knew he was reminding her of the intimacies they had shared in India. She ignored him and instead asked Nicholas questions about St. James's Park as they drove past it. He pointed out the magnificent façade of Buckingham Palace, then proceeded with a detailed account of its history, style of architecture, and the various personages who had lived or died inside its massive walls. She listened dutifully but felt pinned like a never-before-seen butterfly specimen under Stuart's azure eyes. He stared at her so intensely, she wondered if he ever took time out to blink.

"Here we are, and it looks like Marian's party is already in full swing." Nicholas peered through the window as the driver slowed the coach to a stop.

Anjelica bunched the soft white silk of her full skirt and stepped out, enjoying the rustling sounds made by the layers of satin petticoats underneath her gown. All the lace and ribbons made her feel feminine and ladylike, and reminded her of the way her mother used to look when she sat in front of her mirror and combed her hair into elaborate coils and twists for an evening out with her father. She had always kept such memories close to her heart. Her mother would be so happy to see her dressed in silk with Nicholas at her side.

Nicholas led her up a wide stairway that curved gracefully from the drive to the impressive Georgian portico. She didn't have to look around to know that Stuart was right behind them. She wouldn't look at him, she vowed, she wouldn't think of him; she would free herself of his hold on her. She channeled her concentration solely on Nicholas—listening intently to every word he uttered, watching his expressions, responding to him with just enough flirtation.

Somehow it was strange to look at him and know he was her legal husband, that he had been such for years. She was finding him to be a very nice man—one who would make a good husband and father. Her mother had made a good decision, after all. Anjelica would have been content to succumb to her duty wholeheartedly, if only he had chosen someone else to fetch her back to him.

Nicholas kept up an eager chatter as they entered a large white foyer with twin chandeliers glittering with crystal teardrops. A white double staircase led to a second-floor mezzanine.

"I have so many friends here tonight to whom I'm eager to introduce you." Nicholas's smile was rueful. "I suppose the truth of the matter is that I can't wait to show you off."

As he helped her off with her short black velvet

cape, Anjelica waited for Stuart to insist that he should tag along with them. To her surprise, he did the opposite.

"I'll leave Anjelica in your care now, Nick. Have a good time. I'm going to find Marian."

With some degree of surprise, Anjelica watched Stuart wend his way through the foyer crowded with men in black evening jackets with formal tails and ladies in glittering gowns of every color and elaborate feathered coiffures. Nicholas, on the other hand, made no secret of his relief to be rid of Stuart.

"Thank goodness he's gone. I feared Mr. Delaney would want to waltz with us, too, if I dared to ask you."

Anjelica had to laugh, but her gaze longingly followed Stuart's progress. She had never danced with Stuart. She wondered if he were good at it.

"He's in love with you, isn't he?"

When Nicholas searched her face for the answer, Anjelica veiled her eyes with her lashes. She realized she wasn't sure of the answer. She knew Stuart desired her, he certainly made no bones about that, but was there any love involved? Would he want her for his wife if she were free to wed him or just for his mistress?

"I didn't mean to offend you, Anjelica. There's just something disturbing about the way he looks at you." Nicholas paused as if unwilling to continue. "Of course I wouldn't blame him. I suspect many men fell in love with you when you lived in India."

"Everyone in Udaipur knew I was married to you." Anjelica started to tell him that she had been decreed a man by the maharajah for most of her adult life, but quickly decided against it. He wouldn't understand anything so bizarre. No one in England would. In truth, there were many things she had done while in India of which he could never conceive. She wondered if they were too different to have a happy life together. She wondered is she could ever forget Stuart long enough to learn to care for Nicholas.

"There's John Raulton and Edward Constant. Both of them are physicians who worked with me in Africa."

Anjelica accompanied him to a spot near a tall arched window overlooking the back lawn. A group of young couples stood there chatting, and all were friendly and polite when Nicholas introduced Anjelica as his bride.

It didn't take Anjelica long to realize that Nicholas associated with a learned, erudite crowd. Each person seemed informed on every subject discussed, be it the politics of France or the discovery of new heavenly bodies. Anjelica listened as attentively as she could to their worldly discussion but did not feel a part of the group. Chagrined, she realized that she was constantly scanning the room for Stuart's imposing six-foot-three frame. She chastised herself vigorously, but her annoyance with her weakness didn't stop the alarm she felt when she spotted him in an intimate conversation with Marian near the buffet tables.

Half hidden by a white pillar, Marian was looking up at him in a way Anjelica herself had done on more than one occasion. When the raven-haired beauty caressed his cheek with a loving brush of her fingertips, pain struck so hard and fast at Anjelica's heart that she felt it had been gouged with a knife blade. What if Stuart married Marian? Then he would be her in-law. She would see them as a couple often, at every family gathering, at balls, and at other social functions. She would have to watch him hold Marian's hand, smile at her, and perhaps even become father to her children someday. Such thoughts shredded more holes in her already tattered emotions.

"Would you like something cold to drink?" Nicholas was asking her, oblivious to her inner suffering. "Champagne? Or some cold cider?"

"Thank you, yes. Either sounds wonderful."

While he meandered through the milling guests, Anjelica took refuge on a tufted velvet bench near a pair of open French doors. Even as she vowed not to search out Stuart, her gaze roamed the dance floor with no interest for anyone else. She found him whirling Marian around the floor, her flowing black chiffon gown billowing as she laughed up into his face. She watched them as long as she could, forlorn of heart and diminished of spirit. What was she going to do? She loved him, and she couldn't stop.

"I hope champagne is all right. It's been chilled so it'll be refreshing."

Nicholas sipped from his own long-stemmed goblet as he sat down beside her. "My friends all think you're charming and beautiful."

Anjelica glanced at him. "It's kind of them to say so." She realized that everything she said to him sounded stilted and strange, even to her. She was uncomfortable with him because her own thoughts continued to betray her.

"You don't even realize how lovely you are, do you?"

The conversation was becoming embarrassing and so was the way he continually smiled at her. She hastily strove to change the subject. She wanted to know more about Stuart's unknown family. Maybe Nicholas could help her unravel the mystery of his past.

"You said you once knew Cassandra Delaney. Was she a beautiful woman?" She attempted to make her question sound nonchalant but had a distinct feeling that she had failed.

"Oh, yes. She's a redhead, an unusual copper color that was quite striking. All of her colleagues, including myself, were even more impressed with her knowledge. In fact, a friend and I had considered going to the United States to study under her mentor. His name is Joseph Henry and at that time he was at the Smithsonian Institution in Washington. Unfortunately, the American conflict disrupted our plans, and we weren't able to go. Cassie was planning to stay at her brother's house while there, I believe."

"Stuart has a house in Washington? I understood he was from the southern state of Virginia."

"Not Stuart. Their older brother. Harte was his name, I believe. Hasn't Stuart ever mentioned him?"

"No." In fact Stuart had denied having a brother, she remembered, but why? "Did you ever meet Cassie's older brother, Nicholas?"

"No. He didn't visit London. Now that I reflect on it, Cassie rarely said much about her family. I got the idea somehow that she didn't know Harte particularly well. She mentioned Stuart more often, now that I think about it, but only references to the fact that she hadn't seen him in some time. It's quite a coincidence that I happened to make her acquaintance, isn't it?"

Anjelica nodded. "Have you kept in touch with her?"

He shook his head. "Actually I considered her quite a good friend, but we began to lose touch after the Confederacy seceded. She was vehemently pro-South."

"Stuart fought for the South, too."

Nicholas's gaze roamed the ballroom until he found Stuart's place on the far end of the floor. "You're fond of him, aren't you?"

Anjelica wanted to stay as far away from that topic as possible. "I'm grateful to him, and so are my sister and brother. It was not easy to get us out of India."

Nicholas's amber eyes seemed to look deep into her heart where she had hidden her guilty secret. "I owe him for bringing you home to me. I should have gone after you myself a very long time ago."

Anjelica smiled slightly, thinking he was an easy man to like. Her reaction obviously made him happy, too, because he jumped to his feet, took her hands and pulled her up after him. "Come dance with me, Anjelica. I want to show you off some more."

Anjelica pulled back her hands. "No, wait! I'm not even sure I remember the steps, Nicholas. Mother taught them to Suzannah and me but that was years ago."

"Let me show you. Waltzing is the easiest of all. I'll just hold on to you and swing you around in time to the music. All you have to do is follow along."

With reluctance, she went into his arms, and Nicholas grinned, looking boyish and happy as they twirled together in time to the refrains of the orchestra. She held her skirt with her right hand as all the ladies were doing and laughed with pleasure as they made the first circuit of the shiny oak floor. She loved music and dancing, and although the violins and cellos were very different from the sitar and drums, she enjoyed the lilting melody. She was finally happy with her betrothed, she realized, just as she ought to be. Stuart was making no secret that he preferred Marian's company, and Anjelica meant to quit thinking about him and get to know the man she was bound to.

The rest of the evening progressed quickly. As the hours passed, Nicholas proved to be as agreeable and amiable an escort as she could want. She enjoyed herself immensely and her mood flew high with optimism that perhaps they could share a happy life together. But all her good intentions and determination collapsed miserably when she once again saw Stuart. He was leading Marian down the marble staircase from the second floor where the bedchambers must be located. Where had they been so long? What had they been doing? Her good spirits plummeted; so did her expression.

Nicholas noticed at once. "What's wrong, my dear? Are you tired?"

"No, of course not. I'm having a wonderful time." She forced a smile that had to look stiff and wary because now Stuart and Marian were coming straight toward them.

"Anjelica, darling! I'm so sorry I haven't had a chance to welcome you and Nicholas," Marian whispered softly after giving Anjelica a light peck on the cheek. "Stuart whisked me upstairs so quickly that I've hardly been a good hostess to anyone. Not that I'm complaining." She smiled invitingly up at her tall escort, but Stuart was staring at Anjelica with an angry frown.

"It's time to leave," he muttered brusquely with no explanation as to why.

"So early?"

"I've had enough. Let's go."

"If you please, Mr. Delaney, I would be happy to escort her home later," Nicholas offered eagerly. "Really, it would be my pleasure."

"That won't be necessary," said Stuart peremptorily. "I'll see her home myself."

His tone was faintly civil, she supposed, but held little room for compromise. Nicholas didn't argue though he acted as though he wished he could. "May I at least escort her to the carriage? After all, she is my wife."

"Not yet, she isn't," Stuart said rudely.

Marian had stood silently by but she frowned slightly at these last remarks. "Now, Stuart, darling, aren't you being a bit overprotective? Nickie only wants to walk her to the carriage."

Stuart finally conceded, albeit reluctantly, and Nicholas hastened to take Anjelica's arm and lead her downstairs to the outside portico.

"I've had a wonderful time tonight," Nicholas told her as he draped her cloak over her shoulders. "I wish you could stay longer."

"It's nearly dawn, but I've had a wonderful time, too."

"When can I see you again?" he asked eagerly.

"Whenever you like."

"I've business to attend to out at our country estate tomorrow afternoon. But I'll only be gone for a few days. May I call on you Wednesday and perhaps take you on a carriage ride through Hyde Park?"

"Of course, I'd like that."

Nicholas lifted her gloved hand and kissed the backs of her fingers in his boldest act of courtship so far. He let her go as Stuart strode up and retrieved his own cape and gloves from the waiting maid.

"Good night, Anjelica. I'm counting the days until the wedding. Just eleven more."

His suggestive whisper was the closest he'd come to alluding to their forthcoming marital state, and she felt herself blush. The last thing she wanted to think about was the wedding night they would share together.

"Good night, Nicholas," she murmured, hoping Stuart had not overheard.

Stuart gave no indication he had, but he did show a good bit of impatience as he assisted her inside the coach. Without a word to the hovering Nicholas, he called to the driver to proceed. He settled into the seat across from her and stared at her as if he wished to throttle her.

"From what I could tell you're settling rather well into your role as Nicholas's betrothed."

"He's nice to me, and I like him very much."

"I thought he was going to break down in tears when you had to leave," he observed sarcastically.

"At least we didn't disappear for half the evening without any regard for appearances," she retorted before she could stop herself.

In the dusky light she saw his lips curve into a grin. "I wanted to be alone with Marian."

He had made love to Marian, she thought jealously. "Does that mean you're going to marry her?"

"It means I wanted to be alone with her just like Nickie boy wanted to take you home tonight so that he could seduce you in the carriage."

"That's not true. And quit calling him a boy. He's a grown man."

"Did he have the guts to steal a kiss tonight?"

"He's too much of a gentleman. Besides, he's probably afraid you'd shoot him dead if he touched me."

"He's not far off the mark."

"You have no right to tell him what to do. He's the one who's my husband. Perhaps I should insist the wedding date be moved up so that you can be relieved of your duties and spend more time with Marian."

Across from her, Stuart sat very still. "Is that what you want?"

Anjelica couldn't bring herself to say yes. She turned her head and gazed out the window. "Does it give you pleasure to be cruel to me?"

Suddenly he moved, crossing the carriage and taking her by the arms. She could smell the faint scent of his manly cologne, the aromatic scent of his cigars. When a trace of Marian's sweet perfume wafted into her awareness as well, she tried to jerk away.

Stuart held her too securely. He stared challengingly into her face. "What if I told you that I made love to Marian tonight, Anjelica? Does that bother you? Does that make you want to go to your husband even more?"

"Yes," she lied breathlessly. "I'd go to him tonight if I could."

He stared into her eyes, and his fingers closed tighter around her shoulders. When he spoke, his voice was calm, low, intense. "I took Marian upstairs tonight because I didn't want to see Nicholas touching you. I took her up there and pretended I was back in India with you. You don't want Nicholas, you want me, just like I want you, right now, tonight—"

She closed her eyes as his mouth found hers. She wanted to surrender to him, to agree with everything he said. She wanted to give in, to forget that she had ever even heard of Nicholas Sedgwick.

She fought her desire desperately during the long, thorough kiss, then she heard him groan, deep in his throat as if he realized what he was doing. He loosened his grip and pulled back away from her, but she was clutching the lapels of his coat. They stared at each other, the faint flickering of the coach lamp outside the window illuminating their faces, glowing with naked need.

The awful, helpless feeling of being on fire, of being completely out of control took over, and she slid her arms around his neck, hopelessly the aggressor now and his mouth attacked her again, tasting her bare skin where her breasts swelled at the top of her bodice. His mouth burned red-hot against her flesh, and Anjelica's heart thundered with the passion they had denied for so long. He pressed her back against the seat, his fingers sliding under the edge of her low bodice. She moaned with low, helpless pleasure, no longer interested in fighting him.

"End it with Nicholas, Anjelica," he muttered so low she could barely hear him. "You've got to before it's too late." Stuart held her at arm's length for one endless moment.

"I can't, I can't, you know I can't—"

He didn't give her time to say more but backed away from her as if she had turned into an ugly crone before his eyes. He banged the roof to stop the coach. Once the carriage rattled to a standstill, he jumped out without a word. Anjelica fell back into the corner in a rumpled heap of satin and lace as he harshly ordered the driver to take her the rest of the way home. Her sobs came freely and she made no effort to hold them back. She wept with all the pain she had held contained since they sailed away from Bombay, sure now there would never be an end to her tears.

Chapter Nineteen

"Look, Sanj, there he is, down there sitting on the garden bench. We gotta scare the stuffing out of him before Anjelica gets back from that tea party at Julia's house."

Suzannah ran down the steep flagstone steps leading from the formal terrace toward where Nicholas was reading a book in the shade of a big oak tree. Farther down the lawn on the riverbank, she could see Stuart polishing the brass rails on his sailboat. He hadn't taken them out in it yet, but she was going to see if he would just as soon as they finished frightening off Nicholas Sedgwick.

Something drastic was needed for sure, because yesterday when Stuart had taken Anjelica and Sanjay and her sightseeing around London they had said some pretty awful things about Nicholas Sedgwick, but Anjelica had ignored them, even when Sanjay said Nicholas looked just like a sick mongoose. Why, Suzannah herself had objected to his ugly hair color, his sissy way of dressing, and his soft, girly voice, but Anjelica just looked sad and sick to her stomach.

"Why, hello there, Mr. Sedgwick, sir," she murmured with a great show of surprise as if she had happened upon him by chance. "It is so nice to see you again."

Nicholas Sedgwick came to his feet at once, as if she were going to hit him with a stick or something. He looked warily at her, then at Sanjay, tagging along behind. "I trust you haven't been bludgeoning your little brother lately," he said.

Suzannah wasn't sure what that word meant, but she gave a real authentic-sounding laugh as if she thought he were incredibly witty. "Oh, no, we were just playacting with you. Are you still mad at us?"

As she intended, her remarks put him off his guard. "Oh, no, not in the least. I understand children's games. I have five brothers and sisters myself."

"You do?" Sanjay piped up. "Any of'm my age?"

"The twins are five."

"I'm just four."

Nicholas reached out and patted Sanjay's head, then he grinned like a chipmunk in Suzannah's direction.

"What's that you've got in the basket, Suzie?"

Oh, goody, he was walking right into her plot, she thought happily. "It's a peace offering for you, Mr. Sedgwick. Anjelica got real mad at us for playing that trick so we want to make it up to you."

"Well, aren't you nice?"

Suzannah and Sanjay exchanged sly grins. "It's sugar candies Stuart got us yesterday when he took us to that big sweet shop down on Regent Street. Wanna try a piece? They're real good to eat."

"Why, thank you. I do like confections."

With silent glee, Suzannah handed over George's basket.

"I'm so glad the two of you have come down to see me. I want us all to be friends, for Anjelica's sake." Nicholas resumed his seat on the bench and took the basket onto his lap. Suzannah glanced up at the house to make sure Anjelica wasn't watching or anything, then turned back to Nicholas just as he lifted up the lid.

"The best ones are in the bottom, Mr. Sedgwick," Sanjay said, in just the words Suzannah had coached him to use.

Nicholas smiled at her brother as he reached for a piece of candy. Suzannah held her breath, ready for the fun.

"Why, what's this?" Nicholas murmured with a slight frown, then to Suzannah's overwhelming disappointment, he brought out George. When he held the snake expertly by the head and didn't act scared at all, her jaw dropped like a rock.

"So this is George, I suspect." Nicholas examined the writhing cobra without one ounce of horror. "You really shouldn't try to frighten people with him like this, Suzannah. It scares him just as much as it does your victims, you know."

"Hey, how'd you know about George anyways?"

"Anjelica told me the other day when I mentioned that I used to be a herpetologist at the Zoological Gardens in Regent's Park."

"Her pet what?" Sanjay asked, his green eyes wide with wonder.

"That's a man who studies reptiles such as George here," Nicholas informed them, carefully draping the snake around his neck, then rubbing George's back just the way Suzannah always did.

"You mean you aren't scared of him?" Suzannah demanded suspiciously.

"I was only surprised that he got into the candy when you weren't looking." Nicholas gazed straight into Suzannah's eyes. "I know you wouldn't have dared to put him in there just to scare me, not after Anjelica told you to be nice."

Suzannah felt like he was sitting on her chest and holding her down until she said peacock like Shashi used to do in Udaipur. His liking snakes sure was surprising. "How come you like him so much? Most people don't like him at all, and you know it. Even Stuart didn't like him at first, and he's as brave as Vishnu."

Nicholas smiled. "The Hindu god? I had a pet snake when I was little, too, but he wasn't nearly as impressive a specimen as George here."

Suzannah eyed him intently. He was probably just telling her lies to make her like him better. "Did not."

"Did, too."

Sanjay was quick to back her up. "Did not."

"Mine was just a water snake because we lived on a big lake up north near the border of Scotland. I used to scare my snooty old tutor with him because he always boxed my ears when I misspelled my words."

"Really?" Spelling wasn't her best subject, either. "Did you keep yours in a basket, too?" Suzannah asked, her curiosity taking over until she remembered that she didn't like him enough to have a civil conversation. "Just give him back," she demanded curtly. "He doesn't like other people to hold him."

Nicholas carefully lifted the cobra off his shoulders. "You'll have to be real careful with him this winter and keep him in a serpentarium—that's a warm tank with leaves and branches for him to wind himself around. It's too cold here for the Elapidae, you know."

"Just hand him over," she demanded sharply but his warning did worry her a trifle. She knelt down and gently replaced George into his basket. "C'mon, Sanjay, let's go down to the boat and see Stuart. We just love Stuart, Mr. Sedgwick, he's like a big brother to us already. No one else could ever be as good as him, not to us anyways."

"We don't want no other man around, neither," Sanjay added over his shoulder as Suzannah took his hand and led him away.

"That wasn't near as much fun as you promised it'd be," Sanjay complained in a whiny voice as they hurried off down to the riverbank.

"Who would've ever thought he'd like snakes as

much as me?" Suzannah muttered, downright depressed over their continuing inability to send Nicholas into hysteria.

When they reached the river, Stuart looked up from where he was buffing the brass rails with a soft white cloth. "Why the long faces?"

"That Nicholas man likes George," Sanjay told him as he jumped aboard. "Suzie's mad about it, too."

"What happened?" he asked as Suzannah dropped down cross-legged on the deck.

"He had a pet snake so he wasn't scared off at all. Isn't that a shame? George nearly always scares people to death."

"Yeah, I remember." Stuart tugged her pigtail. "We've got lots of time left. You'll think of something else to do to him."

Suzannah glanced up the lawn at her intended victim and saw that Anjelica had just joined him. She wondered if Nicholas Sedgwick would tell on them. Anjelica didn't turn around and come after them, though, so she guessed he didn't tattle.

"Just look up there, Stuart, now he'll spend all afternoon with Anjelica instead of her coming down and helping us clean up the boat."

Stuart's gaze followed her pointing finger and she saw how his expression got all hard and mad when he saw Nicholas kissing Anjelica's hand. She felt bad inside because they had let him down. Well, she would come up with some other thing to drive Nicholas away, even if it took her forever. Anjelica wasn't going to marry Mr. Sedgwick, not if Suzannah had anything to do with it. Even if he did have a pet snake when he was a little boy.

Stuart was growing more and more short-tempered with everyone and he knew it. He was chafing to drive his doubled fist straight into Nicholas's simpering, nice-guy face, but he knew well enough that was the last thing he could do. Anjelica would eventually come to her senses and end the stupid charade.

The man was at the house constantly now—asking for her, following her around, bringing her flowers and gifts. Hell, now he had even resorted to bringing the kids toys in an effort to win their support. A couple more dolls and red wagons filled with candy, and the kids were going to start wavering.

Today Nicholas had come to take Anjelica riding along the Thames. From where Stuart stood on the terrace, he watched them walk their mounts down the path toward the river. He wanted to follow them and make sure Nicholas didn't take too many liberties with her, but then he wasn't sure Nicholas knew how to seduce a woman. On the other hand, Anjelica would no doubt make up for his inexperience. Unlike most unmarried ladies he knew, she had memorized the *Kama Sutra*. She could teach Nicholas more than a few tricks.

He grimaced and shook his head. Good God, he'd never seen such a mild-mannered man who refused to take offense about anything, not even a cobra hidden in a basket with the express intention of scaring the hell out of him. Suzannah was at her wit's end, having tried a whole list of ugly pranks that would rile anyone in their right mind.

If Stuart hadn't been in such a bad mood, he might have grinned. He and Anjelica's little sister had gotten off to a rough start in Udaipur, but now they were pals. He did not want to see her or Sanjay living at the Sedgwick mansion any more than he wanted Anjelica to be there. He wanted to keep them around a while. There, he admitted it.

Muttering a curse under his breath, he moved farther down the wall where he could better observe Nicholas and Anjelica. He felt helpless and not a little frustrated by his inability to sway Anjelica's determination. Her sense of duty was so ingrained that he was beginning to worry that no one could ever change her mind.

Sullenly, he raised his Confederate-issue field glasses and watched their slow progress downriver until Nicholas's horse suddenly balked, then reared his front legs and pawed the air. The hapless scholar went sprawling onto the rocky path, and his spooked mount galloped furiously up through the grass toward the stable. It was then he caught sight of Suzannah's perch in the gigantic oak tree not far from the accident. As usual, Sanjay was close by. When they saw Stuart watching them, they held up the pair of identical slingshots that Nicholas had brought to them only the day before.

Stuart was afraid they'd gone a bit too far this time. Nicholas was still lying on the ground, and Stuart hurried down the path and found Anjelica helping Nicholas onto a bench directly beneath the leafy bower where the children were hiding. If she saw the culprits secreted in the bough above, they'd all be in trouble. He sought to distract her.

"Are you all right, Nick, my man?" he asked as he approached them. He reached down and pulled the smaller man to his feet.

Anjelica whirled on him and presented him with a narrow-eyed, distrustful glare which informed him that she thought him to blame for the skittish horse. "How did you know Nicholas was thrown from his mount?"

"I happened to be on the terrace and saw the mare bolt for the house. Are you all right, Sedgwick?"

"Yes, I believe so." Nicholas appeared to be a trifle groggy. He placed his hand to his temple.

"He hit his head when he fell." Anjelica knelt gracefully and retrieved her lace handkerchief from the sleeve of her brand-new burgundy riding habit. She tenderly dabbed at a tiny trickle of blood on his right temple. "You poor thing. I can't imagine what could have frightened your horse."

Stuart heard a guilty rustling of leaves overhead and hastily spoke up before one of the pint-sized assassins dropped into their midst. "Let me help you back up to the house, Sedgwick. Should I summon my driver to fetch you home?"

He took a firm grip on Nicholas's elbow, then pulled the man's arm around his shoulder.

"I don't believe I'll need a doctor, but I daresay I'd better go home and lie down. I do feel a bit woozy."

"Are you quite sure, Nicholas?" Anjelica was asking solicitously. "You could lie down in the parlor for a while if you wish."

Stuart didn't think so. "I'm afraid Nicholas is right, Anjelica. He needs to go home where his mother can tend to his injury."

"Yes, she's quite used to my falls and sprains. I must admit I'm not much of an equestrian." Nicholas sighed. "You will see that Suzannah and Sanjay get the book on serpents I brought with me, won't you, Anjelica? They really must take proper care of George this winter or he'll surely perish from the cold."

"Yes, of course, Nicholas. It's thoughtful of you to be so concerned."

Stuart rolled his eyes skyward, disbelieving the man was actually worried about Suzannah's damn snake. And Anjelica was babying him as if he had been thrust through the chest with a bayonet instead of merely scraping his head on the ground. He hurried his step until he was half dragging Nicholas Sedgwick up the path, eager to get rid of him before Anjelica spotted the children.

When they reached the house he called for the carriage, then propelled Nicholas through the foyer with the utmost haste. Anjelica continued to hover and fret as the coach was readied and brought around, dabbing at the small cut and soothing the man until Stuart decided perhaps feigning a mortal wound might be the best way for him to win her over to him.

"I'm so sorry that our afternoon had to end this way," Nicholas murmured just after Stuart had shoved him bodily into the coach. He leaned out the window, looking melancholy and pale. "I'll make it up to you as soon as this headache fades away."

"Just take care of yourself," she called as Stuart slammed the door shut and slapped the horse's flank.

The carriage rattled off down the drive, and Stuart turned to Anjelica with a suitably sympathetic expression on his face.

"You put a burr under his saddle, didn't you?" was her heartless accusation.

"I didn't do a thing, I swear."

"Nicholas doesn't deserve to be treated this way," she insisted.

"He's not much of a horseman."

"I do hope he'll be all right." She looked after the coach when Nicholas's voice drifted back to them with one last farewell.

Stuart grimaced. "Hell, Anjelica, it's just a scratch. Now we can take that voyage upriver to Blake House. You've been wanting to go there. Pack some things and let's go for a few days while Nicholas is recuperating from his massive injury."

The kids had arrived in time to hear his suggestion, and they quickly let their feelings be known.

"Yes, yes, we want to come, too!"

"Please let us!"

To his pleasure Anjelica looked more than willing. "I'd love to see the old place again," she said wistfully. "But isn't it too late to leave?"

"If we leave soon, we'll get there by nightfall. We can come back any time you want."

"I should tell Nicholas."

"Send him a note."

Anjelica hesitated a moment longer, then smiled up at him. "All right, it won't take me a moment to pack a few things."

As she and the children headed back into the house, Stuart moved down the path to read the *Virginian*. Once they got upriver he would keep her there for a while. He would finally have some time alone with her where he could wear her down in his own way. She wanted him as much as he did her. All he had to do was touch her and she melted into his arms. And that was an idea that appealed to him.

Chapter Twenty

Down deep in her heart where she could admit her real feelings, Anjelica was relieved to be sitting in the bow of Stuart's sailing yacht, the wind blowing against her face. Down even deeper she was glad to be leaving behind London and Nicholas's constant attentions. She was wicked, wicked and ungrateful, and undeserving of her mother's lovingly laid plans to secure her future.

If only Nicholas had been a horrid person, a swine or blackguard, she might have had reason to annul the marriage, but he had turned out to be a sweet, mild-tempered, and highly educated man who would do just about anything for her and her siblings. She knew full well that he would be an honest, faithful husband who would treat her brother and sister with kindness despite their nonstop harassment of him. On the other hand, he wasn't Stuart. Nobody was like Stuart, and nobody could ever take his place in her heart.

Reluctantly she turned her head and looked at him where he sat in the stern manning the rudder.

The breeze ruffled through the layers of long black hair. He smiled at her, obviously as pleased as she to be away from the city and other people. Her heart melted. *You are so wicked,* she chastised herself again, but she smiled, too, unable to hide the contented glow in her eyes.

"You see, you're happy now that the bookworm isn't hanging around. You'd rather be with me. Admit it."

"You know I would," she said softly, her heart aching with conflicting emotions. He grinned again, gripping the rudder as a gust of wind filled the sail but he maneuvered the craft skillfully, as if he'd had a great deal of practice. "You're a good sailor. Why weren't you in the Confederate navy instead of the army?"

"I should've been. I like the ocean and the feel of wind and spray in my face. I always have, even when I was a lad."

Anjelica could visualize him as a little boy, a dark-haired daredevil skimming over the blue water of some river in a small sailboat, a red one perhaps. His sons would look like that someday. Would Marian be their mother? Would Stuart marry her after Anjelica took her place at Nicholas's side? The thought actually made her sick to her stomach, and she quickly changed the subject. "How long will it take us to get to Blake House?"

"It'll be awhile yet. You might as well sit back and relax. The kids are going to help me with the sails.

I imagine you're tired with the social schedule Julia Sedgwick's had you on."

"Yes, I am," she admitted, "and I haven't been sleeping well." She didn't say that she tossed and turned in her bed, thinking of Stuart and wishing he would come to her room. *Wicked,* she berated herself once more, but she was so tired of being polite and trying to behave as the stuffy Londoners expected her to. She was exhausted from parties and teas and receptions all designed with the express purpose of introducing her to the city as Nicholas's wife. How could she back out of the wedding now, even if she wanted to? How could she humiliate Nicholas in such a way?

What she really wanted was to lie in the grass in a loose tunic and a silk sari and look at the sky the way she had done so often in the fields of Udaipur. She wanted to meditate and wave garlands of amanthus and marigolds and swim naked in the river while the elephants wallowed and trumpeted their pleasure. She squeezed her eyes shut. She wanted Stuart to hold her and kiss her the way he had done on their wedding night. She wanted to forget all about her duty to her parents.

Her thoughts were so distraught that she tried to empty her mind and concentrate on enjoying the journey upriver. The water was calm, the day sunny and warm with flocks of birds wheeling over the river. People waved from the water pavilions of the big houses that occasionally loomed on the tree-shaded banks. Stuart said little, busy with the handling of the yacht, and she went below into the cabin and changed into the pale blue sari and tunic she had brought along with her. The moment the silk settled against her skin, she felt as if she had returned home where she belonged.

When she came back topdeck, Stuart whistled with appreciation, and the children laughed from where they sat in the bow pointing out deer and otter along the banks. Filled with long overdue contentment, she climbed to the flat roof of the cabin and lay down on her back. The sun shone hotly down upon her face, and she was pleased she could release her hair from the staid coils required in London and let it blow about wildly in the moist breezes. She hated the elaborate, constricting bonnets that Mrs. Sedgwick deemed necessary for any proper lady to wear every moment of the day until precisely five P.M. when the evening rules took over. Anjelica had always hated hats anyway, even the turbans she'd had to wear when she was a man.

Tears came up from some deep well within her, grief she had tried to will away during the last few weeks. She was tired of crying. It only exhausted her and made her feel empty. This was what she needed, time alone to meditate on what was happening to her so she could see the wisdom and harmony her marriage to Nicholas would bring into their lives.

She closed off her thoughts and let her mind grow quiet, let the silence of the universe calm her unhappy thoughts, let herself feel nothing, think nothing. She was so tired of the strain of getting to know Nicholas and hiding her feelings for Stuart from him. Feelings so acute they could sever her heart like the blade of a saw. She needed time to relax and not worry.

For a long time thoughts of Udaipur and the maharajah impeded her progress toward that serene state she sought. She wondered if Prafulla Veda had reached the cool mountains of Bhutan, wondered how long the prince had cried when he had found them gone, wondered if she would ever see the palace again, until she finally slipped deep into the dark and dreamless realm of unconsciousness, the only place where peace was offered to those as weary of the world as she was.

When she awoke much later, Stuart was leaning over her, his lips softly brushing her mouth. At first she thought she was having yet another erotic dream where he came to her at night, slipped into bed with her, made love to her, tenderly, sweetly, endlessly. Instinctively she slid her arms around his neck and clutched him closer, never wanting to let him go. Her eyes opened wide when she heard Sanjay's cackling laugh.

"Look, Suzie, he's kissing her and she's kissing him back, too."

That brought her upright, and she rubbed her eyes, realizing it was much later because the sun no longer warmed her bare skin. She realized then that they were already tied up at the boathouse of Blake House. Looking up at the big half-timbered house on the hill, a deluge of memories flooded her. The last time she had seen it was nearly ten years ago. Her father and mother were both with them, Suzannah had been a crawling baby, only recently adopted from the Ursuline Convent in New Orleans when her father had worked there in the British diplomatic corps.

"It hasn't changed," she murmured as Suzannah and Sanjay climbed over the starboard rail and ran up the path toward the house that had seen the birth and death of generations of Blakes. "It looks exactly like it did the day we left. We took a packet barge to London, and I stood right here and wept into the folds of my mother's skirt because I didn't want to go live in India."

Stuart smiled at her. He had the most wonderful smile. "Let's go inside. I sent word a week ago for the caretaker to air the rooms and ready the place. I knew you'd eventually need some time away from Nicholas's smothering. God knows I needed time alone with you."

"We're not alone," she reminded him.

"The kids'll do what I say. You see, they want me for a brother-in-law."

Anjelica had to steel herself against such talk. How easy it would be to simply stay here at Blake House with Stuart, to tell Nicholas and his family that she didn't love him and didn't want to marry him. Inside, though, where duty and honor dwelled, guilt rose and pricked her conscience.

"Let's just enjoy our visit and try to forget everything else while we're here," she entreated Stuart quietly.

He returned her serious gaze. "All right. We'll be together this one last time before you go to Nicholas."

Somehow his resignation shook her more than anything else he could have said. When he reached out to help her from the boat, she put her hand inside his and allowed him to hold it as they walked together toward the house. She allowed the intimacy because she well knew she might never have another opportunity to feel his long, brown fingers entwined with her own. This was probably the last time they could ever be together without other people around, without her husband around. She wanted to savor each and every moment so that she could remember it after she lived in the marble mausoleum that was Sedgwick Hall.

Later that evening they brought out the cold mutton and bread packed in a hamper by Stuart's cook and had supper down on the river landing. All through dinner in tune to the rippling of the river, she listened as Suzannah and Sanjay reiterated their adamant refusal ever to live with her in ugly Sedgwick Hall. They intended to stay on with Stuart at his house on the river, they informed her, and learn to sail and swim in the river and have a wonderful life with him.

She was going to lose them as well as him, she thought with a desperation that cut a gash of loneliness into her soul. The more they spoke, the more determination she heard in their voices. They really meant every word, but underneath their childish threats and anger she could hear the more subtle threads of vulnerability and fear. She had ripped them away from the place they both loved so much and brought them to a strange land that they neither liked nor understood. She had hurt them, and she knew it.

"You can stay with Stuart, if you like. If he is agreeable to have you at his house." Her voice broke slightly but she forced herself to go on. "I understand how you must feel. But I want both of you to know that all I want, all I've ever wanted, is for you to be happy and have a secure future."

After her quiet concession, Suzannah and Sanjay abruptly ended their complaints. Stuart watched her silently for the remainder of the evening, no doubt mocking her honorable intentions. His knowing look stayed with her even when she tucked the children into their beds and kissed them good night.

For a long time after they fell asleep, she sat in a chair between their beds and stared at them. She was hurt that they truly wanted to live with Stuart instead of her, but she understood their feelings, understood them only too well.

Sighing, she rose and wandered back into her own bedchamber. She stared out the open doors of the second-floor balcony and watched the moon rising above the river, white and ghostly, casting a long shimmering path down the river water as it had over Lake Pichola in Udaipur. Stuart would come to her soon. She knew it, and she wanted him to. She was waiting for him.

She sensed his presence without hearing any sound of his approach. She turned slowly. He stood silhouetted in the threshold, his broad-shouldered form nearly obliterating the doorway. His face was hidden in shadow.

"I knew you'd come to me—" She got no further because he was already at her side. His fingers clamped down over her shoulders, and he held her body tight against his own as his mouth found hers, gently, tenderly, but hungrily, too. She was going to give in, let him do whatever he wished, let him do what she wanted him to do.

Moaning softly, she felt his arm lock around her waist and lift her bodily, until she hung against him, her arms entwined around his neck. Her mind began to spin and tilt, her every nerve alive with love and pain and joy and need. His fingers tangled in her hair and forced her head back to where she had to look at him.

"Don't say no to me, dammit. This is the only chance we'll ever have to be together." His voice was gruff, almost tortured, and her answer came breathlessly but resolutely.

"Make love to me, Stuart, give me that much to take with me—"

"Oh, God help me," he muttered, then his mouth found hers again, softly, searchingly, tasting her as she was savoring the taste of his skin.

"I love you," she murmured, knowing she had to tell him, wanting desperately for him to hear her say the words.

Stuart swung her into his arms and carried her to the bed. He lay her down against the pillows and she watched him undress, watched the hard, molded muscles of his chest emerge from his shirt, reached out to him when he was naked, wanting to touch his body, touch his skin, touch his hair and lips.

He lay down atop her, holding her head cradled in his palms and his mouth found hers, hot and eager. He groaned as she opened her lips beneath his probing tongue, groaned as her fingernails raked the muscles of his back. Her body turned into a column of fire, her mind unable to reason. His breathing was loud, a labored rasp next to her ear, but she could barely draw breath at all, her thoughts banished by a maze of erotic response that she had withheld and denied for days, and weeks, and months.

Vaguely, somewhere far away she heard a rip of silk, felt his mouth on her bare flesh, but when his mouth closed, warm and moist, over the erect tip of her breast, she cried out with pure pleasure. She clutched his black hair in her fingers. She couldn't stop, didn't want to stop when he touched her body with his hands and mouth, couldn't think about it being wrong when it felt so right.

She felt his palms on the flat plane of her belly, sliding over her thigh then between her legs. His finger touched her and she jerked with ecstasy, with a feeling she had never experienced before. She couldn't push him away, couldn't even think that she should. She was weak when it came to him, unable to remember honor or duty, unable to think at all.

Suddenly his mouth left hers and he was on his knees, looking down at her. His face was harsh with emotions, his breathing heavy, but his eyes were what held her, filled with a kind of pain she had not seen in them before.

"No," he muttered hoarsely, then slid off the bed. He stopped a few feet away and looked back at her. Weakly, Anjelica pushed herself up on an elbow and their eyes locked for an instant, hers confused, his tortured as he turned and walked toward the balcony.

Shaken, disappointed, afraid of what he meant to do, Anjelica climbed from the bed and pulled on her wrapper. She found him outside, bracing his hands on the wall as he looked down over the moonlit river. He had not put on his shirt, and she lay her palm gently upon the lean muscles of his back.

"Stuart?"

He jerked around so sharply that her hand was knocked away. She took a step back but was not prepared for the way he lashed out at her.

"Don't touch me. Just get the hell away from me. I'm sorry I came here. I'm sorry I love you. I'm god-damn sorry I was ever born. Is that what you want to hear? That I'm suffering. Well, I am. I'm miserable but I've got enough honor left not to seduce you, then send you on to explain it to your husband on your wedding night. I swore I'd never touch another married woman and so help me God I'm not going to, even for you. Maybe you can be content with some kind of sordid affair behind your husband's back, but I can't. Do you understand that, Anjelica? I want more than that from you and so should you."

His words cut deep. She was trembling all over. "I know I'm betraying Nicholas, but I can't help it. I love you so much—"

He grabbed her arms. "Then tell him. Tell him about us and end this farce before it's too late."

"I can't, you know I can't—"

Stuart's hands dropped away. He stared at her, then shook his head.

"Then go to your husband and to hell with both of you."

He moved away down the balcony, and she stared after him until he was swallowed up by the darkness. Her knees began to tremble and she sank back against the balustrade, fighting her desire to run after him, to grab him, beg him not to leave her. He was trying to do the right thing, for himself, for her, for Nicholas, because she couldn't do it herself. God help her, she would never have the strength to turn away from him.

Chapter Twenty-one

Anxious to see Anjelica again, Nicholas kept his hand on the coach's door handle as he was driven into the stone-paved front courtyard of Blake House. He loved the rambling Tudor mansion almost as much as he did his own ancestral estate, which lay not ten miles away at Sloandrake. Soon both great houses would be his to share with his lovely bride. He had never expected to meet a woman so beautiful and sweet, much less have the privilege of taking her as his wife. For years he had put off and dreaded meeting the woman he had wed by proxy, only to discover that she was exquisite in every way.

As soon as the driver brought the coach to a standstill, he jumped down onto the paving stones, then took the front steps two at a time. One hearty clang of the shell-shaped brass door knocker brought May, the old housekeeper, running to answer his summons. He beamed brightly at her but in his eagerness looked past her into the house.

"Miss Blake's still here, isn't she, May? She hasn't returned for London yet, I hope?""

"Oh, no, sir, Master Sedgwick, they've barely just gotten here yesterday evening and gotten themselves settled into their rooms."

"Good, good. I was afraid they'd just come for the day. Where is Anjelica now?"

May's ruddy, country-weathered face took on a worried look. "It be strange, I know, but she's not showed herself all day. I'm fearing that she might be feeling a bit under the weather because she's lay abed near all morning and wouldn't eat naught a bite of the breakfast I took up to her."

Nicholas frowned in alarm. Their wedding vows were to be read in just five days. He certainly didn't want to delay them. "Is she ill, you mean? What's wrong with her?"

"I don't rightly know, sir. Mr. Delaney said she just needed some rest but I did notice she's been weepy and sad, but I don't think it's nothing serious enough to worry yerself with, sir."

Nicholas was not convinced. Anjelica had been fine just yesterday when he'd taken the spill and bumped his head. He wanted to see her himself, just to make sure she was all right. "Where is Mr. Delaney? Perhaps he can tell me more about her condition."

"He done closed himself up in the library office with the door shut. He said he don't want no intrusions, and he didn't want nothin' to eat at midday, neither. The two little ones were more'n a mite disappointed 'cause he promised them a fishing trip down on Rotham Creek. I think he might be gettin' ready to go back downriver."

"Thank you, May. I think I'll speak with him before I seek out Anjelica."

Impatiently stripping off the spotless white gloves he wore, Nicholas hastened his step through the dim rear entry hall to the double doors leading into the library. As May had said, the door was closed. He hesitated, not particularly wanting to disturb Anjelica's imposing guardian, if for no other reason than the man would probably insist on tagging along during every minute of his entire visit. Still, his concern compelled him to tap a knuckle against the oak panel.

"I say, Mr. Delaney, are you inside there? It's Nicholas Sedgwick here, sir. I do have a need to speak with you."

No answer ensued. He knocked again, then frowned with frustration until the door suddenly swung inward. He stared at Stuart Delaney, startled by the other man's appearance. The big American was dressed casually in dark trousers and a full-sleeved white shirt, but to Nicholas's consternation, he was haggard and unshaven, as if he had slept in his rumpled attire. It was a far cry from his usual impeccable dress, and Nicholas tried to hide his shock at finding him thus.

"Good morning, sir. I'm sorry to disturb you, but May just told me Anjelica's not feeling well. I'm quite distraught and wondered if you could assure me that she's all right."

Stuart looked wearily at him out of bloodshot eyes. "Anjelica's fine. Come in, Sedgwick, we have to talk."

Nicholas obeyed, as always completely intimidated by Stuart Delaney. Anjelica's guardian seemed such an unpredictable man at times, despite his well-mannered ways. As he crossed the room toward the desk and several upholstered chairs, he remembered that it was inside that very chamber where he and Anjelica had been wed by proxy.

"Sit down, Sedgwick."

Nicholas seated himself on a leather chair, becoming slightly alarmed by the unusual gravity of Delaney's manner. "Is something amiss, Mr. Delaney?"

Delaney had remained standing but had turned to gaze out the window. He stood very erect, his hands clasped tightly behind his back. He didn't speak for several moments, then he turned around slowly and latched his rather arresting blue gaze on Nicholas's face. His expression was so peculiar that Nicholas fought the impulse to stick a finger between his collar and his neck.

"I'll give you anything I have, Sedgwick, money, my house in London, my boat, any of it—if you'll release Anjelica from that ridiculous marriage contract you're holding over her head."

Nicholas was too stunned to utter a word. When

he finally found his voice, he stammered like a schoolboy before the cane. "W-w-why, sir, I don't understand your meaning!"

"Then listen to me closely. She doesn't love you. She loves me, but she won't marry me because she's bound and determined to do the honorable thing and live up to her parents' wishes. All this is to her is a duty she feels obligated to perform."

His words had become harsh and brittle as he finished his appalling speech, and Nicholas bristled under such an outspoken insult. "I beg your pardon, sir, but I have every reason to believe that Miss Blake is quite agreeable to our wedding plans. I assure you that she holds me in quite high regard as her betrothed—"

"High regard's a far cry from being in love with you. She loves me. If you don't believe me, ask her."

Now thoroughly offended, Nicholas rose to his feet and fixed Delaney with a haughty stare. "I will do so, sir, I can assure you. Furthermore, I suspect that she will be as offended as I that you attempted this outrageous bribe to entice me into reneging on my wedding vows. I do realize that you are yet to know me especially well, sir, but I am one to hold the concepts of duty and honor close to my heart, and to be guided by my conscience. If Anjelica shares these virtues, I can only applaud her."

"Then you're as big a fool as she is."

Stuart stared at him a moment longer, then turned and strode from the room, leaving Nicholas to gape after him in dismay. Doubts had already begun to nag his mind. Could he have been wrong about Anjelica's feelings toward him? Was there something more than friendship between her and the guardian hired to bring her back? He had sensed as much at first until Anjelica had assured him otherwise. She had certainly seemed pleased enough to be with him. He would have to find out, now, today. But if it were true, did he really want to know?

At the front of the house he ran into Suzannah and Sanjay who wore old pants and ridiculously oversized blue shirts. They wasted no time venting their rage on him.

"Stuart's leaving because you're here!" Suzannah cried furiously. "He's on his way down to his boat now, and it's all your fault!"

"And he was going to take us fishing, too!" Sanjay added with less viciousness but with a sheen of tears in his green eyes.

"Now look here, children, I didn't ask him to leave like this. I only came down to visit your sister."

"Well, we came here to get her away from you, and now here you are, butting in again and causing Stuart to go off and leave us. Why don't you just go home and, and, and jump in that big old funny-looking urn on your front porch? That's right, just jump in it and stay there. J-u-m-p i-n i-t!"

With that the little girl ran away at full speed. Little Sanjay rushed away on her heels, unsuccessfully trying to manage both fishing poles as he went and knocking off a vase by the door in the process. Despite Nicholas's efforts to catch it, it fell and shattered into a million pieces.

Nonplussed by the unsettling events of the morning, Nicholas followed the children outside and watched them run down the grassy lawn toward the dock. He could see Stuart there, readying his yacht for departure, and he couldn't help but feel relieved to know the man was taking his leave. Delaney had obviously deluded himself into thinking Anjelica harbored romantic notions concerning him, but he had no doubt mistaken her gratitude for affection.

Determined to find her so that she could verify his conclusions, he turned and was about to reenter the house when he caught a glimpse of her running down the far side of the lawn where the trees thickened into a hunting park on the north perimeter of the property. She, too, was watching Delaney depart from the river landing, and he hurried down the stone stairs and took the path that would provide the shortest access to her position.

As he walked he could hear Suzannah yelling for Delaney to come back but a glance showed him that the American was ignoring her boisterous outcry and was already hefting sail at midriver. Nicholas was pleased to see the last of him, positive that he would have a much more productive heart-to-heart talk with Anjelica without Delaney's ever-vigilant, distracting presence.

As he reached the grassy glade where he had

seen her from the house, he found that she had disappeared. He was ready to make the trek down into the lower portion of the gardens in search of her when he detected the sound of muffled weeping. He stopped in his tracks and listened, then followed the wrenching sounds to a leafy bower made of blooming lilac bushes.

Anjelica lay facedown on the ground, hidden by the lush green and purple foliage. As he inched closer he could see the way her shoulders heaved under sobs of despair. He swallowed down a lump of pure, congealed fear. Oh, God, had Delaney been telling him the truth?

"Anjelica, dear, what is it?" he asked gently as he knelt and touched his hand to her shoulder.

Anjelica lurched up into a sitting position, her face red and ravaged by tears and torment, but the surprise evident in her expression told him that until that moment she had no idea he was anywhere nearby.

"Go away, Nicholas, please, I don't want to see you right now," she murmured, her voice quavering. She dropped her face into her folded arms where he couldn't see it.

He wasn't to be dismissed, however, and he sat down in the grass, not sure what he should say. "Why are you crying, Anjelica? Tell me the truth, please, I beg you."

"I can't. Please don't ask me questions. Just go away for a little while." She dabbed at her tears but still wouldn't look at him. "I'll be all right if you'll just let me compose myself."

"You do love him, don't you?" he asked bluntly. "Delaney was telling me the truth."

She froze in the process of pulling out her lace handkerchief, then looked at him, her guilty expression confirming all his worst fears. More tears welled in her eyes. "What did he say? Did he say where he was going?"

Nicholas shook his head and watched with sinking heart as she turned her tearful attention to the sailboat in the distance.

"It's for the best," she finally said, wiping her eyes and trying to quell her overwrought emotions without a lot of success. She looked again to the departing craft, then burst into a fresh deluge of tears.

"Now, now," he consoled her in a thick voice. He put a comforting arm around her shoulders but he shut his eyes, filled with pain as she wept openly against his chest. It seemed as if a floodgate had opened, and she spoke against the crisp fabric of his shirtfront, her voice muffled with agony.

"I'm so sorry I fell in love with him, Nicholas. I didn't want to. I was true to you in my heart, for years and years I thought only of you. I always wanted to come here and be your wife, but then he and I were thrown together for weeks and weeks and I couldn't help it, I just couldn't. How can you ever forgive me?"

"Shush now, there's nothing to forgive." His

words came hard, however, and for a moment, he nurtured the thought that he could change her heart given time, that he could make her love him instead of Delaney. He longed for that chance, wanted it more than anything he could ever remember as she clung to him, tears for another man wetting his coat.

He sighed heavily and stroked her back until she calmed, but after each pause a fresh onslaught of tears would overtake her until he thought she couldn't possibly have that much water inside her. But as he held her shivering body and felt the depth of her grief, he began to realize the extent of her suffering. Although every need and desire of his body and mind resisted, he knew he would be a fool to hold her to the contract made by their parents. Their marriage would be doomed before it even began. Did he want that?

"Anjelica, please, stop this. There's no need for such distress." He swallowed hard while she valiantly tried again to collect herself. "The truth is that I've secretly had some misgivings myself about going through with this wedding."

That pronouncement stilled both her tears and the trembling of her body. She lifted her face, stupefaction written plainly over her features, and he couldn't stop himself from reaching up and wiping away a tear trickling down her cheek. God, he loved her as much as Delaney did, maybe even more.

"What do you mean?"

Nicholas desperately tried to conceal the disappointment that had begun to squeeze like a vise around his heart. "I think you're the most wonderful woman I've ever met, truly I do. And I would be honored to take you as my wife, but the truth is, Anjelica, I'm not really ready to settle down. I have my studies, you know. I was planning to go to Rome with some of my friends and study in the university there." The next words came hard, dredged up out of his soul like anchors of iron. "I was only going through with this to please Mother. She so has her heart set on us being wed. She adores you, as she did your mother before you."

Anjelica was searching his face with a look of total disbelief. "What are you saying, Nicholas?"

"I'm saying that if you truly love Delaney so much, I'll free you to marry him. An annulment is always possible in a marriage by proxy. It'll be the best thing, I suspect, for both of us."

He nearly choked on that last ridiculous lie, and for a moment she only stared at him incredulously. Then he saw the relief dawn deep inside her eyes, followed by joy and a wave of gratitude so warm he could almost feel it.

She put her arms around him and hugged his neck tightly, only intensifying his agony. "I'll never forget what you've done for me, Nicholas. You're the most wonderful man I know. You'll find a perfect woman someday, I know you will, someone who's not so wicked as I am."

Pulling back she smiled tremulously into his eyes, and he managed a stiff nod, well aware that

that could never be true. No one could ever replace Anjelica in his life.

"You'd better go after him," he said in a brusque, brave voice, but knew at once his attempt at strength was false. "You can take my coach, if you wish. The driver's waiting with it in the front court-yard. I'll stay here with the children until you send for them."

"Oh, Nicholas, thank you so much," she murmured as she scrambled to her feet. She dashed away the remainder of her tears, then bent down to kiss his cheek. Then she was gone, raising her skirts and running up the path that led to the house. He watched her go, feeling as if someone had grabbed his heart and ripped it violently out of his chest.

Chapter Twenty-two

Anchored just upriver from his own London dock, Stuart leaned back against the stern rail and tipped the nearly empty whiskey bottle to his mouth. He drank deeply, then balanced the bottom of the bottle atop his bent knee. The river current lapped soothingly against the hull, and he shut his eyes. When he saw Anjelica's face hovering stubbornly inside his mind, he took another swig, wondering how much liquor it would take to dull his senses into the dark oblivion he sought.

The sun had dropped low through a twilight sky swirled with layers of mauve, gold, and indigo. The familiar fog was settling in over the Thames, obscuring the calm river surface and tracts of woods hugging the shores. Good. He liked the idea of being enclosed in a coat of gray nothingness where he couldn't see or hear anything.

Why the devil had he ever gone to India? he asked himself as he took another hearty draught and let the potent brew burn down the length of his gullet and put a fire in his gut. Why did he have to meet her in the first place? His life had been bloody hell since the first time she had smiled into his eyes. Damn her.

He wasn't drunk yet, he mused objectively, not enough to suit him anyway, because he could still think, could still see her in the misty edges of his consciousness, could see Sedgwick stroking her silken flesh and burying his hands in the flowing softness of her silvery hair, just like Stuart had done that one perfumed night in Udaipur, just like he could have done last night if he hadn't been so damned honorable.

"Oh, God, am I ever a fool," he muttered in supreme disgust. Furious with himself, he cursed and raised his arm and hurled the empty bottle the length of the boat. It smashed against the cabin wall and sent glass shards flying over the rail to make little plinking sounds in the water. He dropped his head into his hands. He wanted to sob, he realized in utter humiliation, like some kind of wretched baby.

"Stuart? Where are you?"

His head jerked up, and he stared blearily to stern, not sure if he had really heard the soft voice. Anjelica seemed to materialize like a wraith in the blowing mists. His jaw dropped when he realized that she was totally nude, her long hair wet and slicked down her neck. He blinked hard, looked at the broken bottle and decided he was obviously a lot drunker then he thought. He was having a hallucination, he had to be, but oh, God, it was one hell of a good one.

"Stuart? I know you're out here," the uninvited apparition called softly as if she didn't know she wasn't real.

Groggy-headed, Stuart wondered if he could talk with a dream, if it could keep him company when he was so damned lonely. Maybe he had just had too much to drink, maybe he should stumble belowdecks and sleep it off. But apparently the ghostly form had seen him. She was smiling Anjelica's smile, walking her walk, coming straight toward him.

"Stuart, I've been looking everywhere for you. I heard glass break out here in the river, and I knew you'd moored the boat somewhere in the fog."

Now she was standing in front of him, close enough that he could easily touch her. Her naked flesh glowed with droplets of water until she shone in the faint light like a marble statue of Venus. He wanted to reach out his hand but was afraid to, for fear his hand would pass through the shining illusion. He didn't have to. She knelt in front of him and cupped his jaw in her palms.

"I had to come to you. I couldn't stand to wait. I was afraid you wouldn't come back home, that you'd just sail away to America and leave me behind—"

The minute she touched him he knew she was real. He came unsteadily to his feet and tried to shake clear his liquor-addled brain.

"Damn you," he mumbled harshly. "Why did you come here? Do you get pleasure out of torturing me?"

"No, no, of course, not," she cried, coming closer. "You don't understand. I love you—"

"Hell, no, I don't understand." He ought to just grab her up and hold her, give in to his own desire. That's what he wanted to do, God help him. He sucked in deep gulps of the cool night air and came back to his senses.

"Look, Anjelica, just get the hell out of here and leave me alone! Go back to your husband. I don't know why you came here, and I don't want to know. I'm leaving the country tomorrow, and that's not soon enough." His jaw clamped. "Now go on, and get off my boat."

For a moment she stood so still that he wondered momentarily if she really was some lifelike figment of his imagination. Her face was hidden in shadows now but he could see that she was shivering.

"Listen to me, Stuart, please. Don't you understand? Nicholas released me. I don't have to go through with it."

At first he couldn't believe his ears. Sedgwick would never do that. He had said so just that morning. What's more, Stuart didn't blame him.

"Why are you lying to me?"

"It's true, I swear it is." When she came up to him again and pressed herself close, his anger fled him. His arms went around her and he pulled her in tightly against his chest. "I want to be with you,

Stuart. I don't even care if you marry me, I just want us to be together."

Something inside Stuart gave, a bubble of pure joy that expanded slowly until he was filled with it. He crushed her to him, shutting his eyes with relief, still plagued by lingering disbelief.

"I love you so much," she was whispering until he quieted her with his mouth. If it were true, he didn't want to talk about it, he only wanted to touch her, hold her, enjoy her in case it was some horrible kind of mistake.

She put her arms around his neck, and he lifted her against him, carrying her through the gangway and down the steps into the living quarters. He fell with her onto the bunk, rolling until he was atop her, bracketing her face with his palms and forcing her to look at him. Her beautiful face was illuminated by the dim lantern in the window. She smiled, her gray eyes filled with happiness.

"I thought you were some kind of apparition my mind dreamed up to help me get over you," he whispered, stroking the elegant contour of her cheek with his fingertips.

"I want to make you happy."

"It's working," he muttered, raising up on his knees and jerking off his shirt. She stared up at him as he removed his clothes, their eyes locked as he came down atop her, bracing his elbows on the bed and capturing her hands on either side of her head.

"I ought to punish you for putting me through all this," he whispered hoarsely against her ear. "I ought to marry someone else and make you suffer for a change."

"No, I couldn't bear it," Anjelica moaned, her chest heaving breathlessly as he smiled down into her eyes. He looked at the soft swells of her breasts, then he bent his head and took one taut nipple into his mouth.

She cried out and arched her body and he touched his tongue to the tip and felt the current jolt through his entire body, heating his blood until his heart throbbed with fire. He let go of her hands, and she buried her fingers in his hair, clutching her fingers there as he moved his mouth across her satiny skin to her other breast.

"I love you, I love you, I only want to be with you," she was murmuring in a muffled whisper that only intensified his own desperate need.

"It's about damn time," he managed to say as he moved lower, trailing his tongue down the flatness of her belly. She writhed beneath him and he thought he should stop and leave, make her suffer and crave him the way he had her for months on end, but he knew he couldn't, not when his every nerve ending was alive and tingling with an acute awareness that he had never felt in his life.

Anjelica came up on her knees and pushed him backward to the bed. He smiled at the sober look on her face, at the way she was breathing so rapidly. She straddled his loins and held his wrists down as she gazed into his face.

"Torture me forever, if you must, but please don't

ever go away without me," she whispered, her eyes smoky with desire as she fitted herself to him. He felt the resistance of her maidenhead, heard her low gasp of pain, then both of them groaned as he entered her fully.

He held her waist as she lifted herself and undulated with him, her head thrown back in pleasure, then swinging forward as she leaned down to burn his lips with a kiss. He caught her hair and held it snarled in one hand as he kissed her hard and long.

His heartbeat thundered harder, and he rolled with her again, bracing his hands on the bed and watching her face as he leaned deep into her. She arched to meet him, moistening her lips, then catching his with her teeth as he thrust deep into her again. They moved together, arms and legs entwined, bodies tightly together, and when the explosion of climax came, it was like nothing he had ever experienced before. He heard her cries of joy mingled with his own and he held her pressed against him afterward, never wanting to let her go again.

"God help me, I've dreamed of this a million times," he managed hoarsely, his cheek against her bare breast. Her heart was still beating wildly beneath his ear, and he turned to press a kiss against her soft skin.

"I love you, I love you," she kept saying, and he laughed because that was all she had said since they had begun to make love. He raised on one elbow and looked into her face. They both sobered as they realized what had just happened, how close they had come to losing each other.

"Marry me."

"We already are by my Hindu law."

"I want it legal in England, too, before Sedgwick the Saint changes his mind and reclaims you."

"He won't. He knows I love you."

"We can sail down to London and have a clergyman marry us."

"Whatever you want."

"That's what I want."

Their kiss was tender, gently caressing, but it soon deepened with passion until their breathing came in ragged gasps and Stuart's words were harsh with need.

"Maybe it can wait until morning." Then he was lost to her, to the wonder of loving a woman in a way he never had before, succumbing to a kind of happiness that delved deep into his heart, that transcended anything else in his life.

Anjelica opened her eyes and stretched luxuriously. She was happy, deliriously happy, and the reason why lay stretched out naked beside her, his suntanned arm thrown behind her on the pillow. She snuggled in closer to him and inhaled the masculine essence of Stuart, never wanting to leave his embrace again. His arms held her possessively, even though he slept peacefully, his chest rising and falling with even breathing. She didn't move, didn't want him to let her go, not ever. They had made love all through the night, over and over until they both were exhausted but sated of the desire they had denied so long.

Their relationship had followed a complicated path but one with its destination ordained in the stars. She had known that the night Chandran had read his charts and told her they were married in the soul. She had waited for the inevitable to happen and it had, but she had been very frightened for a while that they would not fulfill their destiny.

She turned her head, just a little, so she could see Stuart's face. Smiling, she admired the fine features of his profile, the strength of his jaw, and black softness of his hair. He was the most beautiful man she had ever seen, and he was hers. Pride filled her to have such a man actually love her and want her for his own. He could have so many others if he wished, had had them, but he had chosen her because they shared one heart and soul.

Filled with warmth and tenderness for him, she placed her palm lightly on his chest, felt the crisp hair beneath her fingers. Despite the gentleness of her touch, he awoke and opened his eyes and found her face. He smiled and put his hand to her cheek.

"I'm glad you're still here," he whispered softly. "I was afraid I'd passed out on the deck and dreamed all of this."

"I love you, Stuart. I really, really do."

He chuckled as he ran his hand down her bare

back. "And I'm really, really glad. Now hush because I really, really want to make love to you."

His blue eyes warmed and his lips found hers, and she let the magic begin, let their bodies touch and join in the way she felt their souls had done so many other times through the course of eternity. It filled her with hope, that thought, that they would always be together, forever more.

"I love you," she whispered, her mouth muffled against his neck.

"I'm beginning to believe you," he answered, then their mouths met and their thoughts disintegrated into the swirling stars of their lovemaking.

The wedding that Anjelica had feared would never take place was held on the deck of the *Virginian*. She stood beside Stuart in her red wedding sari as she had done so long ago in the palace of Udaipur. This time she wore no painted flowers on her forehead and had no fear in her heart. This time she was at peace and content within her soul.

Stuart held her hand tightly, possessively, and she smiled up at him as the clergyman spoke the solemn vows. Suzannah and Sanjay were standing as their witnesses, both displaying proud smiles. Suzannah held George instead of a bouquet, much to the dismay of the minister who continually darted fearful glances at the serpent.

She felt a laugh bubble up from deep inside her. The feeling of pure joy was a heady, wonderful sensation. She felt free for the first time in her life, free of promises, of duty and honor. Now her duty was to make Stuart happy, and she wanted to do that more than anything else in her life.

"You may now kiss the bride," the reverend said at last, and Stuart did so, tenderly, completely, as the children cheered and jumped about until the preacher got worried about George enough to lift his black robe and flee the boat.

"See, I told you you'd like being married to me," Stuart said, squeezing her close.

She laughed and joined him and the children in readying the boat to sail upriver. More than ever they seemed a family, and Stuart could easily take the place of a father to both her brother and her sister. They were going to have a wonderful life in England and perhaps they would even return to India someday, as Suzannah wanted to so desperately.

Later, when they had anchored in a calm inlet and the children were splashing and swimming in the shallows, Anjelica lay in the cabin's bed, close in Stuart's arms and let herself enjoy the warmth of his embrace.

"I'm so happy," she whispered. "This is what I really wanted, from the beginning, from our first wedding night."

"I think I'm going to like the second one better," he said, nuzzling the side of her throat.

"That's because we had to wait so long."

"No more waiting. We're already halfway through the *Kama Sutra*. Thirty-seven, if I remember."

"No, thirty-eight. Remember on the way up here when the kids fell asleep in the bow."

He laughed and his hand came up to bracket the side of her head, turning it until he could capture her mouth under his. The kiss was long and leisurely enough to arouse them both and Anjelica wet her lips in anticipation of what was to come.

"Let's try thirty-nine now while the kids are busy."

"Yeah, and forty, too, and maybe even forty-one, forty-two, and forty-three—"

Their lips fused again and he raised her and brought her slowly down upon him until she felt the hardness of him inside her. She arched her back, her lips parted with a moan as he moved upward into her, holding her firmly by her waist. The sensations were exquisite, and she leaned down, gasping with each thrust, her hair brushing his chest until his mouth caught the tip of her breast. The explosions of pleasure began then, spiraling deep like molten lava until she writhed with the ecstasy of loving him. She barely heard his groan of release as she collapsed onto his chest, weak and sated, and delirious with joy.

Chapter Twenty-three

Sarah Delaney did not relish the idea of what she had come to London to do. She hadn't seen her youngest grandson since long before the war began. Now she had to reveal to him the most terrible secret of her life as well as the fact that she had been manipulating him for years to gain her own end. His brother, Harte, had been enraged over her machinations concerning Camillia. He still had not fully forgiven her. She had wronged Stuart even worse. He would have more reason to hate her.

Thomas Stonegate had given Sarah the address of Stuart's home. Afraid that he would refuse to receive her, she had not sent word of her arrival but had her driver search out the isolated forest tract where he lived. As she entered the drive she saw the resemblance of the river-edged estate to Twin Pines, his mother's plantation in Virginia and knew why the boy had chosen the residence.

Now that she stood at the front portal waiting for someone to answer the door, however, an overpowering sense of dread held her in its grip. After perhaps fifteen minutes, she frowned and leaning tiredly on her cane made her way down the porch steps, then slowly around the corner of the house. From there she could look down the grassy, tree-dotted expanse of rear lawn and see a group whom she assumed to be the family of the house frolicking near the bank of the stream.

A narrow flagstone path blazed the way to the water, and she used her cane to steady herself as she went, wondering where all the servants had gotten to. Incompetent staff was one thing she had never tolerated at the Oaks. As she drew closer to the river she realized that there was a picnic lunch set up on the grass. Three or four uniformed servants were cleaning up leftover food and utensils and folding a portable table and chairs.

A boathouse was built not far away from the knoll where the servants busied themselves, and she saw several children splashing and cavorting in the water off the end of the dock. She smiled slightly, remembering a long ago time when all three of her grandchildren lived with her. A vision drifted into her memory—of Harte and Stuart racing each other across her front drive while a toddling Cassandra, her beautiful red hair gleaming in the sunlight, tried to keep up. Her heart ached for what had transpired among those three children after their father died, especially the two boys and their tragic association with Camillia.

"Hello, there," a pleasant feminine voice called from somewhere close by.

Sarah turned and watched a young woman agilely lift herself out of the water and onto the dock.
Soaking wet from head to toe, she wore a black
bathing costume that seemed unspeakably scandalous to Sarah's old-fashioned sensibilities. Goodness
gracious, she was even barefoot! Why, her ankles
and a goodly portion of her calves were completely
exposed for anyone to see! What was the world
coming to? The girl was smiling, though, and was
wonderfully attractive despite the way the sun had
browned her face as if she never wore proper headgear to shield her complexion.

"Good afternoon," she greeted the young woman.
"I am Sarah Delaney, Stuart Delaney's grandmother.
Is he home today?"

"Mrs. Delaney! I'm so happy you've come! My
name is Anjelica Blake—" The girl stopped in
midsentence and gave a rueful smile. "Actually, it's
Anjelica Delaney now. Your grandson and I have recently wed. Didn't he send word to you of our marriage?"

Now Sarah could see the resemblance, of course.
Anjelica had the shape of her mother's face and the
same sweet smile. Though a good many years younger, Mary had been Sarah's dear friend all through
her days at boarding school, but that was so long
ago, so very long ago.

"Your mother was a dear friend of mine," she replied, "I was devastated to learn of her premature
passing."

"Mama's only regret was not living her last years

here in England, but I know she would be so grateful to you for sending Stuart to fetch me and my brother and sister from Udaipur. I was afraid we'd never get to return here."

"Stuart sent word through my solicitors that he had successfully found you and returned with you to England. That's why I came."

"Yes, he did." Anjelica's smile was dazzling. "We're very happy now that we're married."

Sarah felt her heart clutch and wondered if what she was about to reveal to Stuart would threaten the happiness he'd finally found. Perhaps she should just go back home and let the past die, but she had tried that with Harte and had nearly lost him forever. She couldn't take that chance again. Besides, more than anyone on earth, Stuart had a right to know what she had done.

"Is that your little sister swimming there in the water?"

"Yes, and our little brother, Sanjay. Would you like to meet them?"

"Yes, very much."

Anjelica called them out of the water, and as they ran up, dripping wet and smiling, Sarah gazed intently at the ten-year-old girl. Tears swam in her eyes, and she felt her throat dry and close until she couldn't speak. She looked remarkably like her mother, too. Had Stuart not noticed the uncanny resemblance?

"How do you do, ma'am. I'm Suzannah Blake," the child said matter-of-factly as she reached out a bare brown arm for a handclasp, much as a man would do.

Sarah clasped her small hand and held it a moment. "I'm very pleased to meet you, Suzannah."

"And this is Sanjay. He's four," she added, pointing to her brother.

"Hello, young man," Sarah said, realizing at once the boy was of Indian heritage. Anjelica answered her unasked questions.

"His mother was my father's second wife. They're both gone now, too."

"I see."

A small silence ensued during which time Sarah could barely take her eyes off Camillia's child. Oh, dear lord, what a lovely product from such a tragic scandal. Would it be better never to let them know the truth? But if she didn't tell the sordid tale herself, could Harte and Stuart ever regain their kinship as brothers?

A shout caused them all to turn toward the house. Up on the rear terrace, a tall man was waving his arm, then he ran easily down the flight of steps to the grass and headed toward them.

"There's Stuart now! He'll be so pleased to see you. I think it's so sad the way he'd lost touch with his family."

Sarah wasn't sure at all that he would be pleased, but as he approached he was smiling. When Suzannah ran to meet him, he laughed and scooped her up into his arms. A hard lump formed in the back of Sarah's throat. They were already so fond of each other. Surely that would soften the blow to both of them.

A sense of pride leapt inside her breast as Stuart came toward them carrying Suzannah. He was almost as tall as Harte with the same raven black hair and striking good looks of all the Delaney men. He smiled at his wife, then threw a curious glance at Sarah. There was no spark of recognition in his pure blue gaze, so like the color of her own eyes.

"Your grandmother just arrived today from America, Stuart. She's been waiting for you to come home."

"Grandmother Delaney?" Stuart put down Suzannah and turned his full attention on Sarah. "I didn't think you would arrive this soon."

"I came as soon as I could to thank you in person and give you your recompense for finding the girls."

Stuart put his arm around his wife's shoulders. "I should be thanking you," he said a bit stiffly. "I wouldn't have met Anjelica if it weren't for you."

"I'm glad things worked out so admirably," Sarah replied with the utmost truthfulness, but inside her breast, her nerves quivered with trepidation over telling him the truth about Suzannah. She hesitated. "I don't mean to be rude, but I need to speak with you alone about a family matter. It's really quite important."

To Sarah's relief, Anjelica had the grace to excuse herself. "That's quite all right because the children and I must bathe and dress for dinner. You will join us, won't you, Mrs. Delaney? You're the only family any of us have here in London, you know."

"Thank you."

"Then we'll see you later."

Stuart took Anjelica's hand and pressed a kiss on the backs of her fingers. Anjelica returned a tender smile, then called to the two children who were playing with an oval basket near the dock. The time had come. Oh, God help her find the right words to explain her actions to Stuart.

"I really don't know how to begin," she said in a halting manner quite unlike herself. "Is there a place we could sit down for a moment? I'm afraid this might take some time to explain to you."

"Is it Cassandra?" he asked, leading her to a small stone bench.

"No, it's about Harte," she said, glad to sit down in the cool shade.

Stuart looked away and gazed out over the river. "Then I presume he survived the war. Did he go back to work for the Pinkerton detectives?"

Sarah took a deep breath. She shook her head. "No. He has remarried. A lovely young girl named Lily from Melbourne, Australia. She recently bore him a son."

"I hope he'll be as happy with her as I am with Anjelica."

"He's very happy now." She hesitated again, loathe to broach the real purpose for her long voyage across the Atlantic.

"What about Cassandra? Is she well, too? I

haven't heard from her since I left Virginia with my unit."

"From what we know she's just fine. She's been in Australia with Lily's brother, Derek Courtland."

"Then it appears everyone's doing fine."

"Is there any chance that you might come home now, Stuart? The war's over, maybe we could all get together and become a family again."

His face sobered. "I'm not sure that would be possible after all that's happened. Besides, I've started a new life here with Anjelica and her family. I really don't have any desire to return to the United States."

Sarah steeled herself and proceeded in a low voice. "I'm an old woman now, Stuart, and I've lived with a terrible sin on my conscience for many, many years." She paused briefly as Stuart turned surprised eyes on her. "Recently I bared my soul to Harte and Lily, and now if I am privileged to meet my Maker with a clean slate I must do the same with you."

"Surely you have no need to confess anything to me. With all due respect, Grandmother, we hardly know each other."

"It's about Camillia."

At the mention of Harte's first wife, Stuart's expression froze with shock, then quickly changed into an unreadable mask. The pain darkening his eyes, however, was all too real. "Camillia died a long time ago," he said stiffly. "Harte's remarried so I see no need to discuss the past."

"I wish that were true, dear, and perhaps Camillia's secrets would have remained buried with her if Harte had not found out the truth."

"I really don't want to discuss this, Grandmother Delaney. Come, let's go up to the house and join Anjelica and the kids."

He was not going to let her tell him, she realized, but she had to. She could not leave London without him knowing the truth. She spoke bluntly. "I know about the love affair you had with Camillia. She confided it to me before she died."

Stuart turned and took a few paces toward the river. He stopped a short distance away. When he spoke, he kept his back to her. "I was young and in love with her, and I've regretted what we did every day for the last ten years." There was a moment of silence, then he asked the question she had been waiting for. "Does Harte know?"

"Yes."

"Oh, God. I'd hoped he would never find out."

"There's more, I'm afraid."

The gravity in her voice brought him back to face her. All she could do was say it. Nothing could ever soften the blow. "Camillia had a child before she died, Stuart."

"What are you trying to say?"

"The child was yours."

A stricken look overtook his face. He began to shake his head. "No, that's impossible. We were only together one time, I swear it. One night."

"She conceived a baby, a little girl."

"I don't believe you. I would've known. She would've told me."

"Would she, Stuart? When she was married to your brother? When he'd been away from home for months?"

Stuart only stared at her.

"I hid the knowledge from everyone, you and Harte, everyone. That's my sin, Stuart, I hid the existence of my own flesh and blood to save Harte's honor and our family name. Yes, and my own sense of propriety." He was staring at her in astonishment and she rushed on before she changed her mind. "I arranged everything for her because she begged me to. She was ashamed and guilt-ridden about what the two of you had done to Harte. She didn't want him to find out, didn't want you to find out. She threatened to kill herself if I didn't help her."

"My God, what are you trying to say?"

"I sent her to a convent in New Orleans. She died from childbirth fever."

"And the child?" His voice was hoarse. "What happened to the baby?"

For the first time Sarah could not face him. She looked down at her lap. "I arranged for some friends of mine to adopt the child. I knew they would take good care of her." She swallowed hard. "Stuart, I gave her to James and Mary Blake."

Stuart's face blanched and he stumbled back a step as the truth dawned on him. "Suzannah? You're talking about Suzannah?"

"She's your daughter, Stuart. That's why I insisted

that you be the one to go to India and bring her back home. I thought if you could meet her and get to know her, then the truth wouldn't be so hard to bear—"

"No, I don't believe you," he muttered, his voice cracking.

Sarah nodded wordlessly, and Stuart turned and fled her presence with long, jerky footsteps. She bowed her head. The last of her burden and shame had been lifted from her heart, but now her grandson had to deal with the demons that had haunted her for so long. God help him. She sighed deeply, then let the tears flow, tears which she had left unshed for many, many years.

Chapter Twenty-four

Anjelica looked back at Stuart and his grandmother as she reached the house, hoping Sarah Delaney had brought good news about Stuart's troubled family. The old lady had appeared unnecessarily reserved, as if she were nervous, which seemed strange because she was obviously a well-bred lady of standing.

"Run along and get ready for your baths," she called after the children who had raced ahead. She lingered a moment longer at the terrace wall wanting to watch the two people conversing down by the river landing.

Stuart had led his grandmother to a bench and seated her there in the shade of an oak tree, and they seemed to be completely absorbed in an intense discussion. Anjelica sighed and turned away, fearing that Sarah's tidings were not welcome to Stuart, after all.

"Come on, Anjie, you've gotta help me unbraid my hair so I can wash it!" Suzannah was yelling at the top of her lungs from well inside the house.

Anjelica hastened upstairs, intending to hurry through their baths so she could talk with Stuart. She hoped his family members in America were well. What if it concerned the brother he had so mysteriously denied? How would he react to such news?

In the children's room, Suzannah sat before the fireplace where Willie the butler had instructed the maids to prepare a hip bath full of warm sudsy water. Sanjay was playing contentedly with his tin soldiers atop the windowsill. She would help them bathe and dress, then she would hurry through her own toilette in case Mrs. Delaney did decide to stay for dinner.

"Hurry up, Anjie, I'm cold and my hair's dripping down my back. I'm hungry, too, 'cause I didn't like that kind of lamb pie we had for lunch."

"I think you're just in a complaining mood," Anjelica scolded quietly as she untied the ribbons at the ends of Suzannah's pigtails. She carefully began to undo the tight plaiting she had woven so diligently just that morning. "If Mrs. Delaney does stay and have dinner with us, I don't want to hear any whining or impolite talk at the table, is that clear?"

"Yeah, we know all that. Will that old lady leave in time for Stuart to help us start our tree house on the riverbank after supper? We wanna pick a tree close to the water so we can hide and spy on people in the boats coming past the dock with Stuart's big army spyglass."

"That certainly doesn't sound like a very nice thing to do—"

Anjelica's rebuke was interrupted when the door was thrown open hard enough to bang on the wall. All three of them jumped and turned in surprise to find Stuart standing in the doorway. His face was twisted into an awful, unfamiliar expression that Anjelica thought was either anger or distress. Whatever it was, it was frightening enough to send her instantly to her feet.

Apparently Suzannah wasn't intimidated because she immediately launched into a conversation with him. "You're still gonna help us with the tree house, aren't you, Stuart? You promised you would. Anjelica will talk to that old lady while we're working on it. Won't you, Anjie?"

Stuart crossed the floor in three long strides, hunkered down in front of Suzannah and bracketed her small, heart-shaped chin firmly between his thumb and forefinger. He didn't answer her questions or say a word but stared at her with such brutal intensity that Suzannah became frightened.

"What's the matter, Stuart? Why are you looking at me all mean like that? What'd I do?"

"Oh, my God," Stuart muttered in such an anguished voice that a chill undulated to the base of Anjelica's spine. When he suddenly dropped his hand away from Suzannah's face and lurched upright, Anjelica took hold of his arm.

"Stuart, what's wrong? What is it?"

He jerked his arm so hard it was torn from her grasp. "Leave me alone. I've gotta get out of here."

"Why?" she cried after him as he rushed out of the room. "What happened? Where's your grandmother?"

Suzannah looked up at her with a hurt expression, then puckered up and began to cry, something she rarely ever did. Anjelica put her arm around her as Sanjay came running over.

"What's wrong with Stuart?" Sanjay asked fearfully. "Why's he being so mean to Suzie?"

His remark caused Suzannah to cry harder, and Anjelica patted her back in an attempt to calm her.

"Now, now, Suzie, don't cry. I suspect he's just upset about seeing his grandmother again. I'm sure he didn't mean to hurt your feelings."

"But he squeezed my face with his fingers and didn't even say he was sorry or if he was still gonna get us some nails for the tree house—" Suzannah ended in a loud wail muffled against Anjelica's skirt.

"I'll help you look for some nails. He probably won't be gone too long anyway. Now let's get your bath over with so we can pick out a good tree to build in."

"We already got the tree picked out," Suzannah told her in a thick, hiccuppy voice, but was obviously slightly reassured by Anjelica's explanation.

Sanjay went back to his toys, and Anjelica pulled the bathing screen into place and helped Suzannah unbutton her dress. She tried to hide her own distress over Stuart's uncharacteristic behavior. Even in Udaipur when he was most put out with the children, he had never touched one of them in anger. Though he hadn't really hurt her, his hold on Suzannah's face had not been gentle. What could have compelled him to do such a thing?

Much later that evening as she made her way to the house from the dock, she still had not come up with a reasonable explanation. She was so worried about him. He had been gone for hours. It was nearly midnight. Where could he be so late?

His penchant was to take out his boat when he wanted to be alone but he hadn't done so this time. She had just come from the river where the *Virginian* lay quietly moored as always. She was puzzled and upset, enough to consider seeking out Sarah Delaney and questioning her about what had happened. According to Willie, Sarah had left immediately in her waiting coach just after she finished speaking with Stuart. What on earth could she have told him that could send him into such a state?

She let herself through the terrace doors and stood in the back foyer, listening for any sound. The house lay in heavy silence; all the servants had retired to their quarters and the children were tucked into bed hours ago. She held her lamp before her to light the way and peered into each room she passed to see if Stuart had returned. All was dark and quiet, and she slowly climbed the steps, alarmed now that he might not come home at all tonight.

At the top of the stairs, she turned down the hall

and walked to the door of the children's room. They
had been restless and keyed up over Stuart's behavior, and she had left a lamp burning low on the table between them until they fell asleep. Intending
to extinguish the wick, she entered and found both
Suzannah and Sanjay snuggled in their beds, the
lamp casting only enough light to distinguish them
huddled beneath the quilts. She tucked the covers
around them, hoping Stuart would come back before they woke up. They loved him dearly. They
wouldn't understand his unexplained absence any
more than she did, she thought sadly, as she
reached down to turn off the lamp.

"Don't turn it off."

Her hand stilled at the sound of Stuart's voice.
The command had been muttered low from the
chair opposite Suzannah's bed. Anjelica turned
quickly and barely ascertained his shape in the
deep shadows hugging the wall.

"Where have you been?" she whispered as she
rounded the footboard of the bed.

"Don't ask me questions, please. I don't want to
talk about it yet."

Anjelica wasn't about to let the subject drop
without some kind of explanation. "Tell me what's
wrong. I think you owe me that."

"Dammit," he hissed softly, pushing himself to
his feet. "I said I didn't want to talk about it."

Shocked by the anger in his voice, she followed
him from the room. Quietly closing the door be-

hind her, she turned and watched him descend the staircase and enter the library.

When she entered the same room a few minutes later, he stood in the dark in front of the liquor cabinet. While she turned up the gas jet beside the door, he tossed down a straight shot of whiskey, then quickly refilled his glass.

"It must have been terrible news," she remarked calmly, determined not to let him shut her out.

Stuart drank in silence and kept his back turned on her. She moved closer to him. "Was it about your brother? The one named Harte whom you told me you didn't have?"

His broad shoulders tensed under her pointed accusation but he still refused to look at her. "Just go away and leave me alone, Anjelica. Please."

Anjelica was very close behind him now. "No, I want to help you. You need to let people help you—"

He whirled around and grabbed her so quickly that she barely had time to gasp. His face was ravaged with pain, agony such as she had never seen on him, or anyone else. Filled with fear, her heart thudded to a standstill. He must have seen the expression in her eyes because his face relaxed, all emotion seeming to drain out of him. He pulled her inside his embrace, held her gently, his voice gruff against the top of her head.

"Oh, God, I'm sorry, I'm sorry . . ."

Anjelica put her arms around his waist and shut her eyes. He was in such distress that she could feel it in his body; his muscles were taut and quivering. "I can't stand to see you like this," she whispered, pressing her cheek against his chest. "Please let me help you."

"Nobody can help me," he muttered thickly, releasing her and pacing a few steps away.

Anjelica watched him sink down on a settee near the window and wearily drop his head into his hands. She sat down beside him and laid her hand lightly on his knee. "You aren't alone anymore, Stuart. I love you. I want to help you. I want to comfort you when you're in pain like this. Please let me, please, I beg you."

Stuart sat still, his face hidden by his hands. "I can't tell you."

"But why? Nothing can be so bad as that."

"This is."

"I can't believe that."

Raising his head, he stared at her. "If I tell you what I'm capable of, you'll hate me."

Shocked by his words, she shook her head. "No, I couldn't hate you, no matter what you've done. I love you. I know what a wonderful man you are. You've proved that to me."

Anjelica had never seen such suffering. Stuart had always been so strong, so silent and enduring in the past, no matter what problems they had faced. When he couldn't seem to speak, she voiced the fear she had contemplated throughout the night.

"It's something to do with Suzie, isn't it?"

Stuart's head jerked up. "Did you talk to my grandmother?"

"No, of course not. But I saw how you stared at her like she'd grown horns. What is it? I don't understand what Suzie has to do with this."

Stuart pulled her head down against his chest. She could hear his heart thundering beneath her ear. She shut her eyes, terrified to hear what he was about to reveal to her.

"I did something terrible when I was a boy. When I was too stupid to know any better."

Anjelica was afraid to speak, afraid to move for fear he would stop. Each word seemed torn from his throat. She held her breath.

Stuart swallowed, his fingers threading into her hair and gently holding her head against him. He couldn't bring himself to look at her when he told her, she realized suddenly, her heart aching for him. He waited a long time before he finally continued, so low she could barely hear him.

"I was sixteen. I went to Grandmother Delaney's house to have my portrait painted for her gallery. I didn't know her very well, and I hadn't seen her since I was a little boy. I didn't know Harte, either. After my father died, my mother took Cassie and me back to Virginia with her, but Harte stayed in Rhode Island."

He was finally telling her about his past, his family, the things Anjelica had waited so long to hear, but each of his words came harder than the last. She wasn't sure he could finish and didn't know

how to help him. All she knew was that he needed
to tell someone, to get the agony out of his mind
where it had festered for so long.

When the silence lengthened and he didn't
speak, she lifted her face and looked at him. He
was staring across the room into the darkness as if
revisiting some long-buried ghosts.

"What happened to cause you such suffering,
darling? You can tell me."

The muscles in his cheek were working, growing
taut, then relaxed, taut, relaxed, over and over until
he jutted his jaw. He stood up, paced across to the
shadowy fireplace where he leaned his arm against
the mantel and stared down into the empty grate.

"Harte wasn't there. He was off playing detective
in Mexico." His voice hardened contemptuously.
"He was always off risking his neck in dangerous
places. The Mexicans almost hanged him once
when he was down there."

Anjelica couldn't understand yet, couldn't quite
string all the things he had told her together in her
head. Her mind worked desperately as she tried to
sort it all out.

"That's where he met Camillia."

A woman, she thought, her heart constricting, he
and his brother had fought over a woman. That's
why they'd been estranged for so long. Who was
Camillia? What had happened? Though she braced
herself, she wasn't prepared for the answers.

"She was his wife."

Anjelica stared at him aghast and knew without

being told what he had done, knew it as if he had said it out loud. Oh, God, no wonder he was so tortured with guilt.

"You loved her, too?" she asked gently.

Stuart turned around. His face was haggard but his eyes were intense, inexorably holding her gaze. "I was the only one who loved her. Harte didn't give a damn about her. He only married her because she saved his life." He sighed and shook his head. "Then he brought her to Newport and left her there without a backward glance while he roamed with the Pinkertons for months on end. And my grandmother made her life hell while she was there because she didn't consider a Mexican peasant like Camillia good enough to be a Delaney."

Stuart was filled with fury now, Anjelica could hear it in his voice when he finished. "She was sixteen like me, beautiful and sad and lonely. I wanted to make her feel better, I wanted to make her happy so that awful look would leave her face." He gave a cold laugh. "All she wanted was to pretend I was my big brother."

Anjelica suddenly felt the most terrible premonition that he hadn't even begun the story yet, that the worst was yet to come. She was right.

"I made love to her once, that's the only time, I swear to God." He looked away from her. "We both were appalled after we realized what we'd done. So I left and went home to Virginia. I never saw her again."

Anjelica tried to comprehend. "What happened to Camillia?"

Stuart came back and sat down beside her. His eyes held an almost frantic look. "That's what Grandmother came here to tell me. She's lied to us all these years. She told us that Camillia died in a fall, a couple of months after I left, but it wasn't true, Anjelica, goddamn her, it wasn't true."

"Are you saying that Camillia's still alive?" she asked slowly, still confused.

"No."

Stuart had become very calm, so much so that Anjelica felt unnerved. Something awful was coming. She felt like covering her ears so she wouldn't have to hear it.

"She died giving birth to my child. She died giving birth to Suzannah."

Anjelica's mouth fell agape, and she was unable to speak as Stuart took hold of her arms, his words gruff and unnatural.

"Suzannah's my own daughter, and I didn't even know it until today."

"How? Why?" was all Anjelica could croak out.

"Grandmother knew your mother wanted another child. She arranged the adoption. Took my child from me, and you know why? To save the great Delaney name, to save Harte's bloody reputation."

"No, no, it can't be true. How could it be true?"

Stuart heaved a shuddering sigh and shook his head. "It's true. Grandmother's good at manipulating people. She did it again when she hired me to go to India and find you. She wanted me to bring Suzannah back so she could tell me the truth. My mother hated that about Sarah. She said Sarah Delaney manipulated her family like a spider spinning a web."

Anjelica was so astounded by his revelation that she wasn't sure yet that she believed him. It was too strange, too enormous to contemplate.

"Are you saying she didn't tell you or your brother about Camillia's baby before she put her up for adoption?"

"That's right. She's been playing God with us all. For ten years now."

"Suzie's yours? Your daughter? Oh, my God, Stuart, this can't be happening!"

Stuart's face went white as a sheet. He shut his eyes. "I told you how sick it was. I knew you'd hate me."

"Hate you? Stuart, no, you're a victim, too. And Suzie, and Harte. How could Sarah do such a thing to her own family?"

Stuart mutely shook his head. Anjelica stared at him, beginning to understand so many things. Why he had disowned Harte, why he never wanted to see his family again, why he had fought so hard against making love to her when she was married to someone else.

"Suzie will be thrilled," she said at length with an unsteady smile, a sense of disbelief still holding back her acceptance. Sarah and her mother had been good friends. That's why her family had adopted Suzannah when they lived in New Orleans. Everything now made a terrible, horrible kind of sense.

"And what are we going to tell her?" Stuart's voice was harsh with self-disgust. "Guess what, Suzie? Stuart's your father. He committed the deadly sin of sleeping with his brother's wife so you were kept a dirty little secret by his family and given up for adoption? Oh, God, I never want her to know about this. She will hate me, even if you don't."

Anjelica forced down her burgeoning fear. Stuart was right. It was all so complicated. Suzannah would never understand. "We can't tell her now. She doesn't even know she's adopted. We never have to tell her at all, Stuart, if you don't want to. Why should we? What good would it do us? If we change our minds then we'll wait until she's older and can understand. She already loves you. That's what Sarah intended, isn't it? For the two of you to get to know each other? It worked out better than she could have imagined."

Stuart pulled her back against his shoulder. "I found you. That's the only good thing Grandmother's ever done."

Anjelica lay silently against him, still able to feel the tension riddling his body but he was better now that he had told her. She, however, still reeled with shock. They would find a way to deal with the truth. They would go on and live with what had happened. Oh, lord, but could they ever do that?

Chapter Twenty-five

Stuart stepped aboard the *Virginian* as the first misty rays of sun crowned the eastern bank of the river. Fog lay like a low, ethereal blanket over the surface of the Thames but soon the sun would burn through the haze and glisten off the water. Forcing himself not to think about the events of the previous day, he went below and made a pot of strong coffee. While the brew simmered atop the small potbelly stove, he leaned against the wall and stared unseeingly out the galley porthole.

He had hoped the familiar rocking of the boat would soothe his mind but the agonizingly painful refrain of Sarah's words began afresh inside his head like one of Anjelica's Hindu mantras. He wondered if the damning litany would never end its torture. He had buried his sins against his brother for so long, had even denied Harte's existence to assuage his guilty conscience. But he could no longer run from the past. Now every time he saw Suzannah's face, he'd remember Camillia and those few stolen moments when he had held his brother's wife in his arms.

Even the thought made his blood rush through his system with bitter self-loathing. He bowed his head and tiredly pressed the bridge of his nose between his thumb and forefinger. He had lain awake all night, thinking about nothing but Suzannah, wanting to believe that it wasn't true, that she wasn't his child. But inside he knew she was. He knew he would have to accept it and bear the responsibility of his actions. The ramifications of Sarah Delaney's treachery stretched out endlessly before him like some awful black ocean filled with angry demons.

Thank God he had Anjelica with him. If he made it through this ordeal, she would be the only reason why. If she had turned on him and looked at him with disgust and condemnation, he wasn't sure he could have borne that pain, not on top of everything else. Instead, all through the night she had whispered reassurances when he had grown restless and so overwhelmed with guilt that he found it impossible to bear the truth.

When she had finally fallen asleep in his arms, he held her close and tried to take comfort in her belief in him but sleep had been impossible. He had left her in peaceful repose and escaped the house for the familiar security of the river. Now he stood alone and forced himself to stare down his own devils.

Not only had he injured Harte so unspeakably,

he had wronged Camillia even more. He had fled her side like an escaped felon, leaving her to deal with the result of their adulterous affair, with his bastard child growing inside her. Camillia had been a devout Catholic, a simple peasant whose faith was ingrained in her existence. If only he had known she had conceived, he could have done something to help her. His mind mocked his own good intentions. What could he have done? Gone back, confronted Harte with the ugly truth, taken Camillia somewhere far away where the scandal wouldn't reach them? He had loved her enough to have done just that, he realized. She had been his first true love and the first woman he had ever made love to. But she never would have gone away with him. She had never loved Stuart; he had been a mere substitute for her wandering, philandering husband.

Afterward, the war had begun and Stuart had thrown himself into the bloody fighting, defending the Confederacy with his life and caring little if he lived or died. And he had made sure he had steered clear of any committed relationship with a woman until Anjelica had come into his heart and taught him what love really was.

Anjelica kept insisting that everything would be all right, that the truth had prevailed for a purpose—so that he could make up his past mistakes. Thoughts of his child sent him staggering again—guilt slamming into the walls of his mind like some great battering ram against a castle keep.

Now he had that crime to add to the guilt crusting his soul with black decay. His own daughter, given away to strangers without his knowledge or consent. Damn Sarah Delaney! He shuddered to think what Suzannah's life could have been like if Anjelica's family had not welcomed her as a beloved family member. She didn't even know she was adopted. And she shouldn't, not now. She couldn't handle any more changes in her young life, not when she had just left Udaipur and everything she loved so much. How could they tell her that he was her father and expect her to understand? They couldn't, he realized, she could never know, because the truth was too damned hideous.

Straightening, he stepped to the stove and tried to concentrate on pouring the boiling coffee into the white cup he took from a hook beneath the shelf. He carried the steaming mug above decks, hoping the crisp morning air would help him think straight. He had always liked early morning on the water when his mind was clear and fresh. Oh God, what was he going to do about this mess?

After years of suppressing any thoughts or affection for his brother, Harte's face imprinted itself stubbornly on Stuart's brain. He hadn't seen Harte since long before he had met Camillia at his grandmother's house a decade ago. They had been close when they were very young children but had not seen each other after their mother had left Harte behind to live with Sarah Delaney. They had nothing in common now except their bloodline. And Camillia.

Stuart cringed to think that Harte knew everything now, that Stuart had slept with his wife, that she had conceived Stuart's child. Harte must hate his guts. No one would condemn him if he did. Hell, no one would blame him if he elected to put a bullet between Stuart's eyes. Not even Stuart. How would he feel if Harte had made love to Anjelica?

Rage hit him at the mere thought, then nausea made his stomach roll over. He forced down another swallow of coffee. He shouldn't worry about facing Harte; he'd probably never see his brother again. It was Suzannah with whom he had to come to terms. She was his daughter, his own flesh-and-blood child. How could he not have known it, not sensed the bond between them? After months and months of seeing her every day, of talking with her, of playing with her?

"Goddammit," he muttered harshly. With one angry jerk of his arm, he slung the contents of his mug out into the water and turned around. Every muscle went rigid when he saw Suzannah sitting cross-legged on the dock a few yards away. No words were possible as a maelstrom of boiling emotions filled his chest. Now he could see Camillia in her. She had the same long dark hair, the large brown eyes with straight black lashes, the fragile build, the heart-shaped face. Once in Udaipur he'd noticed a vague familiarity about Suzannah that had plagued him momentarily, but how could he have guessed who she really was?

"You still mad at me, Stuart?"

Suzannah watched him warily, and Stuart's throat went raw. He wasn't ready to face her yet; he might not be able to hide the feelings tearing up his guts. That was why he had left the house before anyone had arisen. He wasn't prepared to deal with Suzannah.

"I'm not mad at you." Even he could hear how unnatural his voice sounded. He couldn't stop himself from examining every inch of her face. My God, how could she be his own child? It just wasn't possible!

"That old lady told on me, didn't she? She told you I did something bad and now you don't like me anymore. But I didn't, Stuart, I promise, not anything real bad, anyways. I've been pretty good since you and my sister got together. Was it about that extra gumball I filched from the candy store when the clerk was counting them out for Anjelica?"

Her lower lip began to quiver, and she came close to puckering up. "I'm real sorry I took it, Stuart. I know better, I do, Anjelica always taught us stuff about what an awful sin stealin' is. But it was just one gumball, a cherry one, and I won't do it again. I got another penny right here in my pocket that Anjie gave me day before yesterday for running down here to the river and fetching Sanjay back to the house so he could do puja to Vishnu." Suzannah paused for breath, then fixed him with her big, tearful eyes. "I'll give it back to the candy store man, I will, and I promise I won't do it anymore." Finally the tears brimmed over. One followed a trickling path over the brown freckles scattered across her nose.

A different kind of pain clutched Stuart's heart, squeezing like a belt around his chest until it seemed impossible to breathe. He cleared his throat.

"Do you still like me as much as you like Sanjay and Anjie?" Now she was wringing her little hands in distress.

Stuart could only nod, and a great flood of relief released Suzannah's worried frown. She smiled, jumped down onto the deck, then flung herself against him. Stuart hesitated for one brief moment, then picked her up. The instant he did, her thin arms encircled his neck in a stranglehold. For one inexplicable moment, joy at finding his daughter mushroomed until it eclipsed even the guilt lodged so solidly in his heart.

"I like you just about better than anybody else, Stuart," she whispered with her face hidden in his shoulder. "I'll be real good from now on, too. I won't cause no trouble. You're my best friend after Anjie and Sanjay. After Shashi and George, too, I guess. But then you're next, after all them."

Still holding her close, Stuart sat down heavily on the wooden bench. He felt so strange. Everything in his life had changed overnight, everything now seemed different, as if he had stepped into someone else's soul. "I guess I scared you a little last night, grabbing you like that, didn't I? I'm sorry."

Suzannah rearranged herself atop his lap until she could look up into his face. He stared into the luminous depths of her wide brown eyes. She was beautiful, he thought as if seeing her for the very first time. She would be a lovely young woman someday. Pride rose in his heart to think he had sired this bright, lively little girl.

"What'd that old lady tell you then? It must've been pretty awful to get you so riled up. You don't usually show people how you feel so much, you know. Usually we all have to guess what you really think about things, even Anjelica says so."

Stuart sighed at the truthfulness of her observation. "It's nothing you need to know about right now. I just had a shock, and I had to get used to the idea, I guess."

"I bet you told Anjie what that lady told you. What'd Anjie say about that shock you had? I bet she was real mad, too, for you staying out so late and not telling her nothing about where you were going. Where'd you go anyways? I watched out of my bedroom window for you for an awful long time before I got too sleepy to stay awake anymore."

"I walked down the riverbank. I wanted to be alone where I could think about it."

"We woulda helped you think, if you'd just asked us. Sanjay and me are pretty smart for little kids. Anjie says we're all family now that she married up with you, and that we gotta stick together when we're in trouble. You gotta remember that, Stuart."

Her innocent remark hit Stuart hard. He nodded a little. "I'll try to."

He found he couldn't say more but Suzannah didn't seem to care. She gave a gigantic yawn and laid her head on his shoulder. "I didn't get much sleep last night. I was worried you wasn't coming back, and it was all my fault. That's why I woke up and came down here so early. I had a feeling you'd come to your boat like you do sometimes when Sanjay and I start fussing with each other and getting on your nerves."

"You know me pretty well."

"Yeah . . . you still gonna help us build that tree house, aren't you, Stuart?"

"Sure."

Stuart leaned back against the wall and listened as his daughter told him all about her plans concerning the river fort. She was so young and innocent. She looked up to him, thought he was someone special. In the years to come, he could be a parent to her, could love her and take care of her, but she could never learn the truth, he realized, his heart burdened with the worst kind of sorrow. He could not let her know how dishonorable a man her father really was.

"So Ham, So Ham, So Ham—"

After one last deep exhalation, Anjelica opened her eyes and gave up her recitation of the ancient

Sanskrit mantra. Unfortunately, her daily meditation had not given her the answers she sought. She
could not concentrate on emptying her mind because her thoughts were on the letter that had
come in the post yesterday evening.

Retrieving it from her skirt pocket, she gazed
down at the neat, slightly slanted script. The envelope was addressed to Stuart and the return desig-
nation indicated that the correspondence had
originated at Twin Pines Plantation in Virginia. She
transfered her attention to the riverbank.

About twenty yards down the hill from where her
blanket was spread out on the grass, Stuart was
nailing small boards into a tree for the children to
use as a ladder up onto the platfrom he had fash-
ioned between a pair of willow trees overhanging
the water. As usual, her brother and sister were
with him, watching his every move—Sanjay holding
a bag of nails and Suzannah handing them up to
Stuart as he required them.

Anjelica smiled tenderly. They looked like a family. The kids loved him so much, and neither
Suzannah nor Sanjay seemed to realize that anything was amiss with Stuart, at least not after those
first few awful days when he had struggled so with
the knowledge of his paternity.

Now it was mid-August and nearly a month had
passed. Though Stuart seemed to have accepted his
grandmother's startling revelations, Anjelica's heart
ached for him. He attended his duties at his office
on the wharves, spent the evenings with them, then

shared exquisitely tender lovemaking with her in their bed every night. On the surface one would think he had handled the dilemma well, but Anjelica knew differently.

Though Stuart said little about his problems, she sensed the distance in him, often caught him gazing silently into space. At those times she knew exactly what he was thinking. Although he had not talked with her about Suzannah again at any length, nor discussed any of his other family members, she knew better than to push him into confiding in her. From the very beginning she had recognized the fact that he was a proud self-contained man. He preferred to work things out in his own mind. She feared she could be of little help anyway in such a complicated personal matter.

If only he were a more religious man, he could turn to Jesus Christ for comfort, or even to the vast Hindu pantheon of deities. She prayed often to the gods of both religions and encouraged the children to do the same. Perhaps with divine help Stuart could end his pain and become whole once more. But now there was the letter from America. What if it contained more bad news? How could he deal with anything else while caught in his present state of mind?

Down on the bank Stuart was putting the finishing touches on the steps. The kids rewarded his efforts by clapping their hands and jumping up and down in a gratifying show of appreciation. In the blink of an eye, however, they had disappeared up the slatted steps and behind the drooping willow fronds to take possession of their fort. When Stuart turned and looked in her direction, she smiled and waved for him to join her.

Moments later he lounged down on the quilt beside her. He smiled absently as she picked up his hand and entwined her fingers with his long ones, but the terrible haunted look was still evident in his beautiful blue eyes. Would that awful expression never go away? He stared out over the river. Still reluctant to mention the letter from his home in America, Anjelica strove to distract him with a lighter subject.

"I see you've finished the great fort."

He nodded. "It's not much but they seem to like it. I had one overlooking the James River when I was about Suzie's age."

His eyes seemed to look through her, and she knew he was remembering his youth. Had he shared his boyhood tree perch with Harte? Was that the reason his jaw worked so with suppressed emotion? Sorrow pierced her own breast because she felt so helpless. Everyday he seemed to turn his mind further inward until he was a solemn shadow of the man she had fallen in love with.

"I've made a decision. I'm not sure you'll like it."

Stuart's statement had been uttered very low. When he refused to look at her, Anjelica's heart clutched with fear. What if he couldn't bear the pain of being around Suzannah? What if he had decided to go away and leave them?

"What do you mean?" Her trembling voice revealed her worry.

Stuart glanced at her. "I've done nothing but think about what's happened—about—everything." He shook his head. "I've turned it over so many times in my mind that I'm about to go crazy. I just can't deal with it anymore, Anjelica. I can't live my life so torn up inside." When he paused, Anjelica held her breath, terrified about what he was going to say. He was still wrestling with the decision, even now as he continued in a reluctant voice. "Every time I look at Suzie, I see her mother, and then I see Harte and think about how I betrayed him."

Anjelica couldn't stand it any longer. "Please don't leave us, Stuart. I know what a strain it is for you to be around Suzie, but she loves you so. We all do. You belong here with us."

Stuart jerked his face back to her, a look of shock twisting his expression. "Leave you? Good God, Anjelica, you're the most important person in my life. How could you even think I'd do such a thing?"

When he pulled her against him, Anjelica's whole body went limp with relief. That had been her greatest fear, she realized, that he would have to leave her. "I just can't stand seeing you so unhappy. I want to help you, but I don't know what to do."

His chest rose and fell with a heavy sigh. "I don't either, but I think I'm going to have to go home. At least long enough to see if Cassie's all right. We were close until the war started. Maybe she can help me figure all this out. She knows Harte better than I do. I think she even lived in Harte's home for a time during the war. I'm worried about her anyway. No one seems to know if she's all right, or not."

Anjelica knew the time had come to show him the letter, but what if it concerned his sister? What if she were dead, God forbid? Could he bear that now that he looked to Cassandra to help heal his heart?

"Stuart? The postman brought a letter yesterday evening while you were gone to the city."

"What letter?" Already his shoulders had tensed as if he expected to be attacked. His gaze questioned her as she brought the envelope out where he could see it.

"It's from Virginia."

"Is it from Cassie?"

"I don't know. It just says Twin Pines Plantation."

"Maybe that means the house is still standing. I'm surprised the Yankees didn't burn it down since they set fire to damn near everything else below the Mason-Dixon line."

Anjelica cringed at the fierce resentment threading his voice as he took the letter from her.

"This is my sister's handwriting," he said with sudden excitement.

Anjelica was pleased when he smiled. She watched him slit open the wax seal with his thumbnail. As he removed the folded piece of parchment

and began to read, she placed her palms together
and mentally repeated an urgent prayer to Ganesh,
the Hindu god of good fortune. *Please, please, let it
be good news, let it be a way to help him end this
horrible ache in his heart.*

"Good God, she got married when she was down
in Australia."

"Married?"

"Yeah. The man's name is Derek Courtland.
Sarah mentioned him, too, come to think of it." He
stopped and stared at Anjelica. "Wait a second, I
know that name myself. Courtland's one of the best
blockade runners the South had, at least toward the
end of the war. Good God, I used to procure supplies for his ship during the war."

Anjelica was surprised, too. "Really? Have you
met him?"

"No." He read some more, then frowned. "She
goes on to say that Courtland is Harte's brother-in-
law. That's how the two of them met—through
Derek's sister, Lily."

At least Stuart's family were all still alive,
Anjelica thought thankfully as her husband turned
over the sheet of parchment and skimmed the remainder of the letter. When he refolded it and
placed it back into the envelope, Anjelica prompted
him gently.

"What else did she say?"

"She wants me to come home. She wants me to
meet her husband."

"Why, that's wonderful. You'd already decided you needed to go there."

Stuart fixed his gaze out over the water. "She said she wronged Harte during the war, and she wants to make it up to him."

"How did she wrong him?"

"She didn't go into detail but she said she wrote a letter to him."

"Does that mean she's invited him to come to Twin Pines?"

"I guess so."

Anjelica laid a comforting hand on his arm. "Maybe it's for the best. Maybe it'll be easier if you're all there together."

"It'll never be easy," he muttered, agitatedly tunneling his fingers through his black hair, "but I know I have to face him or I'll never get rid of this damn pain." He suddenly took hold of her hands. "Come with me, Anjelica. I can't do this without you."

"Of course, I'll come," she said without hesitation. "We can leave any time you want. Today, if you wish."

"Then it's settled."

Anjelica cupped his jaw with her palms. "You're doing the right thing, sweetheart. Once you get there and see your sister again, everything will fall into place, I know it will."

"I don't deserve you," he whispered hoarsely, touching her lips with a gentle kiss. "You're too good for a man like me."

Anjelica's lips twitched with a rueful smile. "You didn't think so when we first met. Remember?"

Despite her attempt at levity, the expression in his eyes remained serious. "Well, I think so now."

Anjelica's lashes drifted closed as the loving kiss deepened, somehow knowing in her heart that he was making the right decision. Somehow she knew that once he was back in America, he would find peace of mind. That's what she wanted more than anything else in the world.

Chapter Twenty-six

Derek Courtland perched a hip on the banister of the side veranda of Twin Pines Plantation and watched his wife Cassandra and little boy play with ten frisky gray and white kittens frolicking inside a big wicker laundry basket sitting at the foot of the stairs. Big Roscoe sat on the ground nearby, holding the mother cat and wearing a huge toothy white grin that split his rugged black face from ear to ear.

Roscoe had good reason to be happy now, and Derek was glad. The former slave had been abused by more than one master until the day Derek won his freedom in a card game. Now Roscoe played the incongruous role of gentle, protective nanny for Joey, their two-year-old adopted son.

The scene before him was a happy one, and Derek smiled fondly at his family. They had been in Virginia for over a month now, but he had yet to miss his cattle station in the outback of Australia. The time they had spent there earlier that year had been full of danger and hardship. He forced a swal-

344

low over the lump that rose in his throat. He had come so close to losing Cassandra to the quicksand pits in the sacred caves. And by the hand of Becky Strassman, his childhood friend.

Pained by the unsettling memories, he gave a brief shake of his head. Even though the Strassman woman was dead now, and had been half crazy at the time she had attempted to murder his wife, he didn't like to think about what she had done to them. Despite the fact that his family still owned valuable land near Melbourne, he was just glad he had taken Cassandra away from Australia soon after he had foiled Becky's brutal plot.

Cassandra had wanted to come home to her war-torn country and that's exactly what they had done. All through the voyage he had worried that her plantation house would be in ruins, but they had been lucky. The northern army had used it as their headquarters in the area. Though it was dilapidated and many of its furnishings had been stolen or destroyed, the structure still stood intact.

Now Cassandra waited impatiently for the return of her brothers. She had written to both of them in care of their last known addresses, but as yet she had heard nothing from either Harte or Stuart. Even as she played with the scampering kittens, her eyes darted constantly down the entrance lane. But the road from Richmond was always empty.

On the other hand, Derek had heard from his sister, Lily, soon after Cassandra had written to Harte. She was excited to find them back in the

United States but couldn't travel because her new baby was so young. Since she was happily married to Cassandra's older brother, Derek hoped she could persuade Harte to come when she was ready. At the moment, making amends with her family was what Cassandra needed more than anything else.

As a Confederate secret agent, Cassie had wronged Harte during the course of the war. She had spied on his activities as a Union agent, lied to him, used his importance in the Federal government to gain access to military secrets. The American war had been bitter, both sides had been ruthless in their intrigue and espionage, but now Cassandra was wracked with guilt over the actions she'd committed for the South. She wanted to make amends to Harte, needed to, before she could make peace with herself.

"Look, Derek, there's a carriage coming!"

As she called his attention to the conveyance moving swiftly toward them in the distance, Cassandra put down the kitten she held and shielded her eyes against the glare of the afternoon sun. Little Joey squealed and chased the tiny creature into the low-hanging branches of a fragrant rhododendron bush edging the porch. Derek ran down the steps and squeezed Cassandra's shoulders. "Maybe it's Harte and Lily."

"I'm afraid to hope so," she whispered under her breath. "It's been so long now. I've about given up on them."

Derek knew differently. He had seen her walk to the end of the road only yesterday and gaze west toward the city. She tensed when the coach turned into the long magnolia-canopied driveway that led to a semicircle at the front of the massive sandstone portico.

"They're coming here," she murmured. Under Derek's palms her body trembled, and he remembered how often she had lain in his arms in bed at night, haltingly confessing her nervousness over meeting her brothers again. Unlike his own close-knit family composed of Lily and his parents, Cassandra's had been separated often and for long periods of time. She came from a broken family with broken relationships, and he felt certain her unhappy upbringing caused much of her recklessness and unscrupulous behavior during her tenure as a Confederate spy.

"Then let's go out to meet them. Roscoe, you'll watch the baby, won't you?"

The big Negro nodded, but Cassandra seemed reluctant now that the time was at hand. Derek put his arm around her shoulders and drew her down to the drive.

"Don't worry, luv, I'll be right here with you. I have a hunch Harte and Lily have come with their new baby."

Cassandra looked up at him out of turquoise eyes that he had found could implore him to give her just about anything she wanted. She'd had that effect on him from the first day he had met her. He still wasn't used to it.

"Thank you, Derek, for being so good to me."

"You'll do fine once your brothers get here. Just let things come naturally."

Derek pressed a reassuring kiss against the top of her soft coppery hair, then kept his arm around her waist as the carriage rolled to a stop in front of them. He felt Cassandra's body tense as the door swung open.

Surprised, he watched two children scramble out without even dropping the boarding steps. A little girl with long brown braids pulled the iron bar down for her fellow passengers, then brushed dust off her royal blue skirt and shirtwaist top. She looked around nine or so, and the little boy with her was much younger, probably not much older than Joey. He stared mutely at them out of his wide green eyes.

An instant later a big dark-haired man appeared in the open door. He looked nothing like Derek's flame-haired wife but the stranger bore a close resemblance to Cassandra's brother, Harte, whom Derek had met on several occasions during the war.

"Stuart! It's you!" Cassandra cried joyously as her brother stepped down.

Obviously forgetting all about her nervousness, she lifted her skirt and ran the rest of the way down the path. To Derek's relief, Stuart opened his arms and welcomed her with a bear hug. *I owe you a fa-*

vor, God, Derek muttered with an inward sigh of satisfaction.

"Oh, Stuart, I'm so glad to see you! I didn't know if I mailed my letter to the right address!"

"We got it in London," Stuart answered, smiling down at his sister. "But I want you to meet my wife." He turned and assisted a slender young woman from the interior. She was blond and beautiful but with skin as brown and tanned as Derek's own sea-bronzed face.

"This is Anjelica, Cassie. We've been married several months now."

"How do you do, Cassie," Stuart's pretty bride said politely. To Derek's surprise, she put her palms together and touched them to her forehead in the greeting of the Far East.

"Anjelica and her family grew up in India," Stuart explained quickly, gazing down at his small wife in a way that told Derek just how important she was to him.

"And who are these darling little ones you've brought along?" Cassandra was asking Stuart now, beaming at the two children who had stood by patiently while the adults exchanged greetings.

Derek thought he glimpsed a peculiar expression on Stuart's face for a bare instant and wondered about it until Anjelica spoke up and answered the question for her husband.

"They're my brother and sister. They live with us in London."

"I see. What are your names, children? I guess that makes me your Aunt Cassie now."

"This is Suzannah," Stuart said, drawing the little girl in close against his side. Almost protectively, Derek noticed.

"How do you do, Suzannah. I bet everyone calls you Suzie, don't they?"

"Yes, ma'am, they surely do."

"And I'm Sanjay. I'm very pleased to meet you, Aunt Cassie."

Smiling, Cassandra glanced up at Derek as she hugged the little boy. "Well, welcome to Twin Pines, all of you. This is my husband, Derek Courtland. I told you about him in my letter."

Derek moved forward with an outstretched arm to greet his new brother-in-law. Stuart took his hand in a firm grip. Their eyes locked for an instant, and when he spoke, Derek decided by his first words that he was a decent enough bloke.

"You're a lucky man to have caught my sister. She's always been a very special lady."

"I found that out."

"Though she used to have a tendency to get in trouble a lot," Stuart added, grinning at Cassandra.

"I'm much better behaved now that I'm a married woman." Cassandra defended herself quickly and with more seriousness than was really called for since Stuart had made the remark in jest.

Stuart looked at Cassandra briefly, then turned his gaze to the once-grand facade looming behind them. "It seems strange to be back here after so many years. I can't believe the bluebellies didn't burn it to the ground."

Cassandra nodded. "Me, too. We owe the survival of the plantation to Harte's intervention, I think. They did burn the barns, but Harte somehow got an order issued forbidding the army to destroy the house. I'll always appreciate that."

Derek saw a ghost of emotion flash across Stuart's face, noticed how quickly his wife, Anjelica, looked up at him. Stuart and Harte had lined up on opposite sides of the American conflict. Did he still harbor resentment that his older brother had fought for the Union?

"Come, please, let me introduce you to Joey and Roscoe," Cassandra was saying as she led them up the steps. "And I'll show you to your rooms so that you can rest awhile before supper. It won't be like the old days, you understand. I'll be doing the cooking instead of Pansy and Ruth."

"I'll help you," Anjelica Delaney offered at once. "I'm not the best cook around, either, but I'm learning more every day."

"Thank you, Anjelica. We'll use the time in the kitchen to get to know each other. We all have so much to catch up on."

Derek followed the small party through the double front doors into the house, both pleased and relieved that things were going so well. It appeared that Cassandra and Stuart would be able to reunite with relatively few hurdles. He just hoped to God that Harte's arrival would go as smoothly.

* * *

Later that evening they gathered on the back porch to catch the cool breezes off the river. Cassandra sat in her favorite old rocker, listening to the conversations going on around her. Now that Stuart had come home, she felt better than she had in a long time. She looked at him where he sat on the steps enjoying a smoke with Derek. They discussed the exploits of Derek's ship, the *Mamu*, which was docked at the wharves of Richmond.

Once she and Derek had agreed to take the Oath of Allegiance to the United States, they had not been hassled by the Yankee soldiers swarming the streets of the former Confederate capital. She had a feeling Harte had been instrumental in paving their way home, too, and she was glad for his help though it broke her heart to see the South crushed in defeat.

She wouldn't think about that, she decided, willing herself to change the direction of her thoughts. Her brother was home after years and years away, and he seemed relatively happy although she had sensed a certain amount of uneasiness in his manner, as if he were distracted.

Of course, she couldn't ask him what was troubling him, not yet anyway. They were still getting used to each other again. He had been reluctant to discuss Harte, she had seen that right off the first time she'd mentioned their older brother's name.

One thing she did know for a fact, though. Stuart was crazy in love with his bride. Cassandra liked

Anjelica, too. She was a very sweet and amazingly worldly girl, and she obviously loved children. As a matter of fact, she was playing with them now. Cassandra smiled as her own tow-headed Joey and dark-haired Sanjay got into a rough-and-tumble wrestling match. Bossy little Suzannah jumped right in the middle of the two boys, much to Anjelica's embarrassment.

Cassandra hadn't even been able to tell her brother that Joey was adopted and the horrible circumstances that brought the darling little boy into their family. At the thought of his mother, Becky Strassman, a delicate shiver inched across her flesh. She didn't want to think about that, either. She wanted only to think about the future.

Stuart and Anjelica planned to stay a month or more; she would have plenty of time to talk seriously with her brother and find out what had transpired in his life since the war had separated them. She was content to wait. Now if only Harte and Lily would come.

Coming together as a family again would be difficult at first but they could all be reconciled, she knew they could. The war was over; their political beliefs didn't matter anymore. If Harte refused to come to Twin Pines to join them, she vowed, then they would all go to him in Washington. All they had left was one another, and somehow, some way, she was bound and determined to make them see that.

Chapter Twenty-seven

"This was my river fort when I was a boy, Suzie. See the ladder? I built yours the same way."

At Stuart's words, Suzannah and Sanjay took off for the ancient gnarled oak. Anjelica watched Roscoe lumber behind them in a slow trot, his tiny blond-haired charge sitting high atop his broad shoulders. The black man and toddler were a strange twosome, to be sure, but both so sweet and good-natured. Suzannah and Sanjay were already fast friends with them.

She looked at Stuart, pleased that Cassandra had welcomed him back to Virginia with such pleasure. He had dreaded coming to Twin Pines but he had visibly relaxed some during the three days they had been at the plantation.

"Is it strange to be back home?" she asked gently.

"Yeah, like being propelled into the past. I can't get used to it. It does seem deserted now. My mother had three hundred or more slaves who worked the cotton and lived back there in the slave quarters."

Anjelica gazed out past the back of the house where burned-out cotton fields stretched for a mile or more. In the distance she could see a grouping of tiny brick cabins. She attempted to visualize how it could have looked when Stuart was a small boy perched in his tree house and hundreds of Negroes such as Roscoe worked in the fields and around the great, airy mansion.

"Mother always had guests afoot, too, relatives and friends from the surrounding plantations. Cassie said most of those people are gone now, their places either destroyed or sold to the murdering Yankees for a pittance of their worth."

Again she heard the bitter anger in his voice, in a way she hadn't heard it until they had come to Virginia and Stuart had seen the destruction first-hand. "This war was a terrible thing, wasn't it? I mean, everyone fighting one another when you were all citizens of the same country."

Stuart nodded without answering. For a moment he watched the kids playing in the old tree house. Big Roscoe stood beneath the limb, ready to catch anyone who overstepped the edge of the boarded floor.

"No matter what Cassie thinks, Harte will never come here."

Anjelica glanced up at Stuart. "Why do you say that?"

"He never once stepped foot on Twin Pines. Did

I ever tell you that? I think he hasn't ever come here because it would be a painful reminder that Mother brought Cassie and me here to live with her when she left Harte behind in Newport for Grandmother Delaney to raise. He was only seven when Grandmother insisted on keeping him but I don't think he ever forgave my mother for abandoning him. She didn't even tell him good-bye. He never saw her again."

"Oh, that poor little thing must have been terribly hurt," she murmured with true compassion for Harte's youth. From what she had heard, Harte Delaney had suffered more than most people during his lifetime. Although she had never met him, although all her loyalties lay with Stuart and his pain, she realized that Harte had faced many betrayals at the hands of his own family members. He had obviously survived such tribulations, but she wondered what kind of person he was now. Had all the heartbreak he had experienced since his childhood turned him into an angry, mean-spirited man?

Frowning, Stuart shook his head. "I don't see how Mother could have done it. I could never go off and leave Suzie now that I know about her, or Sanjay either, for that matter. Mama wasn't a good mother, not to any of us."

His last remark came out very hard, and Anjelica's heart broke yet again for her husband. She tried to comfort him. "The three of you can make amends for what she did to you. That's why we're here. Cassandra told me that she wronged

Harte during the war. She wants to make it up to him, just like you do."

"What she did doesn't compare to my crime with Camillia," he replied in a low voice.

Anjelica wanted to come up with the right words to ease his guilt, but there was only one person empowered to do such a thing. Harte alone had the power to forgive, and until he did, Stuart would never forgive himself.

"Look, Stuart!" Sanjay cried from the leafy bower. "Soldiers are coming!"

Anjelica gasped when she saw a contingent of four uniformed soldiers following their officer down the path from the front drive. Cassandra and Derek had just seen them from where they sat on the side porch and were walking out to meet them.

"Who are they?" Anjelica cried in alarm, grasping Stuart's hand as they hurried to catch up to Derek and Cassandra. "Why are they here?"

Stuart took a firm grip on her shoulders. "They're Yankees. Just stay calm until we see what they want."

Within moments the soldiers had reached them, and the young officer in front looked directly at Stuart. He was young with a sunburned face and a well-groomed handlebar mustache. Great bushy sideburns reached well out onto his cheeks in a way Anjelica had not seen before. "I am Lieutenant John Corbitt, United States Army. Are you Captain Stuart Delaney, sir?"

"I am."

"The Captain Stuart Delaney who served with the Army of the Confederate States of America, sir?"

"The same."

The young officer stepped back. At his signal his men trained their rifles on Stuart.

"Then it is my duty to inform you, sir, that you are now under arrest for treason against the United States of America."

"No!" Anjelica cried in horror as Suzannah and Sanjay rushed up beside them. "How can that be? The war's long over."

"That's right, Lieutenant," Derek Courtland said as he and Cassandra stood their ground before the arrest party. "Mr. Delaney is merely a guest here at Twin Pines. In fact, he is a resident of London now, and only came here to visit his sister."

Lieutenant Corbitt looked back at Stuart. "Then I must ask you, sir, did you procure funds and supplies for the Confederacy during this residency in London?"

"I did," Stuart said firmly.

"Then again I charge you with treason against the United States government. You'll have to come with me, sir."

"This is preposterous," Cassandra cried angrily. "The war's been over for months. Stuart hasn't done anything since he came here."

"Hush, Cassie, don't get yourself arrested, too," Stuart said calmly, then turned to Anjelica. "Don't worry, sweetheart. We'll get this cleared up and I'll be back soon."

"No, no, you can't take him!" Suzannah cried with rising hysteria.

"I'll go with you, Stuart, and see what I can do," Derek offered at once. "I know the commanding officer in Richmond. You'll probably have to take the oath, then they'll release you with a pardon. They've been handling nearly all the Confederate soldiers that way, ever since the war ended."

Anjelica felt better to hear that but her heart twisted with fear as Stuart was marched off in the midst of the blue-coated soldiers.

Three hours later that tiny scrap of comfort had totally disintegrated as Anjelica worriedly paced the floor of the parlor. Cassandra sat by trying to reassure her but both women ran to meet Derek when they heard him enter the hall.

"I've got bad news," were his first words as he entered the door. "Apparently the authorities have solid proof from one of their agents in London that Stuart's been soliciting funds for the new Confederacy in Mexico even after the truce was signed at Appomattox. Is that true, Anjelica?"

"I don't know," Anjelica cried, wringing her hands together. "What will happen to him if he did?"

"He's charged with treason."

It was Cassandra's turn to prowl around the room, her brow knitted in concentration. "Harte can get him out," she said suddenly. "Even with Lincoln dead, he's got influence with the White

House. He can get Stuart a pardon just like he did for Derek and me."

"But will he?" Anjelica was not so sure.

"Of course. He did it for me, didn't he? He'll do it for Stuart, too."

Anjelica trembled with fear, knowing that Harte had good reason not to do so. Cassandra had to know the truth. She took a deep breath. "There's something you don't know about Harte and Stuart, Cassie. Something terrible."

Cassandra stopped and quickly turned. She stared at Anjelica, and Derek waited silently for her to speak again.

"Harte might not agree to intercede for Stuart because of what happened between them."

"What are you talking about? They haven't seen each other in years."

Anjelica sank down on the sofa, glad Cassandra had sent the children upstairs. "I'm afraid you'll be shocked."

"Please, just tell me what you're talking about, Anjelica!" Cassandra cried, sinking down on the couch beside her. "You're frightening me."

"We just found out ourselves a few months ago. Sarah Delaney came to England and told Stuart the truth."

"Grandmother Delaney came to see you? What's she got to do with all this?"

"It's about Harte's first wife, the one named Camillia."

"I never met her. What about her?"

Anjelica began the tragic story in low, pained words, realizing it was hard for her to relate aloud her husband's shame. During her discourse, Cassandra's expressions flitted from shock, to horror, to despair.

"Suzie's Stuart's own child?" she breathed in astonishment. "And he didn't even know until the four of you got back to England?"

"Good God," Derek muttered, rubbing his jaw. "And you say that Harte knows about this, too?"

"That's right. Sarah said she had already told him the truth before she came to see us. That's one reason we came here. Stuart's been having such an awful time accepting all of it. He wanted to face Harte but he said just today that he didn't think Harte would come here, not for any reason."

"Well, he had better come here!" Cassandra cried. "Or I'll go up there and get him myself. Stuart's life could hang in the balance here!"

Anjelica cringed at her words, and Derek draped a comforting arm around her shoulder.

"Try not to worry, Anjelica. Nothing will happen right off. He'll have to have a military trial first. But we'd better get a telegraph message off to Harte and Lily, just in case. Then if we don't hear back from them in a day or so, I'll ride up to Washington myself."

Anjelica fought the tears burning her eyes but she was glad Cassandra and Derek were there to help her. What would she have done if they hadn't been?

"I want to go see Stuart, please, Derek, take me to him."

"All right, get your things."

Anjelica ran to obey but she was frightened, more than she had ever been in her life.

Chapter Twenty-eight

"I believe this is the road to Twin Pines." Lily said, leaning forward to peer out the carriage window.

Harte Delaney followed his wife's example and caught sight of the six great pillars of Twin Pines on a low knoll rising to their left. Cassandra had described the place to him more often than he could remember but he hadn't expected the mansion to be quite so impressive.

Even though he had received Cassandra's telegraph message a week ago, giving him days to get used to the idea of visiting the plantation, unaccustomed anxiety assailed him as they turned in between the two huge pine trees guarding the entrance gate. This was where his mother had gone that long-ago day. This was what she shut him out of.

"Harte, are you all right?"

Lily sounded concerned. She knew how god-awful hard it was going to be for him to set foot on the place. She was the only one in the world with whom he had ever shared the pain of his child-hood.

"I'm fine." He forced himself to smile at Lily, who was holding their twelve-month-old son, Courtland, cuddled in her arms. Courtland was peacefully asleep, but Lily's eyes, as golden as her hair, were troubled. He hated for her to be upset but he had stopped trying to fool her a long time ago. When a man's wife had the extraordinary gift of second sight, he had little defense against her intuition. "I guess I'm still a bit reluctant to see everyone again, especially down here in Virginia."

Lily nodded solemnly. He appreciated the wisdom of her silence. She never pried or tried to make him talk his problems over with her. She was simply there when he needed her. He could trust her. He had never been able to trust anyone else.

As they rounded the curve in the driveway, the mansion loomed large and spacious with double wings stretching off to each side. Now at closer range, he could see the disrepair, the chipped paint, a few broken windowpanes. The war years had taken their toll, all right, but the old house still stood. He had seen to it that the plantation was not touched by his own army. Why he had done such a thing, he still wasn't sure.

Cassandra sat alone on the front steps in the shadow of one of the big pillars. She got up and ran down the steps to meet them as the coach stopped at the base of the portico. The last time he had seen her, she had come to his house with the express purpose of betraying him to the enemy. He tried not to think about that, or anything else in the past, as he climbed down to greet her.

"Harte! I'm so glad to see you! Thanks so much for coming."

As Harte took Courtland and carefully propped the sleepy infant against his shoulder, he knew instinctively that Cassandra had changed since the war had ended. Even her voice was quieter now, more mature than before. Dispassionately, he stood by as his wife and sister embraced warmly, then watched Cassandra admire his son. But they all knew why he had come.

"Where did they take Stuart?" he said, not willing to engage in small talk when there was important business to attend to.

Cassandra clasped her hands together and shook her head. She was a lot more worried than he had first thought. "He's at the prison yard in Richmond. Derek's there now and so is Stuart's wife, Anjelica. I stayed here with the children today in case you came."

"You have children, too?" Lily asked as she reached up to take the baby out of Harte's arms. Carefully cradling him, she smiled at Cassandra.

"Derek and I adopted a child in Australia. His name is Joey. And Stuart and his wife brought along her brother and sister."

The thought of facing his brother hit Harte like the blow of a sledgehammer. Even though he now loved Lily with all his heart and had never really loved his first wife, he had been married to Camillia when Stuart had taken her to bed. Another betrayal, another family member, but this one so much worse than all the others. He gave himself a violent mental shake, furious because he had thought he'd finally come to terms with it. The roiling anger in his gut now told him otherwise.

"The girl's name is Suzannah, isn't it?" Lily asked quietly. Cassandra knew about Stuart and Camillia, too, he could see it in her eyes. All three of them stood there, knowing every wretched detail, but too polite to say the words out loud.

Finally, Cassandra nodded. "Suzie's upstairs. All the children are taking their afternoon naps."

"I suspect we need to talk about this alone, Cassie," Harte said brusquely, wanting to get it all over with as quickly as possible. He had never been exactly comfortable with his sister anyway, and he certainly wasn't under these circumstances. He doubted if he ever would be.

"I'm awfully tired from the trip," Lily said. "Maybe Cassandra could show me to my bedchamber, then you and she can go into Richmond and see what can be done." Lily gave her husband a significant look, knowing instinctively that he would want to confront Stuart alone.

Harte nodded and kissed her on the cheek, and Cassandra led Lily up the wide staircase rising to the left of the front door. He glanced around, mentally trying to picture his mother walking through the hallway, perhaps wearing the lemon dress she always wore when he remembered her. The yellow gown had been the last thing he had seen her wear before she left for Virginia when he was a boy of seven.

When the old ache of sorrow squeezed his heart, he turned abruptly and went back outside. The driver had unloaded their trunk and other baggage, and Stuart helped him carry it onto the portico.

"My sister and I are going back to town. She'll be ready momentarily."

As the driver climbed atop his perch Harte entered the carriage to wait, glad to have an excuse to leave Twin Pines so soon. He already loathed the place.

Within minutes Cassandra had returned, her forest green bonnet tied beneath her chin, her matching serge cape around her shoulders. She sat down beside him and called to the driver to proceed. The moment the coach rolled off down the drive, a cloying, uncomfortable silence ensued.

"I'm glad we're going to have this time alone together, Harte. I've been wanting to talk to you for quite a while."

Harte merely waited for her to go on. She looked as beautiful as ever with coppery curls peeking from beneath her hat and her intelligent silver-blue eyes searching his face.

"I've done so many horrible things to you. I don't know where to begin."

Surprised by her frankness, Harte returned his gaze to the passing scenery. He and his sister had never had a serious conversation. He supposed that was as much his fault as hers. Before Lily had come into his life, he had intentionally kept people at bay. "It was a terrible time. We all did bad things in the name of war."

"Don't try to make it easier for me. It was wrong what I did to you. I used you for my own purposes. I betrayed you when all you had ever shown me was kindness and the hospitality of your home."

Harte didn't know what to say. Since the war had ended, he had attempted to put her deviousness out of his mind and had succeeded for the most part.

"I was almost killed in Australia."

Quickly he returned his attention to her face. "How?"

"Derek went there to find the man who killed his father. I got caught in the middle of his fight with some people named Strassman."

"You're all right, aren't you?"

"Yes, though sometimes I still have nightmares about it. I'll let Derek tell you about it some time. It still bothers me to discuss it." When her voice began to waver, he realized that she was still very shaken by whatever had transpired in Australia.

"Anyway, I came close enough to dying to make me realize a few things. And I want you to know how sorry I am about what I did to you. I'm ashamed, and I'll never forgive myself so I'm not going to ask you to forgive me. I just want you to give me another chance to be a decent sister. I want to make it up. I want us to be a family because we've never really been one. That's why I asked you and Stuart to come here. So we can get to know each other again."

Harte couldn't bring himself to meet the imploring look in her eyes. "I don't know if that's possible, Cassie. Too much has happened between us."

"Will you at least say you'll try? Just for the length of time you and Lily are here?"

Harte set his jaw, more affected by her earnest plea than he would have expected to be. "I'll try, I guess."

"Thank you, Harte."

Harte nodded, and they lapsed into silence for the rest of the drive.

Stuart paced up and down the prison yard outside his cell, waiting for Anjelica to come for her daily visit. The longer he stayed in jail, the more he hated being away from her. Still he dragged his feet about taking the damned oath. He wanted no part of the new order; felt no loyalty to the United States anymore. Hell, he preferred banishment to calling himself a Yankee. He shouldn't have returned to Virginia in the first place. If he managed to get out of the country again, he sure as hell would never come back.

When the door to the cell block opened, he turned quickly, ready for Anjelica to run into his arms. Instead, Harte stood there, dressed in the dark blue uniform of a Federal major. The two brothers stared at each other without speaking.

Though it had been fifteen years since they had seen each other, Stuart recognized Harte at once. The first thing that struck him was their close resemblance to each other. Harte was taller, but not by much. Stuart stared at him, all the guilt inside him slowly rising like a tide to rob him of speech.

"You're a fool not to take the allegiance."

Harte's first words were not the ones Stuart had expected, but his rebuke broke the ice, if not the electrifying tension crackling between them.

"I didn't fight for five years and watch the South destroyed to join up with the enemy."

Harte moved closer, and Stuart resisted the urge to take a step backward. He held his ground as Harte stopped a couple of feet in front of him.

"A lot of other Confederates felt differently, including Cassie and Derek. Most of the rebels are back at home now, trying to reconstruct their lives because they took the oath."

"Under the heal of gloating Yankees like you?"

"Damn right."

Harte wasn't backing off, either, wasn't showing any of the dangerous emotions swirling alive inside Stuart's chest. God, didn't he know about Suzannah? Had Sarah lied about telling him the truth?

"Why are you here?"

"To get you out."

"I'm surprised you came."

"Cassie asked me to help you. She cares, and so does your wife and your—"

Their gazes locked hard. Expectancy hung in the air until Stuart had to broach the subject. He couldn't stand the evasion any longer. He finished Harte's sentence for him. "My daughter? Mine and Camillia's."

Harte looked as if Stuart had slugged him in the stomach but he stood silently and struggled to compose himself. He was so rigid with control that only his jaw worked furiously as he ground his teeth together.

"That's right, Stuart," he said evenly. "Your daughter's worried about you, too. So why don't you think about your family instead of yourself and take the goddamned oath so they can have some peace of mind?"

Stuart couldn't believe his ears. Harte was acting like nothing had happened. Had he cared so little for Camillia that her infidelity meant nothing to him? Rage rose, black and lethal—maybe because Camillia wasn't there to show her outrage at his nonchalance, maybe because he could remember how much Camillia suffered from Harte's long absences. Or maybe it was because he wanted Harte to share the blame for Stuart's own dishonorable acts, he realized in a flash of insight that nevertheless did little to stop his fury. His voice shook with bridled anger.

"You're a fine one to talk about thinking of your

family, Harte. You weren't exactly a dutiful husband, at least not the first time around."

"You bastard."

Despite Harte's low oath, he still showed no emotion, as if he were unaffected, when Stuart had spent his whole life suffering from the guilt of his sin with Camillia. He stepped up to Harte until they stood nearly nose to nose. "You didn't care that she died alone and miserable, did you, brother? I bet you were so caught up being a big, tough detective and sleeping with all those other women you bedded while you were married to Camillia that you didn't even bother to come home when you heard your wife was dead. Did you, Harte, did you even make it back for your wife's funeral?"

Harte moved so quickly that Stuart didn't even see the blow coming. The doubled fist struck him hard against the right cheekbone, knocking him off his feet and onto his back in the dirt. Then Harte was straddling his chest, lifting him up by his lapels.

"Damn you for blaming this on me," Harte gritted out through clenched teeth. "You're the one who wronged me, Stuart. You're the one who slept with my wife in my own home while I was gone."

The bluntness of his words stung because they were true, and Stuart could contain his ire no longer. He exploded upward, thrusting Harte up and off and coming to his knees, both fists held ready for a fight, blood streaming steadily from his nose.

As a prison guard burst through the doors to subdue his prisoner, Harte waved the soldier away. He staggered to his feet and stared down at Stuart. "You want me to fight you, don't you, Stuart? Is that what it's going to take to make you feel better about sleeping with my wife? For me to beat the hell out of you? Well, you can forget it. Find another way to absolve yourself."

Stuart lowered his fists and all the fight drained out of him. Harte was right. They both knew it. His words came out hard, low, gruff, tortured, as Harte was walking away.

"I'm sorry I did it. I'm so goddamned sorry I did it. She wouldn't have died if wasn't for me."

Harte stopped in his tracks. He turned around very slowly. "You think I haven't blamed myself for what happened to Camillia, Stuart? I have so goddamn many times I can't count them all, but it's over, she died a long time ago. You and I might not ever feel the same about each other again, but at least we know the truth. Thank God, I have a woman now who loves me the way I love her, and so do you, I think. And you have a little girl who seems to think you're somebody special. Do us all a favor and sign the oath before it's too late."

Stuart wiped his bloody nose on his sleeve. He looked down into the dirt until Harte walked back and stood over him. When Stuart looked up, Harte reached out his hand to him.

"Come on, let's go. We have a family waiting for us."

Stuart stared at his brother's proffered hand ex-

tended in forgiveness, then raised his eyes to the
face of the man he had wronged so deeply. He felt
an absurd burn of emotion behind his eyes when
he realized they had never clasped hands before,
never had any kind of conversation, not since they
had been ripped apart as little boys. They had never
been brothers to each other, nor to Cassandra.
Maybe they could start now. Or maybe they
couldn't, but it wouldn't be because he didn't try.
He reached up and gripped Harte's hand tightly
and let his brother pull him to his feet.

In the front office of the prison, Anjelica bit her
nails and stared out the window. Harte had been
inside with Stuart for over an hour.

"What can be taking so long?" she cried in agitation, whirling around to face Cassandra who sat on
a bench against the wall.

"Maybe Harte's talked him into taking the oath.
He said that's what he was going to do. I just don't
understand why Stuart won't do it. Derek and I did,
and we both were staunch defenders of the Confederacy."

"Don't you see, Cassie? Stuart's refusal has nothing to do with the war. He wants to be punished for
his involvement with Camillia, I think. He never
has had to face the consequences except in his own
mind."

Cassandra gazed thoughtfully at her. "He won't
think that way long. Once he remembers you and
the children are depending on him."

Anjelica hoped that were true, but she was afraid. Stuart was so distraught and had been since Sarah had come to London. Now she wished they hadn't come to America. She should have refused, and they would still be back in England at the house on the river. Tears sprang up and burned like coals against her eyelids until she heard a key scrape in the locked door at the end of the corridor. She jerked around.

Stuart stood in the doorway, and she ran the length of the hall and threw herself into his arms. She sobbed against his chest, and he held her tightly until she was able to pull back and look at him. It was then she saw the blood on his shirt and the way his eye was beginning to blacken.

"What did they do to you?" she whispered, biting her lip and reaching up gently to touch the bruise on his swollen cheekbone.

"Harte made me see reason," he answered, his gaze finding his brother who was now standing beside Cassandra. "I signed the bloody oath. We can go home now."

"Oh, thank God," she murmured, hugging him again. "I've been so afraid."

"I should have done it in the first place. I wasn't thinking straight until Harte pointed out a few things."

"What about Harte?" she whispered, anxiously searching his face. "Did the two of you have a talk?"

"He's willing to try and so am I."

Stuart's eyes had lost some of the dreadful melancholy that she had seen in them for weeks on end. Her heart soared with new hope and tears glittered as she took Stuart's arm, and they followed his brother and sister out of the awful jail. Everything was going to be all right now, she told herself, and this time she knew it was true.

Epilogue

Suzannah sat at the long oval table in the dining hall of Twin Pines Plantation. They were having a fancy supper but all the children were invited, too, which was a big surprise. Anjie, and her aunt Cassie, and her other aunt Lily had all been cooking all day in the kitchen, and that had been fun to watch 'cause none of them really knew how. Anjie was the best, though, at least in Suzannah's opinion.

Now that Stuart was back she felt a lot better, even though he had an awful shiner that made his eye turn black and swell shut when he got home from the jailhouse. No one would tell her what happened to him but she bet those mean Yankees had hit him for not taking their dumb old oath soon enough.

"Look, Suzie, Aunt Cassie made me a cherry cobbler," Sanjay cried excitedly. "She said she heard about our trick on Nicholas Sedgwick and made it in honor of our engines."

"No, she didn't. She said *engine-new-it-tea*. I

377

don't know what that means, either, but she said she had it, too, and that it runs in Stuart's family."

Aunt Cassie had looked at her when she had said it, then given her a real nice hug for no reason at all. Suzannah really liked Aunt Cassie. She was always telling them things about history and the stars and all that good stuff. She was real smart. And Suzannah liked her little boy named Joey, too. He had pretty white hair and he followed Sanjay everywhere just like Sanjay followed her everywhere. She looked at him where he sat on her uncle Derek's lap. Her uncle was pretty good, too. He had a big ship, and he was going to take them all back to England on it.

"Do you really think you can make a go of it here on Twin Pines, Derek?" said the man named Harte.

Suzannah thought he was nice, because he was always carrying around his little baby named Courtland, but he was the quietest except for Stuart. He looked at her funny sometimes, too, but she didn't know why. But he would always be her favorite uncle because he got Stuart out of jail.

"Yes, if Stuart can use his influence in London to get me some financial backing to reestablish the cotton fields."

"That won't be a problem. That's what I did for the Confederacy. Besides, that's where Anjelica wants to settle." He smiled at Anjelica and she blushed real big. Boy, her sister was always doing that in front of everybody.

"Then it'll be a family enterprise," Cassandra said

happily. "Harte can provide the ships through the Delaney shipping company to take our cotton to the London markets. I knew if we all put our heads together we could work out a family business."

Stuart sat next to Suzannah, and she tugged on Stuart's sleeve as the adults continued to discuss their big plans. "You know what, Stuart?

"What?"

She spoke up loud so he could hear her over all the talking. "I didn't wanna come here much at first, but I kind of like it here now. You got a real nice family, Stuart, don't you?"

When it got real quiet all of a sudden, she realized everyone was listening. Stuart glanced around the table then he smiled. "Yeah, Suzie, I guess I do."

Suzannah grinned back but when she looked at Anjelica she was dabbing a tear away, and so was Aunt Cassie. Good grief, she never would understand adults, she thought as she got down from her chair and followed Sanjay and Joey out onto the veranda for a game of hide-and-seek. They were always crying and moaning, and for no reason at all.

The big man named Roscoe who was always watching over little Joey was waiting for them on the back steps. He was fun. He didn't even mind playing their games.

"You're it!" she cried to Big Roscoe, then ran to hide among the low branches of the magnolia trees with Sanjay and Joey hot on her heels.

If you enjoyed *White Orchid*,
you'll love the rest of the
"White Flower" trilogy
by Linda Ladd. Turn the
page for a glimpse of
the delights in store for you
in *White Lily* and *White Rose*. . . .

THEY CAME TOGETHER
IN LOVE AND WAR

Ravishing, golden-haired Lily Courtland is both blessed and cursed with the extraordinary gift of second sight. But even she can see no way to escape from the men who have abducted her—and from the nightmare of sexual slavery awaiting her.

Harte Delaney has conquered countless women with his virile good looks and braved many dangers as secret agent for the North in the shadowland of intrigue during the Civil War. But he has never met a woman as magically mysterious as this beauty for whom he risks all to rescue and possess.

Amid the flames of war and the heat of passion, this woman who knows all and this man who fears nothing find themselves lost in a heart-stopping adventure with their own fate and the fate of a nation hanging in breathless balance . . .

White Lily

A VICTORY OF THE HEART

With hair as bright as flame and eyes as cool as silver,
Cassandra Delaney is changeable, unpredictable, and a
perfect spy. Her brother, Harte, has sided with the hated
Yankees, but Cassandra is the notorious "White Rose,"
risking her life and honor for the Confederacy in a
desperate flirtation with death . . .

Derek Courtland, rakehell Australian blockade runner,
possesses an uncanny ability to perceive danger, but on
this mission his every sense is taut, his blood on fire. His
job is to abduct the mysterious, sensual woman known
as "White Rose" to Australia to save her pretty neck.
Only she is fighting him, body and soul, to escape his
ship and the powerful feelings pulling them both
toward the unknown . . .

Now, under star-splashed skies, the ocean rising and
plunging beneath them, a man who can see through
deception and a woman who is an expert at lies are
being swept away on a perilous voyage to a distant,
seductive land . . . and to the far more dangerous
territory of deep, fathomless love.

White Rose

Topaz's
Crown Jewels

Get $1.00 back when you purchase

White Orchid
Linda Ladd

To get your rebate, just send in:

- Original sales receipt for your Topaz book
- This certificate
- Copy of book UPC number

Send to:
TOPAZ'S CROWN JEWELS rebate
PO Box 8008
Grand Rapids, MN 55745-8008

Name _____

Address_____

City_____State_____Zip_____

Topaz

ANNOUNCING THE

TOPAZ FREQUENT READERS CLUB
COMMEMORATING TOPAZ'S
1 YEAR ANNIVERSARY!

THE MORE YOU BUY, THE MORE YOU GET

Redeem coupons found here and in the back of all new Topaz titles for FREE Topaz gifts:

Send in:

 2 coupons for a free TOPAZ novel (choose from the list below);

- ☐ THE KISSING BANDIT, Margaret Brownley
- ☐ BY LOVE UNVEILED, Deborah Martin
- ☐ TOUCH THE DAWN, Chelley Kitzmiller
- ☐ WILD EMBRACE, Cassie Edwards

 4 coupons for an "I Love the Topaz Man" on-board sign

 6 coupons for a TOPAZ compact mirror

 8 coupons for a Topaz Man T-shirt

Just fill out this certificate and send with original sales receipts to:

TOPAZ FREQUENT READERS CLUB-1ST ANNIVERSARY
Penguin USA • Mass Market Promotion; Dept. H.U.G.
375 Hudson St., NY, NY 10014

Name_____

Address_____

City_____State_____Zip_____

Offer expires 5/31/1995

This certificate must accompany your request. No duplicates accepted. Void where prohibited, taxed or restricted. Allow 4-6 weeks for receipt of merchandise. Offer good only in U.S., its territories, and Canada.